Praise for Bertrice Small's
Pleasures Novels

Dangerous Pleasures

"A pleasurable erotic tale. . . . Fans will enjoy Bertrice Small's fine character study." —The Best Reviews

"The queen of sensual romance has done it again. . . . Sizzling." —*Romantic Times*

"Erotica has never been done more tastefully, or been more captivating." —Romance Junkies

Sudden Pleasures

"Arranged marriages are nothing new but the spin that Small puts on her contemporary version is hot and different . . . definitely scorching." —*Romantic Times*

"Full of emotions and unruly feelings. . . . An entertaining read. . . . Ms. Small writes every character realistically and with realistic faults." —Romance Junkies

continued...

Forbidden Pleasures

"Small is the queen of steamy romance, and this sequel to *Private Pleasures* is a truly entertaining fantasy that delivers. . . . Fans of erotic romance will not want to miss Emily's sexual awakening."
                                                    —*Romantic Times*

Private Pleasures

"One of the best erotic novels I have read this year . . . with her trademark savvy, sass, and sensuality all wrapped up in one seriously beguiling package . . . a winner."
                                                    —A Romance Review

"A complete success . . . gritty, truthful, and of course, extremely sexy."
                                                    —*Rendezvous*

"[A] XXXX tale . . . fans of erotica will enjoy."
                                                    —*Midwest Book Review*

. . . and for Bertrice Small

"Ms. Small delights and thrills."
                                                    —*Rendezvous*

"Bertrice Small creates cover-to-cover passion."
                                                    —*Publishers Weekly*

Books by Bertrice Small

BERTRICE SMALL

PASSIONATE PLEASURES

NEW AMERICAN LIBRARY

First published by New American Library,
a division of Penguin Group (USA) Inc.

First Printing, August 2010

Copyright © Bertrice Small, 2010
All rights reserved

ISBN 978-1-61664-740-7

Printed in the United States of America

For My Longtime and Dear Friend, Barbara Bretton
This one's for you, kid, with love from ME. Thanks!

🪶

PASSIONATE PLEASURES

His full name was Lucifer Nicholas, but few knew that. He was known simply as Mr. Nicholas, CEO of the powerful privately held company known as The Channel Corporation. He was a charming man, soft-spoken with a slight crisp British accent, graying hair and coal black eyes. He wore custom-tailored suits and beautiful shoes. His interests were wide and they were diverse as well as being successful and profitable. He was a major stockholder in a large tobacco company. Channel Artists represented several important rock stars and actors. His people lobbied to drill for oil on public lands.

And of course he had created the clandestine interactive entity known as The Channel. The Channel was for women, and women alone. It allowed them to live out their wildest fantasies each evening between eight P.M. and four A.M. the following morning. Their husbands and boyfriends knew nothing about The Channel. It was just one of those premium channels on the satellite or cable bill, like Disney. If asked about it a woman would say it was like Lifetime. The man doing the asking would usually roll his eyes and change the subject. Sometimes they would even make a joke about women's television.

Mr. Nicholas adored women. He loved their shapes, their colors, the different scents that surrounded each one. He loved the sounds they made in the throes of passion, their laughter when happy. But most of all he wanted to tempt them into living their fantasies because when they did, he was able to lure some of them under his control. And there was nothing more devious, more dangerous, more exciting than a good bad woman. Many women tired of The Channel sooner rather than later because eventually a surfeit of wonderful grows dull. But not all women did.

The village of Egret Pointe had proved an amazingly fertile ground for Mr. Nicholas. He had culled two women from the village's midst in the beginning of this twenty-first century. But he wanted Kathryn St. John, the town's librarian, more than all the others. The males in her family had been simple to entrap over the centuries. Men with a sense of their own importance, a strong desire for great wealth, and a need for power were easy fodder. And each generation wanted more than the previous generation had wanted.

But a woman of quality cannot be lured from the straight and narrow path as effortlessly as a man can. Kathryn St. John was not an easy woman to tempt. Her character was strong and firm. But like all females of the species, she had a weakness for good sex, and lots of it. Unfortunately she had no way of indulging her lust without causing a scandal.

And so Mr. Nicholas had introduced Kathryn St. John to The Channel. To be able to indulge her fantasies privately while keeping her family's reputation unsullied had delighted her. So she had brought The Channel to the attention of a few other women, who had in turn shared their delicious dirty little secret with other friends. And Mr. Nicholas waited patiently for this lovely ripe plum of a woman to fall into his power. He had all the time in the world. She did not. But then something totally unexpected happened. *Timothy Blair came to town.*

CHAPTER ONE

Kathryn St. John, pronounced *Sin Gin,* could still see forty in her rearview mirror. *But just.* Still, for a woman of her years she remained amazingly youthful. She was tall, standing five-foot-ten in her bare feet. She was slender without being thin. She had breasts and hips and a butt that had caused more wet dreams among men of a certain age than could be imagined. Her features were elegant: with a heart-shaped face; a long, slim nose; and surprisingly sensual lips, which needed no enhancement. Her eyes were the green of a summer forest, and while she wore it in a proper, neat chignon, her hair was still the red-gold she had been born with though whether the color was enhanced now no one knew for certain. Her voice was low and melodious. Her smile quick and sexy.

Many people in her own generation said she looked like Suzy Parker, a famous 1950s model. Kathy had heard that her entire life, and had always been flattered by it. As a teen she had admired the glamorous flame-haired beauty turned actress, who was often quoted as saying that as a model she was nothing more than an animated clothes hanger. It indicated to her a woman of common sense with a solid grip on reality. But then reality was for those who lacked imagination. And if there was one thing Kathryn St. John had in abundance, it was imagination. A very active imagination.

She supposed that, kept in check, an imagination was a good thing for a librarian to have. Miss Kathy, as she was known to her staff, was Egret Pointe's librarian. It was a position to which she had been born. Since her great-great-grandfather had built the library in 1895, all its librarians had been St. John women. There was nothing written into the bylaws of the library corporation that said that had to be so. But it was tradition, and the St. John women had all proved most satisfactory in their duties.

Kathryn St. John had thought she might be the last of the St. John women to manage the library, for her older brother had been late to marry. But then at the age of forty Hallock Kimborough St. John V had found himself a wife. A very young wife, Debora, who had so far produced five little St. Johns—twin boys and three girls—and was newly pregnant with a sixth. Kathryn was rather surprised to find her brother so invested in his paternity, for she had always thought him a bit stuffy and selfish. She couldn't quite imagine Hallock having sex or in the throes of unbridled passion. But she had to admit that he was a very good father and a devoted husband. Go figure.

At least she didn't have to live with him. When she

had taken up her position at the library twenty years ago, Honeysuckle Cottage had become hers. Great-aunt Lucretia, the previous librarian, had never retired, but at that time Hallock was unmarried, so Kathryn had continued living at home even as she pretended to be the assistant librarian. Her great-aunt spent most of her days asleep in a rocking chair behind the checkout counter while Kathryn attended to library business.

Great-aunt Lucretia had been her grandfather's elder sister, born in 1898. She had become librarian of the Egret Pointe Library at the age of twenty. Her fiancé had been killed in the war, and so she devoted her life tending to her family's gift to the town. The St. Johns were after all among Egret Pointe's founders. It was the family's duty, having founded the library, to see it was well maintained and as well run as a St. John would do it.

And so Lucretia Kimborough St. John had remained at her post until she quietly passed away one summer's afternoon in her rocker behind the checkout counter. She was ninety-two. And with her quiet death the library board had officially hired Kathryn St. John as the town librarian at a salary of one dollar a year, as was customary since the St. Johns all had private incomes.

Kathryn would have worked at the library for free because Honeysuckle Cottage came with the job, and she had waited her whole life to possess it. Set on a half acre of gardens directly behind the library building, the cottage was a replica of an idealized English cottage. It had been built in the same year as the library to house Miss Victoria Kimborough St. John, the first librarian. Everything in the cottage had been original when Kathryn St. John came into possession of it. She had waited another year before moving into it while the electric and plumbing were brought up to code, the chimneys cleared of decades of birds' nests. And she had kept it up to date ever since.

Honeysuckle Cottage was a whitewashed structure decorated with vertical light-colored wooden strips and standing two stories tall. The second story overhung the first just slightly. It was typical of cottages found in the Southeast of England. It had a fine slate roof although if it had been totally original, it would have had a thatched roof, the peak and eaves decorated with a design. Its leaded paned casement windows swung out when opened. There were two brick chimneys. The larger could be seen on the outside at one end of the cottage. The other came up through the roof at the other end of the building. An ancient honeysuckle vine climbed over the roof of the entrance to the house and around it. The oak front door had a leaded paned glass window shaped like a beehive.

Inside, the cottage had a charming parlor with a fireplace on one side of the central hall. On the other side was a small dining room with a second fireplace. The kitchen ran across the back of the cottage and had a hearth with an old-fashioned oven to one side of it. There was also a little powder room. On the second floor the cottage contained a large bedroom, dressing room, and bathroom. First-time visitors being given a tour of Honeysuckle Cottage were always surprised by the bathroom, which was light and airy with—among other accouterments—a bidet, a large garden tub, and a glassed-in shower.

Kathryn St. John might have been the town's librarian, but she liked her comforts and could afford to indulge herself, and she did.

She might have married. She was beautiful, and had money. But Kathryn St. John was an independent woman, and she liked it that way. She took several little vacations a year, flying to places like Paris or Dublin. She had been to Rio and to Venice for carnival, climbed Mont Blanc, traversed the Great Wall for several miles; and done a walkabout in the Outback of Australia. She chartered a private sailing yacht to cruise the Caribbean for a week, and even spent ten days at The Channel Corporation's Island Spa, where its manager, Fyfe MacKay, had proved a most satisfactory lover.

She knew his uncle, of course, for he had briefly been her first lover. Nicholas was a charming man, and while obviously much older than she was, no virgin had ever had a grander introduction to pure unadulterated sex than Kathryn St. John had had. It had been Nicholas who had introduced her to The Channel, and cajoled her into presenting a few of her friends and acquaintances with it. She often wondered what their lives would have been like without The Channel. Most women kept it for a time, but then gave it up. Kathryn St. John wasn't one of those women. The Channel allowed her to retain the independence she never meant to give up.

She had taken some of her favorite novels to translate into fantasy adventures. Just last night it had been *The Three Musketeers*. Kathryn loved playing the role of Milady St. Jean, and she played it to the hilt, enjoying every moment of the passionate pleasures she obtained from her lovers. She had programmed her remote, and suddenly she found herself quite naked and in bed, the man atop her fucking her quite vigorously.

"*Mon Dieu! Mon Dieu!* Is there anything finer than a lascivious noble whore?" He groaned as he sank himself deep into her steaming cunt.

"Only a libidinous musketeer with a long, thick, randy cock," Kathryn answered, laughing. She wrapped her slender legs about his sturdy torso. "Go deeper, Porthos, and harder. You know how I like it, *cherie.*"

"Will you scream for me, milady?" he asked softly, brushing her mouth with his own. His dark eyes were alight, the mocking smile touching his lips beneath his small, neat, dark moustache. He was so deliciously dangerous, she thought, as he rode her harder.

"Can you make me scream, Porthos?" she taunted, her fingers caressing the thick nape of his neck and sending chills down his spine. Make me scream, *cherie.*"

"I but live to serve you, milady," and he smiled into her face. Then, delving deep, he found that certain spot that he knew would drive her wild with passion. He worked it skillfully, slowly at first, then more deliberately.

Milady screamed with pleasure. *"Tu es un diable!"* she cried, as her muscles tightened themselves about his throbbing penis, squeezing, squeezing.

He felt her spasming around him, her creamy juices bathing his raging member. *"Sacré bleu! Tu es magnifique, ma belle!"* he shouted as he came.

Ping! Ping! Ping! "The Channel is now closed," the syrupy voice said.

"Oh merde!" Kathryn St. John said as her climax slowly faded away. She had just begun to really enjoy her-

self. With a rueful laugh she turned over, slipping into an easy, restful sleep. She had a busy day ahead of her.

When she awoke, it was a beautiful late-summer's morning. Kathryn St. John wasn't surprised to find several young people waiting for her to open the doors to the library when she arrived. There were those who did their summer reading early, and those who did it late. "Good morning," she said to them as she swung the doors open.

"Morning, Miss Kathy!" each of them greeted her, hurrying through the screen doors and heading back into the stacks. She grinned, hearing them already arguing about who was going to get to read what first. She had known most of them since nursery school. Then turning, she went back into her little private office. There was already a cup of light sweet coffee on her desk. "Thanks, Mavis," Kathryn called out.

Mavis Peabody, her assistant, immediately came into the room with her own coffee and sat down. "Let Caroline handle the checkouts," she said. "It seems more and more of them are waiting till just before school starts to do their summer reading. I always read my stuff first to get it over and done with so I could spend my time at the beach. But not these kids. Everything else comes first for them. Beach. Mall. Movies, and those damned cell phones that do everything except be phones."

Kathryn laughed. "Now, Mavis," she said, "you just have to keep up with it all. Have you seen the new Kindle Two?"

Mavis sniffed. "Not interested. I like the feel of a book in my hands."

"One day libraries could be obsolete," Kathryn said seriously.

"I'll be long dead, and glad of it!" Mavis snapped. "It has to be bad for your eyes, reading a book that way. And how are authors supposed to earn a living?"

"Oh, the agents will keep up," Kathryn laughed. "They have kids to put through college too, you know."

"Speaking of kids, the school board has found a replacement for Mrs. Riley," Mavis said. "She went to the hospital last night."

"So soon?"

"Riley or the new Middle School principal?" Mavis said.

"Both," Kathryn laughed. "Tell me about Mrs. R. first. I thought she wasn't due until late October."

"With multiples you end up delivering earlier, and once that sonogram showed five, it was a sure thing it would be sooner rather than later. They managed to stop her labor, but they're keeping her in bed and in the hospital for as long as they can to give those babies a better chance," Mavis replied.

Kathryn St. John shook her head. "Poor woman. Married ten years without a hint of a baby, and then quintuplets without any infertility help. 'Wow' is all I can say. So who's the new Middle School principal? I'm assuming someone local. They've hardly had time to look around since Mrs. Riley didn't say anything until just before Memorial Day. Please, not Bob Wright. He's such a stuffy jerk. The parents don't like him at all."

"Someone new." Mavis chuckled. "Marion Allison told me that the board decided before that looking in-house was going to cause problems no matter who they chose, so they would check around for someone else."

"And they found her?"

"*Him!* Timothy Blair is his name. He was assistant principal at a small private school in the city, but there was little chance for advancement since his boss was only five years his senior. Marion says he liked the idea of a small town, and he's got all the qualifications the board wanted, plus a few they hadn't even thought of, she says."

"Sounds perfect," Kathryn replied.

"Marion says he's cute, and he's single."

"Probably gay," Kathryn said. "If they get to be a certain age and aren't married, or haven't been married, they're usually gay."

"Hallock wasn't," Mavis pointed out, "and he was over forty when he married Debora. Marion says he's really nice."

"Hallock was my brother. St. Johns are never gay. No, I take that back. Great-uncle Arthur was, although in his day no one bothered to say anything about it, and neither did Arthur or his longtime companion, Harry."

"People wonder about you," Mavis noted. "I mean you're not a kid at this point, and you never date anymore."

"Don't have to." Kathryn chuckled.

"The Channel is fine for a while, Kathy," Mavis said, "but you can't substitute it for reality, and real men."

"Why not? The men are hot and sexually insatiable. They do what I want. They don't pitch hissy fits if I make suggestions, and I don't have to pretend to come, because I do, every damned time. What real man fits that description?" Kathryn asked. "And I don't have to sneak them out of the house before dawn so there will be no gossip."

"There's gossip anyway," Mavis said dryly.

"Small-town America," Kathryn answered with a shrug.

"Emily Devlin is pregnant again, and so is Ashley Mulcahy," Mavis volunteered.

"Where do you get all this information?" Kathryn asked.

"I don't live my life in the library and The Channel," Mavis replied sharply.

"I go out," Kathryn protested.

"To church, to board meetings for Mothers Alone, to the market when Mrs. Bills can't get there for you. That is your life, Kathryn. Duty, duty, and more duty," Mavis said.

"And The Channel," Kathryn said. "Don't forget The Channel."

Mavis shook her head wearily.

Kathryn reached across her desk and patted her friend's hand. "You don't have to worry about me, Mavis. Honestly you don't. I am outrageously content with my life."

"You're still attractive enough to catch a man, Kathy."

"What do you want me to do when I catch one? Broil him? Stew him?" Kathryn teased mischievously.

"You are closer to fifty than you are to forty, Kathy," Mavis said candidly.

"Don't remind me," Kathryn St. John said with a grimace. "Thank God for The Channel, where I can be twenty-five forever."

"I give up!" Mavis said rising from her chair.

"I'm hopeless, I know," Kathryn said, "but don't give up on me, Mavis."

"You're going to live as long as your great-aunt, and you'll be all alone," Mavis wailed. "You have no one, Kathy!"

"I have you, and my brother, and Debora, and all her little munchkins," Kathryn said. "And poor Great-aunt Lucretia had no one either, but she was perfectly happy."

"I despair!" Mavis said with a gusty sigh.

"Go and set up the schedule for the autumn children's events," Kathryn suggested. "That always makes you feel better, and I do want it out the first week of school. You've got two and a half weeks, Mavis."

"Good Lord! I barely have time!" Mavis Peabody exclaimed, and hurried from Kathryn St. John's office.

Watching her go, Kathryn smiled. She and Mavis had been best friends since nursery school. They had never lost touch, even when they had gone to different colleges.

Mavis meant well. She had been happily married for twenty-six years to Jeremy Peabody. They had two children: a boy, and a girl who was now engaged to be married. Mavis loved her job and her family. *She's duller than I am,* Kathryn thought, but she knew that wasn't really so.

Mavis didn't understand what it was like being raised in the St. John household. Kathryn's mother, Jessie, had been a sweet woman who was devoted to her husband and children. She had given up a promising career as a concert pianist when she married Hallock Kimborough St. John IV. She had fitted herself quietly into the male-dominated St. John household, delivering the requisite male heir within twelve months of her marriage. She had miscarried a second son two years later, and when Kathryn had been born two years after that, she was visibly disappointed, especially after the doctor told her that having another child would kill her. And it had, when Kathryn St. John had been six.

After that, there was no strong female influence in Kathryn's life. The household consisted of her grandfather, Hallock III, her father, and her older brother. The house was managed by a houseman, Mr. Todd, who saw that everything in the St. John household was in perfect order, and cooked the meals. A series of cleaning ladies came in once a week over the years. Twice a year they came for five days in a row, to spring clean, and several months later to prepare the house for the winter months.

And no one paid a great deal of attention to little Kathryn St. John. Her brother was the scion of the family. He followed his grandfather and father down the broad center aisle and into the family pew at St. Luke's Episcopal Church each Sunday, never once remembering to hold the door and step aside to allow his sister entry once she came up from the Sunday school. After a month of Sundays Kathryn St. John took to entering her family's pew via the side aisle. The first time she did it, she surprised her grandfather, but then a small smile touched his thin lips, and he nodded his approval to her.

He believed that she had accepted her place in the scheme of all things St. John. Actually that Sunday had marked Kathryn St. John's declaration of independence. She was eight years old, and from that moment on Kathryn ran her own life. She was careful never to clash directly with her male kin. As long as her grandfather lived, he was deferred to as head of the household. Kathryn did not bother with her father, and she ignored Hallock V as much as she could. When she wanted something, she worded her request in such a way that it was unlikely her grandfather would refuse. And the things she could not learn from the male-oriented household in which she lived, she learned from Mavis's mother, grandmothers, and older sisters.

She was a quick study, and Kathryn St. John knew she had learned to be a proper lady the day she overheard Mavis's maternal grandmother say to Mavis's mother, "I just don't know how poor little Kathy St. John survives in that household of men. You would think old Hallock would have brought a nanny in for the child when Jessie died. Not that Jessie paid a great deal of attention to her daughter. It's amazing she's as well-mannered and ladylike as she is. Well, breeding will tell, won't it?"

"I wish Mavis were half as ladylike," Mavis's mother had replied. "I'm glad they've remained friends. I think Kathy is an excellent influence on my daughter."

Hearing those words, young Kathryn St. John smiled to herself. She didn't need anyone but herself to survive in this world. She could do whatever she wanted to do, herself. Let her male relations believe that they were superior just because they had an appendage dangling between their legs. They weren't. She knew she was beautiful, and she knew she was smart. She could do anything, and she could do it without a man.

Kathryn St. John wasn't against men. Indeed, she liked them very much. While her father and grandfather were didactic, they were extremely clever and charming.

So were many of the male friends who surrounded them. At sixteen Kathy found she had a serious crush on one of those men. He was fascinating in a mysterious way that appealed to her intellect. No one really knew a great deal about him except that he was quite wealthy and seemed to make a success out of everything he did.

"You may call me Nicholas, my dear Kathy," he told her one summer's afternoon when the garden was full of men and women laughing and drinking.

"You intrigue me, Nicholas," she had told him, surprised by her own daring.

He laughed. "And you enchant me," he replied with a small amused smile. "However, you are much too young for me to seduce, Kathy."

"When will I be old enough?" she asked him seriously.

He laughed again. "We shall see, my dear," he responded. "You will know when the time is right. In the meantime, we shall become friends." And they had. She looked forward to his visits to Egret Pointe.

There was nothing she couldn't ask him, be it serious or silly. He always answered her, and he didn't scold or criticize as her male relations were wont to do when she asked a question they thought foolish. Kathryn St. John's curiosity was endless. In time she began to query him about sex, because Mavis's mother had only given her daughter and her daughter's best friend the barest knowledge. There had to be more, Kathryn thought. While the girls at school had giggled and gossiped about their adventures with boys, Kathryn could hardly believe some of the things they said. So she asked Nicholas.

Sometimes he had laughed, then explained the misconceptions. Other times he had been most serious and thoughtful in his answers. Kathryn St. John had become more and more curious about what it was like to experience the mysteries of sex.

"You must not allow some careless boy to have your virtue," he had said to her one day. "I want that first time to be special and memorable for you."

"What would my father and grandfather think if they heard you speaking with me like this?" she queried teasingly. Dear heaven, this man excited her passions!

He laughed. "Your grandfather and father trust me to do the right thing," he said.

"Do they mean for you to marry me?" Kathryn asked, curious.

"I'm not a man for marriage, my dear," he admitted. "I enjoy women. I enjoy conversing with them. I enjoy possessing them sexually. Your male relations know that. They know whatever I do I will cause you no harm, nor will I cause a scandal."

"What will you give me for graduation next week?" she asked, turning the subject.

"What do you want, my dear?" he replied.

"Don't you know?" she teased him, moving so close to him that the tips of her breasts brushed against the fabric of his beautifully cut suit jacket.

He took her upturned face between his two elegant hands. Looking into her face, his black eyes seemed to be filled with flames. "Yes, I know," he said softly against her ripe lips. "You shall have exactly what you desire, Kathy. You shall have as much of it as you want, and you will not be disappointed, I promise you."

And once Nicholas had relieved her of her virginity, Kathryn St. John had set about to indulge her lusts. But because she wanted no scandal attached to her family's name, she kept her active sex life to her adventures in The Channel. The single men in Egret Pointe were always available for a dance at the country club or dinner and a movie; however, the pool of men her age grew smaller as the years passed. By the time she was thirty-five, the town gossips had given up trying to match her.

She hadn't even bothered an attempt at catching the bride's bouquet at her brother's wedding, although Debora pitched the flowers directly at her. The delicate roses and stephanotis had ended up in the hands of a squealing teenage relation on the bride's side, who shrieked gleefully as she elbowed Kathryn aside to get to the flowers.

No, Kathryn St. John needed no one. She sipped her coffee slowly, and considered the day ahead. She had her weekly staff meeting at eleven this morning.

It was time to discuss the Christmas Book Fair, which meant getting in touch with all the contacts she had made over the years for new-book donations. And she had to decide on the new Web site for the library. Kathryn smiled to herself. Great-aunt Lucretia would have been very taken aback by how complicated the business of running a library had become.

Libraries were no longer just in the business of loaning out books. The Egret Pointe Library had published a vision statement several years back. In it they set out the ways in which they would and could serve their community. The library sponsored a series of concerts on the village green each summer. They had wonderful programs for children from toddlers on up. Their summer-reading contest for 'tweens would shortly be coming to an end, and the winners announced. They would get the treat of their choice at Walt's ice-cream shop. Each Friday evening in February at seven P.M. the library had what they called Family Movie Night. It was a very popular program with family-oriented films being shown. And the library was far more accessible on a snowy winter's night than the local cineplex at the mall several miles away.

One of the most popular programs, however, was the computer classes that were given for seniors. Many of Egret Pointe's older citizens had children and grandchildren living far away now. Becoming computer literate let them stay in touch. Yes, indeed, Great-aunt Lucretia would have been very surprised by what the library was doing today. And not just books were available for loan now. There were DVDs and videotapes too. This new technology demanded they do more and more to remain relevant. Kathy wondered if it would be possible to loan out Kindle readers. Could libraries get subscriptions to download books for their readers? How would publishers charge for it? A onetime fee? Would there be a discount? She would have to keep an eye on it for the future.

Mavis stuck her head in the door. "Time for the staff meeting," she said.

Kathryn St. John rose from her desk, gathering up a small pile of papers to take with her. The meeting would be held as it always was in the library boardroom. Her staff of six was already there and waiting when she hurried in with Mavis. "Good morning, everyone!" she greeted them.

"Good morning, Miss Kathy," the staff chorused back.

"Anyone have any old or new business?" she asked, knowing the answer but asking anyway. "No? All right then, let's get to the preplanning of our annual Christmas Book Fair. Caroline, I'd like you to continue to deal with the paperback houses."

"No problem," Caroline said.

"Does anyone have an idea of what the Merchants Association is doing this year for Christmas windows?" Kathryn asked.

"Dickens," Mavis answered. "A Dickens Christmas."

"Then I think it would be fun if the volunteers dressed in the appropriate costumes for the fair this year," Kathryn said. "What does everyone think?"

"Once we know who's volunteering to work the fair, I can get the costumes," Peter Potter, the only man on the library staff, said. "I have friends in the city who can help us with that."

"That would be wonderful! Thank you, Peter," Kathryn replied. "Let's put out the call for volunteers right after Labor Day."

There were murmurs of assent.

"We should do something special for the kids," Marcia Merryman, the children's librarian, said. "We may have a few games relevant to the period for them to play, along with suitable prizes. I can research it."

"Perfect!" Kathryn agreed. "Now we have to pick a date, people. How about Saturday, December fourth? It's after the Thanksgiving rush, but before people have bought all their gifts. Remember, this is our big fund-raiser. We can't depend entirely on the taxpayers these days. The budget just squeaked by in May."

"We've always done well," Mavis said.

"We have to do better this year," Kathryn responded. "We should make the Book Fair more interactive. And we need other sources of income from it."

"Food!" Susan Porter suggested. "Hot mulled cider, little mincemeat pies, hearty soup, and tea sandwiches, that kind of thing. Maybe even a corner where we could set up a tearoom. People are always more amenable when you feed them. They'll come. Buy a book or two. Eat, and then buy more books."

"That is very clever!" Kathryn chuckled. "You're in charge of that, Susan!"

"Oh my, me?" Susan Porter squealed turning pink with excitement. She was a short, plump woman with short, tight iron-gray curls.

"You," Kathryn repeated. "Make it profitable, Susan."

"I'll help with the pricing," Mavis volunteered dourly, a little jealous that Susan Porter had come up with such a really good idea.

"I will handle the hardcover houses as usual," Kathryn said. "I think that's all we have to do today. I'll expect reports on your efforts two weeks from now. Anyone have anything else to bring up?"

"The staff bathroom has problems again," Peter murmured.

Kathryn sighed. "I'll call the plumber," she said. "We need a new commode, and I've been trying to avoid the expense. I guess we can't anymore."

The meeting concluded, Kathryn returned to her office. The rest of the day seemed to disappear amid all of the busywork she had to do.

"Closing time," Mavis reminded her at seven P.M.

Kathryn decided she would be glad when summer hours were over, and she could close up the library at five P.M. Locking up, she bid her friend good night, and walked through the library's back garden to her cottage. Mrs. Bills, her housekeeper, had left a cold plate of chicken salad and sliced tomatoes in the fridge. Kathryn poured herself a glass of Duck Walk Windmill Blush and took her plate out to the little brick terrace off the dining room to eat.

The mid-August heat was actually visible hanging in the trees, and the tree frogs were in full voice tonight. They were such tiny creatures, and you rarely saw them. But, oh my, at this time of year you certainly heard them. Kathryn ate slowly, enjoying both her meal and the wine. Windmill Blush was one of her favorites. She lingered with her glass as the light faded and it grew dark. There was a new moon tonight that quickly set, and the moist haze made it difficult to see the stars. Unless they got a cool front in another day the Perseid meteor showers wouldn't be visible this year. Actually there hadn't been a good Perseids in several years. But when it was clear and moonless, the meteor shower was glorious.

The dew was beginning to fall. Kathryn got up, taking her plate and glass with her to rinse and set in the dishwasher. Then, making certain the doors and windows were locked, she went upstairs. She had added central air to the house when she renovated, but being frugal, put in two zones. She pressed the button on the ON switch in the hall outside her bedroom suite before entering, programming it for seventy-two degrees. By the time she got out of her shower the upstairs would be comfortable.

Going into the large bathroom, Kathryn turned the jets on in her glassed-in shower. Then she went back into the bedroom to kick off her leather loafers, peel off her khaki cotton skirt, white tee, silk briefs, and silk and lace bra. Beautiful undergarments were her weakness, and Egret Pointe was fortunate to have a delicious shop, *Lacy Nothings*, that catered to women who loved silk-and-lace underthings. She hung up the skirt and deposited the other garments in her dirty-clothes bin.

Turning, Kathryn looked at herself in the ornate full-length mirror in the room. Not bad for an old broad, she decided. Having never had children, she had managed to keep her belly pretty flat. It had just a hint of roundness to it. Her boobs were still pretty perky and her ass hadn't started to fall yet. Reaching up, she undid her hair, and the red-gold curls spilled over her shoulders. Kathryn St. John smiled at her image. Naked, with that wild hair, she hardly resembled the town's proper librarian. With a chuckle she went into the bathroom, and opening the glass door, stepped into her shower.

The warm water felt wonderful. The shower had a full dozen jets that spurted at her from all angles. Reaching for her apricot shampoo, she quickly washed her hair, then, tucking it up and securing it with a large tortoiseshell pin, she washed herself. What was she in the mood for tonight? Her French fantasy with the Three Musketeers? No. She just wanted a good fucking, not three randy soldiers eagerly probing her every orifice all at the same time. Cleopatra and Caesar or Cleopatra and Anthony? Definitely not! She was not of a mind to deal with strong personalities tonight. Did she want to be Bess, the innkeeper's daughter, entertaining her highwayman lover? No. That fantasy was far too intense, and she didn't want intense tonight.

She wanted fun and games, she decided, as she washed herself with a hard-milled olive-oil soap from Italy. And fun and games usually meant Lady St. John and the eighteenth century. Yes, it was that kind of a night. A lusty and uninhibited young lover, a game of hide-and-seek in the manor gardens, a forbidden tumble in a dimly lit hayloft, and then spying on Lord St. John and a housemaid. She might even join them.

Kathryn giggled. It was perfect, and just what she needed. And it wouldn't even take the entire evening. She would be in and out of The Channel in quick order, relaxed and ready for a good night's sleep. Finished washing, she set the soap back in its dish, rinsed herself off, and turned off the shower. She stepped out of the glass enclosure, reached for a towel, dried herself, and damp-dried her hair before giving it a quick blow-dry. Then, folding her towel and placing it back on the rack, she reentered her bedroom.

Pulling back the coverlet on the bed, Kathryn climbed in naked. Opening her nighttable drawer, she took out the remote and pointed it at the beautiful painted cupboard opposite her four-poster bed. She pressed a button, and the doors to the cupboard swung open to reveal a large flat-screen television. The remote in her hand contained at least half a dozen buttons, marked A through F. There were only a very few of these special remotes, for the majority of them contained only two buttons. A and B.

Kathryn St. John had introduced The Channel to Egret Pointe, and by doing so had unknowingly brought it to all the women who wanted it on the North American continent. The CEO of The Channel Corporation had, although Kathryn certainly didn't know it, a soft spot for her. It was unusual for Mr. Nicholas to show any weakness. The Channel had been created for one reason, and one alone. To lure women to the dark side.

If out of a hundred thousand subscribers he found one woman he could use, Mr. Nicholas counted it a victory. Oddly, ordinary women didn't succumb to his lure, but then he didn't want ordinary women. He wanted clever, intelligent women, who could be useful.

Egret Pointe had to his great surprise given him two women to use for his nefarious purposes. Nora Buckley and Annie Marshall. Both now worked for him. Both owed him their very lives. But Mr. Nicholas wanted Kathryn St. John too, and so he saw that she was spoiled by being given one of the special remotes that would allow her several fantasies to choose from, and not just two. Being well-read, he found she had a marvelous imagination, and quite enjoyed watching the fantasies she had programmed. Having personally taken her virginity years ago, he took great pleasure in seeing how truly lusty and adventurous she had become over the years.

Kathryn paused a moment, making certain within her own mind of the fantasy she had chosen for tonight. Yes, naughty fun and even naughtier games would suit. She pressed the button marked C, and immediately found herself in a green garden maze.

She was wearing a low-necked flowered pale blue silk dress, a line of little bows edging the full skirt's paniers. Her hair was long, and dressed in thick ringlets.

"Kathy? Where are you?" she heard a voice she recognized as that of her stepson, Robert St. John. He was her husband's offspring from his first marriage.

She giggled just enough for him to hear, and moved stealthily through the maze. "Catch me if you can, Robbie," she teased.

"Oh, I can catch you, Kathy, and when I do, you will be given a sound spanking for being such a naughty girl. Does my father know how naughty you are?" he asked.

"Of course." She laughed. "Why else would he have married the daughter of a poor vicar? Your mother, God rest her, gave him three sturdy sons. Henry didn't need another wife. A nice mistress would have suited him well, but I wouldn't settle for being just a mistress. I gave him just a little taste of paradise, and then withdrew myself from him. If he wanted me, he had to wed me, and he did." She listened for his footsteps.

He followed the sound of her voice through the maze. His cock was already straining against the satin of his breeches. The little vixen had been taunting him for weeks now. She was so exciting, so different from his wife, the insipid daughter of their neighbor, the duke of Malincourt. She bored him so greatly it was difficult to get hard for her so he might take his marital rights, and beget an heir. But with his father's young wife he found it difficult to keep his cock from swelling fully. The mere sound of her voice made him hard with desire.

He heard a faint rustling to his left, and turned to see a flash of blue silk. He hurried around the hedge. "I'm coming to get you, Kathy," he repeated. Her laughter tinkled in his ears.

"You're getting warmer," she teased. "And my cunny

is getting wetter just thinking about you, Robbie. Hurry and find me."

He undid the buttons on his breeches, releasing his cock. Ohh, he was going to fuck her hard, but first he would spank her arse until she begged for his mercy. She deserved it for bedeviling him so, ever since he and Jemima had returned from the London season. His eye caught sight of a dainty slipper peeping from a hedge corner. Slipping about the greenery he found her, back to him, listening for his approach. He fastened one arm about her narrow waist while his other hand plunged beneath her neckline to grasp one of her delicious, full breasts.

Kathy squealed. "Ohh, you bad man, you have caught me!"

"Indeed, madame, I have," he agreed. He squeezed the breast, and then, removing his hand, turned her about to kiss her full, seductive lips. Then, grasping her hand, he pulled her along, bringing them successfully out of the maze into the far recesses of the gardens and to a marble bench. Seating himself, he pulled her over his knees, pulled up her skirt and petticoats so he might carry out his threat to spank her. Her bottom was plump and a perfect peach. He wondered if his father had rutted between the twin halves, but that would be for another day. His big hand descended several times.

"Ohhh," she half sobbed, "you are too cruel, Robbie." But she wiggled against him, further arousing him.

He gave her several more hard spanks, enough to know her clit was probably tingling at this point. Then he tipped her onto her feet again, surprised when Kathy picked up her skirts and fled him. He knew, of course, where she was going, and followed her to the cool, darkened hay barn. Catching her again, he threw her down into a large pile of sweet-smelling hay and yanked her skirts up practically over her head.

"Ohh, you are a wicked boy!" Lady St. John scolded him.

"You are a wicked wench," he countered, grasping his engorged cock in his hand.

"Ohh, you dare not fuck me!" she pretended to object.

"Aye, I dare!" he growled at her. "I shall fuck you hard, and I shall fuck you deep, madame. And you will beg me for more when I am finished with you."

"Nay, darling," Lady St. John said. "You will beg me." And she laughed. "I shall make you weep like a schoolboy, Robbie. Now fuck me!"

And he did. Driving his thick length into her over and over again until she came with a shriek of delight. But he was not satisfied, and so he fucked her further. It was then that Lady St. John began to torment him, wrapping her silk-clad legs about him, squeezing the foraging cock tightly again and again until he began to whimper with his pleasure. She held off his release until he was almost mad with his lust. Only then did she let him come, and he flooded her. He sighed gustily. "Great God, Kathy, that was incredible! Why is it I can't wait to fuck you, and my own wife cannot engage my lust?"

"I have no idea, Robbie. Jemima seems pretty and affable enough," Lady St. John answered him. "Try harder with her, please. Your father wants you to have an heir." Pushing down her skirts, she stood up. "That was lovely, darling, but I must go. Your father will wonder where

I have gotten to, for he is most solicitous of my well-being."

"Don't go," he begged her. "I want more!"

"You may have more later, but not now," Lady St. John said, and then she hurried from the darkened hay barn, returning to the great manor house. She knew exactly where her husband would be at this time of day. Entering the house, she hurried up the stairs to the bedroom floor. Reaching the corridor, she stopped and listened. She heard the low pants and the soft grunting coming from the linen cupboard. Opening it, she found her husband, the woman with him on her knees sucking vigorously on Henry St. John's cock. She assumed it was one of the maids, until the woman raised her head slightly, and Lady St. John stared into the startled eyes of Jemima St. John. "Oh, how deliciously naughty," she murmured low. "Well, it can't be comfortable in this cupboard. Get on your feet, girl! Take him by his cock, and bring him along to my bedchamber."

"Lusty wench, my wife," Sir Henry said. "Come on, 'Mima. Kathy will know how to give us all a good time before dinner."

Not knowing what else to do, Jemima grasped her father-in-law's now stiff cock, and following Lady St. John, led him to the suggested chamber. The doors to the chamber were firmly locked and at Sir Henry's suggestion the trio disrobed entirely, although the ladies retained their silk stockings and garters. Jemima was ordered to lie upon Lady St. John's bed. Sir Henry mounted his daughter-in-law as his wife moved so that her cunt was directly over Jemima's head.

"Lick and suck her, girl," his lordship ordered as he began to fuck Jemima. "You'll not come until she is ready to come. And if you don't make her come, I'll see that groom who fancies you, and whom you dislike so, has a go at you. Now use your tongue, girl. I can attest it's a skillful one."

Jemima St. John did indeed have an expert tongue. Reaching up, she pulled Lady St. John's nether lips apart and directed the tip of that artful tongue to Kathryn's clitoris. Her tongue swirled and encircled it, teasing the tiny nub of flesh until it began to burgeon and swell. It occurred to her that she could taste her husband's cum on the lady's flesh. Had the wretch been fucking his stepmother? She nipped at the now swollen bud and Kathryn squealed.

"Make me come, you little bitch!" Lady St. John hissed. "Do not dare to keep me waiting another minute! Ah! Ah! Ahhhhh! Oh, that is good! More! I want more! Release your cream, Henry. She's pleasuring me well. Ah! Oh! Ohhhh!"

Sir Henry found Jemima's special spot, and worked it hard. She shrieked with her delight, and content that they had all been well satisfied, he came with a shout. When they had recovered from their bout of Eros and restored themselves with wine laced with aphrodisiacs, Kathryn sucked her husband's cock to a stand, and then lay beneath Jemima, suckling on her large nipples while Sir Henry ass-fucked his daughter-in-law until she came with a screech.

"It is almost the dinner hour," Lady St. John remarked. "Leave me now so we may all dress." She watched as, gathering up their garments and putting them on quickly, Sir Henry and Jemima left her. "That's enough for tonight,"

Kathryn said. "Channel off!" Back in her own bed, she pressed the CLOSE button on the remote and watched as the doors on the cabinet shut. It had been a most satisfying night, and she was relaxed enough now to sleep. She really loved The Channel. It didn't matter how old she got, it would be there for her. And there were no obligations once she turned it off. It was perfect!

CHAPTER TWO

The twelve-year-old beige-colored Ford Contour eased off the treed parkway at the exit marking Egret Pointe. Timothy Blair's blue eyes took in the countryside as he drove into the village. He had only been here briefly once before. The place was almost too perfect, he thought, with its wide main street edged in tall, ancient trees, and the charming shops that lined it. Hell, there was even an ice-cream parlor. As he slowed down, Rowdy awoke from his place on the backseat and sat up with a low *gruff*.

"Like it or lump it, boy—this is our new home," he said to the dog.

Rowdy whined and thumped his tail.

Tim scanned the main drag, and then he saw it. Country Real Estate. He pulled into the space directly in front of the office and parked his car. Getting out of his vehicle, he opened the back door of it, and Rowdy bounded out.

"Stay!" Tim commanded the shaggy dog, then bending, clipped a leash to Rowdy's collar. "Now behave yourself," he instructed the animal.

Rowdy pulled on the leash, and lifting his leg peed on the trunk of the tree before the real estate office.

Tim chuckled and, dog in tow, walked into the building. "I'm looking for Mrs. Kirk," he said to the woman at the front desk.

"Are you Mr. Blair?" she asked, and then without waiting for an answer added, "I'm Doris Kirk. Welcome to Egret Pointe, Mr. Blair."

"Thanks," he replied.

"I wasn't aware you had a dog," Mrs. Kirk said.

"This is Rowdy," Tim told her. "Rowdy, shake!"

The seated dog offered a paw to Mrs. Kirk, whose serious demeanor suddenly vanished as she took the paw and shook it before patting Rowdy on his head.

"I had several rentals to show you, Mr. Blair, but most of them won't take dogs, I'm afraid," she told him.

"I didn't consider that," he admitted. "I've lived in the same prewar building in the city for years, and there was no problem."

"Well, there is the Torkelsen cottage over on Wood's End Way," Mrs. Kirk said. "Martha was a widow, and she just died. Her kids don't live here anymore. They decided to rent the place out until they can make a decision what to do with it. It's surprisingly up to date. Martha was an incredible cook, and the kitchen is wonderful. It's little. Two bedrooms, one a decent size, the other small. But it does have a fireplace in the living room, and a garage. You can actually walk to the Middle School from there."

"Let's go look," Tim said. "I'll follow you in my own car. I don't want Rowdy shedding all over someone else's upholstery."

Mrs. Kirk took a key from the key rack on the wall by her desk. "My car's the one right in front of yours," she said as she locked up her office.

He got Rowdy back in the car, and followed Mrs. Kirk, who drove a BMW convertible. Business must have been good for Country Real Estate, Tim thought wryly, as he followed her off of the main street, down another street to the right, turning right again, and then finally left onto Wood's End Way. It was a dead-end street that ended in a treed woodland. The few houses on the street were neat and nicely kept. They stopped at the last house on the left, and to his surprise Tim felt an immediate affinity for the dwelling even before going inside.

It was a cottage, but it had charm and had been very well kept up. Getting out of his car, he opened the back door and took up Rowdy's leash to let him out. There was very little front lawn to the house because the garden beds on either side of the structure were wide and filled to overflowing with plants, giving them the appearance of English gardens.

The cottage was white painted brick with a dark slate roof. There was a bay window with a copper roof on its left. The window on the right was a four over four with black shutters on either side. The front door was painted red, and had a large brass knocker.

Mrs. Kirk took out her key, and opening the door, ushered them into a small central hallway. It was painted a cheerful pale yellow and had a white chair rail. "The living room is here to the left," she said.

Tim stepped into the room, which was also painted pale yellow. The bay window had a window seat with a tufted floral cushion. The fireplace mantel and its surround were white. The floors were wide board and varnished. Properly furnished, it would be a charming room in which to entertain.

"The smaller bedroom is directly across the hall," Mrs. Kirk said as she led the way. The room had two windows: the large one facing the front, and a small one on the side of the house. It was paneled in a light wood. "I think this would actually make a wonderful den," the real estate agent said. "Mrs. Torkelsen used it as a dining room because her kitchen is directly behind it." She opened a second door at the rear of the room, and they stepped into a very modern kitchen. The stove had six burners and a grill, along with two ovens. The refrigerator was large. There was a dishwasher and a double sink, one side of which was deep. Mrs. Kirk pulled back a louvered door, revealing a stackable washer and dryer. "As you can see, the kitchen has everything—even granite counters."

"It's very nice," Tim said. He had never expected to find anything quite like this in Egret Pointe.

"Let me show you the master bedroom," Mrs. Kirk said. "It's got a wonderful walk-in closet. Did I mention the house has a cellar beneath it? And there is some storage space above. The entry pulls down there." She pointed as they reached the rear of the center hall. "And here's the larger bedroom."

Tim stepped into the room and looked about. There were three windows: one on the side, and two at one end that looked out into a rear yard with woods behind it.

Mrs. Kirk opened the door to the closet and turned on a light. Then she pointed out the house's single bathroom, which, like the kitchen, was quite up to date, with a claw-foot tub, a separate glass and tile shower, a sink set in a cabinet, and a commode.

"Any thoughts?" Mrs. Kirk asked him as they came out into the hall again.

"How much?" Tim inquired.

"The heirs want a thousand a month," Mrs. Kirk ventured.

"I'll want a two-year lease with an option to purchase," Tim told her.

"They only wanted to rent for a year," Mrs. Kirk said in a regretful voice.

"I have a co-op in the city I have to sell," Tim told her. "The market is poor right now. Two years will give me a chance to see if I like Egret Pointe, and if Egret Pointe likes me. That's the term of my contract with the school board right now. I'll be a good tenant. I'll keep the gardens and lawn up for them. And I'm sure you can recommend a good cleaning woman to help me keep the place inside, although I'm actually a pretty neat guy. And Rowdy is a good dog. Right, Rowdy?"

At the mention of his name Rowdy, who had been dutifully following the two humans about this strange house, whined, cocking his head.

Mrs. Kirk smiled, and patted the dog again. Then she pulled out her cell. "Let's see if we can make the deal now, Mr. Blair." She pressed the numbers, and then said, "Mr. Torkelsen? This is Doris Kirk, Country Real Estate in Egret Pointe. I believe I have good news for you and your sister.

I have a client, the new principal of our Middle School, a single gentleman, who would like a two-year lease on your mother's house." She paused, listening. "Yes, I know, but to be candid with you, Mr. Torkelsen, I don't see the market coming back quickly here. Mr. Blair has a two-year contract with the school district, and if at the end of that term they decide to continue on together—and frankly, I don't see why they wouldn't—he would then purchase your mother's cottage. Yes, a two-year lease with an option to buy." She paused again, listening, then said, "I'm quite certain he could obtain a mortgage."

"It would be an all-cash deal," Tim said softly.

Mrs. Kirk raised an eyebrow, and then said, "Mr. Blair says it would be an all-cash deal, Mr. Torkelsen. I really don't see how you can go wrong. Would you like to speak to your sister, or shall I call her? Yes, I'll call her. We're in agreement then? A two-year lease with an option to purchase. Thank you so much." Mrs. Kirk snapped her phone shut. "He's in agreement, and his sister will do what he wants. I'll call her now. Forgive me for asking, but an all-cash deal?"

Tim Blair laughed. "From a guy driving an old Ford? The explanation is simple. I've been living in my late parents' co-op. I got permission from the co-op board to rent it out for two years with an option to purchase. My tenants are the daughter of the head of the co-op board and her husband. They're expecting a baby, and the parents on both sides are doing an all-cash deal with me in two years. In the meantime the expectant parents are paying me rent. The monthly co-op fee plus a little bit for my goodwill," he explained. "I expect in two years the co-op price will still be more than the price of this little house. I might even buy a new car." He chuckled. "I notice you didn't mention the dog."

"Why complicate matters?" Mrs. Kirk said. "Besides, haven't you told me that Rowdy is a good dog?" She smiled mischievously.

"Thank you," he said.

"Let me call Jean Torkelsen Rich now, and get this settled," Mrs. Kirk replied. She flipped her phone open, punched in some numbers and waited a moment. "Mrs. Rich? This is Doris Kirk from Country Real Estate in Egret Pointe. I've just gotten off the phone with your brother, Donald, and I have good news."

While she spoke Tim took the time to walk about the small house again. Opening a door in the kitchen, he descended into the basement. It was clean and dry. Coming up, he opened another door that led to a short covered breezeway with a flagstone floor. The garage was at its other end. Standing on the breezeway he looked out into the rear of the property. There was a small, neat, fenced-in vegetable garden and pristine green lawn. He wondered if he could adjust to living such a bucolic life.

"Mr. Blair?" Doris Kirk came out to join him on the breezeway. "Mrs. Torkelsen's daughter says it's a deal. I told you she would. Now when would you like to move into the cottage?"

"Today?"

"*Today?*" Mrs. Kirk was more than surprised.

"My furniture's arriving in Egret Pointe tomorrow," Tim Blair said. "I counted on finding a place today, and the Jacobses' lease on my co-op begins September first.

They wanted to paint and paper before they moved in. Lisa Jacobs's baby is due in November," he explained. "I thought I should give them a little time."

"Well, aren't you just the nicest man?" Doris Kirk said. "But where will you sleep, Mr. Blair?"

"I brought my sleeping bag," he said with a boyish grin. "I can eat supper out, and if you'll point me to the nearest market I'll get some stuff in for the morning."

Doris Kirk laughed. "I'll tell you what, Mr. Blair. You go shopping for your groceries, and I will make out the lease while you're gone. I'll need a month in advance, and a month for security. Your rent will be due the first of every month. Now, if you'll follow me, I'll get you to our IGA. There's a large chain at the mall, but that's a bit of a drive today. The IGA is perfectly fine, and most of Egret Pointe shops there unless they need something very special. Come back to my office when you're finished."

He followed her back outside to where their cars were parked, and she led him quickly to the town's local market. Tim parked the Ford beneath a large maple tree in the center of the parking lot. He cracked the windows generously for Rowdy, and filled his water bowl on the backseat from a bottle of water he had been sipping from on the drive out from the city. Then he went into the market and did his shopping. Milk, orange juice, half-and-half, a box of Newman's Own Honey Nut-O's, rye bread, some dry and some moist dog food. He stopped at the deli counter for the honey-maple ham/swiss combination, some cole slaw, and potato salad. He considered a six-pack of beer, but picked up one of Dr Pepper instead. No need starting gossip.

At the register, the girl checked him out efficiently. "Are you visiting?" she asked him, curious, assuming he was a summer person.

"I'm Tim Blair, the new Middle School principal," he answered.

"*Oh!*" the checker said, looking him over more closely. "My son is going into Middle School next month. Nice to meet you, Mr. Blair."

"Who is the owner of the old brown car?" A woman had stepped into the market. She was a tall redhead who looked like a retired supermodel. "There is a dog locked in that car, and he's howling, poor thing," the woman continued.

"That would be my car, and my dog," Tim said.

"This is Mr. Blair, the new Middle School principal, Miss Kathy," the checker said.

"I hope you will treat your students better than that poor dog of yours," Kathryn St. John said. "You ought to be ashamed of yourself, sir!"

"The car is under a large tree. The windows are open, and Rowdy has water," Tim defended himself. "I have been in the market ten minutes. What more did you expect me to do, madam? It was the car, or an empty house with which Rowdy was not familiar. I chose the car." *Damned woman*, he thought irritably.

"Then why is the poor creature howling?" she angrily demanded to know. She hated thoughtlessness toward animals.

"It's his first time in Egret Pointe, and as I'm not settled yet I thought it better to keep him with me. But dogs are not allowed in markets, ma'am. Rowdy is just a little scared without me. I'm going out to my *old brown car* now, and you are welcome to come along and check him out. Are you a veterinarian?"

"Well, Kathryn St. John, I can assure you that Rowdy is spoiled rotten, well fed, loved, and has all his shots," Tim told her, his blue eyes meeting her hazel green ones. Lordy, she was really a beauty. Was that hair color natural? It had to be, given her pale cream-colored skin.

"My last name is pronounced *Sin Gin,* Mr. Blair," Kathryn said. What an arrogant man he was. And that boyish engaging grin was probably used to great advantage. Well, she wasn't about to be taken in by blue eyes and a winning smile.

"I shall remember that in future, ma'am. Now if you'll excuse me, even I can hear Rowdy's howling at this point." Tim gathered up his groceries, and walked from the market. "Good day, Miss St. John."

"How rude! What an insufferable man!" Kathryn St. John said irritably. And how did he know she was a *Miss?*

"I think he's kinda cute," the checker responded, gazing after Tim as he went to his car. "He looks like a nice guy, Miss Kathy."

Tim could feel the women staring after him as he made his way to the car. Rowdy practically turned himself inside out at the sight of him. Tim opened the trunk of the car and put the grocery bags inside, slamming the lid down, and got into the driver's side. He turned and looked at the dog. "When did I ever mistreat or desert you, you overgrown mutt? Here I am telling everyone what a good dog you are, and you howl like a banshee just because I leave you alone for a few minutes," Tim said.

Rowdy licked his face, making happy-dog noises.

Tim laughed. "Go lie down," he ordered the dog. "We have a lease to sign, and then we're going to our new home. You're going to have your own yard, Rowdy."

He put the car in gear and drove back to Mrs. Kirk's office. She was waiting with four copies of the lease for him to sign. His late father had been an attorney. He had taught Tim to read anything he was going to sign. The lease was pretty boilerplate. He noted one small clause that read *the price of the house to be determined by current market conditions at the time of the sale*. He initialed it, signed where indicated, and pulled out his checkbook.

"It's a city bank's account," he told Mrs. Kirk.

"As long as it's good," she told him with a smile. "If you're interested in opening a local account, Egret Pointe National Savings Bank is reliable and safe."

"Thanks," Tim said. "I'll open the account tomorrow. Can you tell me the official address of my new home?"

"It's Sixty Wood's End Way," Mrs. Kirk replied.

Pulling out his cell phone, Tim pressed in a number, waited, then said, "Hi, this is Timothy Blair. Your van can deliver my stuff to Sixty Wood's End Way in Egret Pointe tomorrow. Give my cell number to your driver. My cleaning woman will be at the apartment at eight A.M. to let you in and lock up afterwards. Yeah, thanks." He snapped the phone shut.

"My goodness," Doris Kirk said. "You are certainly very efficient, Mr. Blair. Here are your keys to the house. They are the only set in existence."

Tim took the keys, and then said, "Do you have a cleaning woman you can recommend, Mrs. Kirk?"

"I do. Mrs. Bills, but she's very particular about who she will clean for, so let me give her your number, and she'll call you."

"Fair enough," Tim said. "Thanks so much for finding me such nice shelter. I want to spend the rest of the week getting settled. Next Monday I have to get back to work and meet my teachers. School starts in just a few weeks."

"It was a pleasure doing business with you, Mr. Blair. Good luck!"

When he had left her office and driven off, Doris Kirk picked up her desk phone and dialed a number. The phone rang three times and was picked up. "Evie, it's Doris Kirk. I've just rented the Torkelsen house to the new Middle School principal. He asked me if I could suggest a cleaning woman. I told him you, and that you would call him."

"What's he like?" Evie Bills asked.

"Handsome, well-spoken, and has a little money, from what I can gather," Doris Kirk said. "I liked him. No-nonsense type. Came out from the city today to rent, and his moving van arrives tomorrow. He brought a sleeping bag for tonight. Has a dog. A silly-looking shaggy terrier mix with big brown eyes named Rowdy. The dog adores him."

"Well, that says something," Evie Bills replied. "Dogs don't adore bad guys. How am I going to call him if he hasn't had a phone installed yet? Does he have a cell?"

"He does," Mrs. Kirk said, "but I don't have the number. I forgot to take it down before he left. He called me a few days ago, told me who he was, what he wanted, and said he'd be here this morning before eleven. He was. The Torkelsens agreed. He signed the lease, and went off.

I know he has a cell, because he called his moving company from my office. They're coming in tomorrow with his things."

"I'll take care of it," Evie Bills said. "Thanks for the reference. I'll let you know what I decide to do." Then she rang off. At eight thirty the following morning, Evie Bills knocked on the front door at Sixty Wood's End Way. When it opened she smiled up at the tall man standing in his pajamas. "Mr. Blair? I'm Mrs. Bills. I understand you're looking for someone to clean. I would have called, but Doris Kirk didn't think to get your cell number. May I come in? I've brought some nice strong brewed coffee, and cinnamon rolls fresh from my oven." She stepped past him. "We're going to have to get going if the house is going to be ready for your movers. What time do you expect them?"

Rowdy bounded up to Mrs. Bills.

"About one o'clock," Tim said. "I expect the movers around one."

"Any empty house goes quicker," Mrs. Bills said, going straight for the kitchen. "Can Rowdy have a little treat?"

Tim nodded, slightly dazed by this small dynamo. "Sure," he said.

Mrs. Bills set her large satchel of a bag on a kitchen counter. Reaching into it, she pulled out a thermos, two small china mugs, a square plastic box with a lid, and a steak bone wrapped in Glad Wrap. She unwrapped the bone and handed it to the dog.

Rowdy's eyes danced as he took the bone gently from her fingers.

Tim took the dog by the collar and led him out to the breezeway with his bone. "Stay, Rowdy," he told the animal. Rowdy lay down, gnawing on the bone between his two big front paws. Returning to the kitchen, Tim found the mugs filled with coffee, and the square plastic box opened to reveal the sweet rolls. "He'll be your slave for life," Tim said. He sipped the coffee, and taking a roll, took a bite. "And so will I. These are absolutely delicious, Mrs. Bills. Thank you."

"You have nice manners, Mr. Blair. I charge fifteen dollars an hour. I'll do your cleaning, the laundry, and if you want to leave me a list, I'll do the shopping once a week for you. Hank at the IGA will set up a house account for you. I'll come in twice weekly. Tuesdays and Fridays if that's suitable."

"Yes," Tim said. "Are you an angel?" He smiled at her.

Mrs. Bills chuckled. "Doris Kirk said you had charm, and you do. Now finish your roll and coffee and get dressed. With no curtains on those windows everyone in Egret Pointe will be talking. This is a small town, Mr. Blair, and gossip is the chief entertainment in a small town. Since we're agreed I'll go home and get some cleaning supplies. I don't imagine you thought to pick up any yesterday afternoon at the IGA."

"Guilty as charged, ma'am," he replied.

She nodded. "Be dressed by the time I get back, which will be in fifteen minutes, Mr. Blair. I don't live far." And then Mrs. Bills was gone out his front door.

Timothy Blair laughed, genuinely amused. Mrs. Bills was a character for certain, but he knew right away that she was a godsend, and they were going to get along. He suspected that even if she had had his cell phone number she wouldn't have called. She would have come because she wanted to get a look at him, evaluate the situation. If she hadn't liked him, she wouldn't have offered to work for him. Timothy Blair realized that he was very lucky. He would remember to thank Doris Kirk.

By the time the movers arrived that afternoon, closer to two than one, Tim noted, Mrs. Bills had washed all the windows, vacuumed the floors, dusted the woodwork and the bookshelves on either side of the fireplace, and cleaned the bathroom and the entire kitchen.

"Martha Torkelsen kept a clean stove and fridge," Mrs. Bills observed, "but the house has been shut up for almost six months now. You know where you want the furniture placed?"

"Pretty much," Tim said.

"Do you have carpets?" she wanted to know.

He nodded. "Too many for this house, I'm afraid. I had them cleaned and wrapped before the movers came. I had the cleaner mark the sizes on the wrapping."

"Good," she said. "They can unload the carpets first. I'll tell you which one will fit the living room, which one your bedroom. What are you going to do in the old dining room? Will you need a carpet in there? And what about a runner for this hall? The floors will be ruined if they don't have a runner."

"I'm going to use the smaller room as a study," he said. "And no, I don't have a runner. Is there somewhere I can go and purchase one?"

"I'll take you myself as soon as the movers have left," Mrs. Bills said firmly.

When the van from the city pulled up, his angel, as Tim had begun to think of Mrs. Bills, was outside immediately, directing it to back into the driveway. And then she took complete charge of the movers. "I'll want the carpets before you take a single thing off of that truck," she said.

"No can do, lady," the driver said. "Them carpets was loaded up first."

Hands on her ample hips, Evie Bills looked up at the driver. "Now, my dear," she said in reasonable tones, "I can't have you bringing furniture into the house with no carpets to set them on. You're putting the cart before the horse. I'm sure you can get those carpets out for me, and then set the rolls on the drive so Mr. Blair and I can see which go where. Some will have to go into the cellar, as this wee house isn't as big as his apartment in New York, is it?" She smiled at him.

The van driver considered her words.

"And when you boys are finished, I've a nice plate of sandwiches just made, for I expect you've had no lunch yet, and a fresh batch of cookies I baked this morning for you," Mrs. Bills said.

The van driver laughed. "All right," he said. "I expect we'll get to those sandwiches and cookies a lot faster if we do what you say, lady."

"Indeed you will," Mrs. Bills agreed.

"Mike! Pete! Get them carpets first, and lay the rolls in the drive. The lady will tell you where they go," the van driver said with a chuckle.

Timothy Blair watched in amazement as Mrs. Bills handled the rough movers with all the skill of a lion tamer. The carpets were unloaded, and the cleaning woman identified which ones would fit in the three rooms needing them. None of them would clash with the upholstered furniture. One, an antique green Chinese floral, would go in the living room. A dark red-and-blue antique Persian rug was laid in his study; a beige-and-blue Oriental rug fit perfectly from wall to wall in his bedroom. The three remaining carpets were directed to the cellar.

"I'll have Mr. Bills come in and build you some racks," Mrs. Bills said. "Those carpets have to be off the floor. This is a good, dry basement, but still." She then proceeded to have the furniture off-loaded into the driveway bit by bit, while Tim indicated which would go in which room. Mrs. Bills had those pieces set aside in one spot on the little front lawn. The rest of it was left in the drive.

When the truck had been completely unloaded, Mrs. Bills sent Tim back into the house so he might show the movers where the living room furniture should be placed, then his study, and finally his bedroom. The rest was taken down into the cellar for storage. Her method was surprisingly efficient and quick. When they had finished, Mrs. Bills brought the moving men sandwiches and cookies as she had promised, along with paper cups of iced tea.

The van driver said, "Hey, lady, you want to come along with us on our next job? I don't think we ever got a truck unloaded so fast. And thanks for the lunch. Me and the boys don't usually get treated so nice."

"You're good workers, all of you," Mrs. Bills said with a smile.

Tim then tipped the men and thanked them while Mrs. Bills gave the driver a bag of her cookies for the road. "You really are an angel," he told the cleaning woman.

She chuckled. "Get into my car, Mr. Blair, and we'll go get that runner for your hallway. It's not quite four, and the carpet shop doesn't close until five thirty."

She didn't take him into the village, but rather drove the several miles to the nearby mall. In the carpet store they found a plain beige hemp runner with a geometric design woven into it for the center hall of the house. He purchased it

"Just right!" Mrs. Bills approved when they had gotten back to the house and laid it down on the polished wood floor after she had mopped it free of the movers' shoe prints.

"Now you don't have to pay me today, but so you know, it's eight hours. Once a week, on Fridays, will be fine. Find the draperies and curtains you want hung. I'll send my mister over tomorrow to put up your rods. I opened the box marked bed linens and made your bed, Mr. Blair. And I've left those cinnamon rolls for your breakfast in the morning. Good afternoon. See you Friday!" And she was gone out the door.

Timothy Blair went into his now perfectly arranged living room, and sat down with an audible sound of relief. Rowdy came and put his head in Tim's lap with a sigh. Tim laughed softly. "Well, boy," he said, "here we are. This is home for at least the next two years. I know I did the right thing resigning as assistant headmaster at Kensington Academy. David Grainger was going to remain headmaster there till hell froze over. And then the board would have considered me too old." He scratched the dog's head. "Better we make a fresh start out here in the boonies, but from what I can see, Egret Pointe isn't too bad a place to be. I just hope its citizens aren't all like that starchy librarian we met yesterday at the IGA. Still, it was nice she was worried about you, you old faker."

Rowdy whined, looking up at Tim with liquid chocolate eyes.

"Yeah, she was kinda hot for an older woman, wasn't she?" Tim mused. "Maybe we should pay a visit to the library and find out what kinds of programs she offers for the Middle School students. We all know reading is the key to everything, but with all the distractions these kids face today—cell phones, BlackBerrys, texting, and Twittering—a lot of them forget books. We don't want that to happen now, Rowdy, do we?"

Rowdy barked as if in agreement with Tim. The man stood up and began to look about him. It was amazing. Yesterday this house had been empty, devoid of an inhabitant. Now it was all furnished again. He needed the draperies and the curtains up, true. And there were boxes to be unpacked, but he could fix himself a meal and he would sleep in his own bed tonight, not on the floor in a sleeping bag. With a few more hours of daylight left on this late-summer's day, Tim began to unpack the book cartons and immediately saw a problem.

An only child, he had inherited his family's co-op apartment in a prestigious old prewar building in the city. The apartment had had a big wide foyer, a walnut-paneled formal living room with a working fireplace flanked with floor-to-ceiling bookcases, a formal dining room, a kitchen with a butler's pantry and maid's quarters with a bath, a paneled library with a second working fireplace and built-in bookshelves, four large bedrooms, and four bathrooms.

It was a corner apartment facing west and north over the park. It was the only home he had ever known.

Born to older parents—his mother was in her mid-thirties and his father over fifty when he appeared on the scene—he had first gone to school in the city, then to prep school in New England, and finally college in the same region. From the time he was eight until he was sixteen, he had spent his summers at Mohegan Camp for Boys in the Adirondacks. The summer he was seventeen he had accompanied his mother to Europe for three months. His father had joined them in Tuscany in mid-August.

Timothy Blair had loved his parents. They weren't at all disappointed when he decided to teach English. And they were proud when he gained the position of assistant headmaster of Kensington Academy. His father hadn't retired until he was eighty, and he hadn't died until a year ago. His mother had died three years earlier of bone cancer.

It was after she died that Tim had moved in to watch over his increasingly frail but still mentally acute father. He had been living previously in a condo he owned. He had, on his father's advice, sold it and simply put his profit in bank CDs.

The law firm in which his father had been a named partner saw to the probate of his parents' will. And there Timothy Blair suddenly found himself, rattling about in a large apartment, stuck in a dead-end job. It didn't matter to him that he had money in the bank, and would have a helluva lot more when he sold his folks' apartment. He was bored, and bored was not good. And then one of the lawyers in his dad's old firm, a man with whom he played squash once a week, told him of a job opening out of the city.

"My cousin, Joe, and his wife live in this cute small town called Egret Pointe. The principal of their Middle School has to retire. She's expecting quintuplets. They're looking for a new principal. Think you might be interested?"

"Why would you ask?" Tim said.

"Hey, buddy, you're bored. I can tell," Ray Pietro d'Angelo said. "We both know you'll never be headmaster at Kensington. Your folks are gone. You need a fresh start. Egret Pointe is a nice town. My cousin, Joe, is on the school board. Want me to give him a call?"

Why not? Timothy Blair had thought to himself. It couldn't hurt to interview. He didn't have to take it if they offered. "Sure, go ahead, Ray."

"Hey, as my wife would say, what can it hurt?" Ray replied with a grin.

And so Timothy Blair had driven out to Egret Pointe in late June to interview.

He had liked the school board. They had liked him. As the assistant headmaster of Kensington Academy he had the experience the school board needed. He was young enough to appeal to the kids and the parents. With a Master's in school administration and management, and a doctorate in English literature, he had possessed far more qualifications than they could have hoped for, and they offered him the job on the spot. He accepted without hesitation because deep down something told him this was the absolute right thing to do.

He returned to the city and gave his notice. His headmaster was surprised but understood. He was smart enough to know that he was eventually going to lose Tim Blair. Tim was too smart to be content in an assistant headmaster's position forever. Good opportunities didn't come around that often. He wished his former assistant luck. And now here Timothy Blair was, two months later, sitting in the living room of a little house on a street called Wood's End Way in a town called Egret Pointe.

Rowdy whined, looking toward the door. "Okay, old boy. You want your walk," Tim said. Standing up, he went to fetch the dog's lead, the pooper scooper, and bag. There was still plenty of light as they walked down the street. Neighbors were out watering lawns, sitting on porches.

"Good evening, Mr. Blair."

"Welcome to Egret Pointe, Mr. Blair."

"That's a fine-looking dog, Mr. Blair."

Voices called to him as he and Rowdy strolled by. "Thank you," he replied. "Good evening. Say thank you, Rowdy." Rowdy tilted his head, his floppy ears cocked, and he barked.

"Why, isn't that just the cutest thing?" a woman on a porch said.

How on earth did they know his name already? Tim wondered. And then he remembered Mrs. Kirk's remark about gossip being a form of entertainment in small towns. He grinned to himself as he walked along. A small short-haired Jack Russell terrier bounded off a lawn, yapping. Tim stopped, giving Rowdy a soft command as he did. Rowdy sat down immediately, patiently waiting for the terrier to calm itself.

"MacTavish, come!" A gray-haired woman hurried from a house. "I am sorry, Mr. Blair. Jack Russells are so territorial. Ben," she called to a man obviously her husband, "come and get MacTavish. My goodness, how well behaved Rowdy is. I'm Gloria Sullivan." She smiled, holding out a hand. "I teach seventh grade."

"It's very nice to meet you, Mrs. Sullivan," Tim said, shaking the woman's hand.

How the hell had she known Rowdy's name?

"Ben Sullivan," the man now holding MacTavish said, offering a hand to shake. "I suppose you know you're the talk of the town," he said with a grin. "You a golfer?"

Tim shook his head. "My father was, but it never interested me much. I played squash in the city."

Ben Sullivan nodded. "They got a good court at the country club. One of your perks as the new principal is a membership there. Think you're going to like it here?"

"I don't know," Tim said candidly. "I've never lived out of the city, but I have to admit Doris Kirk found me the perfect house. The apartment in the city was way too big for one man after my parents died."

"No wife?" Gloria Sullivan said. "Heaven help you, Mr. Blair. Every single woman in Egret Pointe will be chasing after you."

"Unless you're gay," Ben Sullivan said. "You gay?"

Tim laughed. "No," he said. "Just a little slow with the ladies. I spent the last three years looking after my widowed dad. Between that and my job there didn't seem to be any time for a personal life." He smiled his winning smile at Gloria Sullivan. "I'll rely on you, Mrs. Sullivan, to help me sort out all the ladies who are going to come after me. Well, I'd best be getting home now that Rowdy has had his walk. Oh, perhaps before I head back, you might tell me something about your librarian. I'm afraid I had a bit of a run-in with her yesterday."

"We heard," Ben Sullivan said. "She's something else, Miss Kathy. Descends from one of the original families who founded Egret Pointe in the seventeen hundreds. Her family built the library, and the librarians have all been St. John women. She can be a bit intimidating at times. I heard your car windows were open, and your dog had water. No need for her to carry on like she did."

"Rowdy got a little frightened when I left him to grab some groceries," Tim explained. "He set up quite a howl, and I think she thought he was harmed. She's obviously not a dog person, I guess."

"Miss Kathy? Nah," Ben Sullivan said. "A pet would spoil that perfect, orderly life she lives."

"Ben!" his wife scolded him. "Miss Kathy isn't your mother's librarian, Mr. Blair. She's modernized the library, added wonderful programs for the children, for the seniors, for young mothers and families."

"And spent the budget on a bunch of silly women's books," Ben grumbled.

"That isn't so at all," Gloria Sullivan said. "My husband doesn't think popular commercial fiction like romance is literature. But it is! And thanks to Miss Kathy you get to read all the latest suspense and thrillers that come out, Ben, so hush up."

"I thought I would go and make my peace with the lady tomorrow," Tim said.

"I think that's a wonderful idea," Gloria Sullivan encouraged him. "You know she runs a terrific summer reading program for the Elementary and Middle School students. Ask her about it when you see her."

"I will," Tim said. "Good night now, Mr. and Mrs. Sullivan." He turned back to his little house. Rowdy was tugging on his leash now, anxious for a bowl of food before settling himself on Tim's bed for a good night's sleep. Tim wanted to make himself a sandwich. He hadn't eaten much today with all the excitement of moving in.

He slept surprisingly well that night, awakening even before his alarm went off at seven. Getting up, he showered, shaved, and let Rowdy out in the backyard. He didn't want to miss Mr. Bills. Draperies and curtains were an absolute must. He'd undressed in the lighted walk-in closet the night before, and dressed there this morning. Putting on a pot of coffee, he reheated several of Mrs. Bills's cinnamon rolls, and sat down to eat.

Mr. Bills arrived at eight o'clock, pulling his truck into the drive, and coming in from the breezeway. " 'Spect you know who I am," he said. "The missus sent me down to get your curtain rods up. Let's see what you got to hang, Mr. Blair."

"I put the cartons over here," Tim said, "opened them last night, and laid everything in the proper rooms before I turned in for the night." He led Mr. Bills to the living room.

The handyman examined how the curtains should be hung, nodded, and grunted to himself. Then he followed Tim into the study and finally the bedroom, where he repeated the same proceedure. "The missus says you should have a small shade for the bathroom. She gave me the size, and I picked it up at the hardware store for you along with the rods you'll need. She told me what rods to put in the kitchen and on the back door. Says she'll discuss what goes there with you on Friday. No need for you to stand around, Mr. Blair. You go about your business, and I'll go about mine."

"How do I pay you, Mr. Bills?" Tim asked.

"I'll leave the bill on the kitchen table," came the reply. "You can give the money to the missus on Friday. She'll give it to me. I'll start in the living room." He picked up the toolbox he had brought into the house with him and exited the kitchen.

Tim fed Rowdy, who had come in with Mr. Bills, then put his dishes in the dishwasher. Going down the hall to his bedroom, he made his bed. Then, going to his study, he began to unpack the rest of the books and get his computer and desk set up.

When Mr. Bills finally came into the study, Tim went to the living room to see how the handyman had fared. The valances were set perfectly. The slim, heavy draperies with their sheer curtains hung perfectly.

Tim emptied the remaining cartons of books he wanted to keep. He quickly discovered there wasn't enough room for all the volumes that had come out of the apartment. He intended donating what he didn't want to the library. He had already given his father's law library to Ray Pietro d'Angelo. Ray's gratitude made him glad he had given those books to someone who would appreciate them. And his father would have been pleased. He had always liked Ray.

By eleven o'clock Mr. Bills had finished the job he had been sent to do. "I'm leaving the bill on the table, Mr.

Blair," he called out. "Give the missus cash if you don't mind. I prefer cash on jobs like these."

Tim caught the handyman before he got out the breezeway door. "You did a spectacular job," he said, complimenting Mr. Bills. "Thanks so much."

Mr. Bills smiled slightly. "Glad to oblige, Mr. Blair. Good morning." And the handyman was gone, out to his truck.

"Rowdy," Tim called. "Let's take a walk to the library." He clipped the leash onto the dog's collar, made certain his keys were in his pocket, and headed out the door.

The mail woman walking her route patted Rowdy on the head, and greeted him by name. Tim smiled and nodded at her, noting she put some mail in the box in front of his house. He'd check when he got back, but right now he had to focus on making a friend of Egret Pointe's starchy librarian, Kathryn St. John, pronounced *Sin Gin*. If he couldn't win her over, then maybe Rowdy could. Rowdy was good at winning women's hearts, even if his master wasn't.

CHAPTER THREE

The sign on the front door of the brick Victorian library said most distinctly SHIRTS AND SHOES. NO DOGS ALLOWED. Of course no dogs, Tim thought. Miss St. John obviously didn't like dogs, even if she had a soft spot for what she thought was an abused animal. Deciding to check out the library anyway, Tim tied Rowdy's leash to the old-fashioned black iron hitching post. "Sit. Stay, Rowdy," he commanded the dog. Then he patted him on the head. "I'll be back, boy. You just wait for me."

Rowdy thumped his tail and whined softly as Tim moved away from him.

"It's all right, boy. *Stay*," Tim repeated. He entered the library, surprised to find given its exterior how light and bright it was. He walked up to the slightly curved walnut front desk. "Good morning. Is Miss St. John available?" he asked the pretty woman standing behind the counter.

"I'll see if she is, Mr. Blair," the woman said. "I'm Mavis Peabody." She held out a hand, which he shook. "Nice to meet you."

"Same here," Tim responded. He had stopped wondering how everyone knew who he was, and knew Rowdy's name.

Mavis Peabody turned and hurried back to Kathryn's office. "Kathy!" she said excitedly. "*He's here!* Mr. Blair, the new Middle School principal. He's asking for you. Do you want me to bring him back here to your office?"

Kathryn St. John was surprised. What could that irritating man possibly want of her? She stood up, involuntarily smoothing her skirt and reaching up to be certain her hair was neat. "No, I'll come out." She moved quickly past Mavis, seeing him almost immediately. She had been so mad about the poor dog the other day, she hadn't really bothered to look closely at him. She took a moment now to do so. Tall. Maybe six three or six four. Unusual. She had never met a man as tall as that. Clean shaven. Nicely barbered chestnut brown hair with just a touch of gray at the sides. Khakis, a dark green tee that revealed a toned body. Good grief! Why was she possibly considering that aspect of the man? "Good morning, Mr. Blair," she greeted him.

"Good morning, Miss St. John," Tim replied. "I thought I'd come by and apologize for any harsh words I might have uttered the other day over our little misunderstanding."

She was surprised, but good manners dictated she accept the apology. "That's very kind of you," Kathryn answered him. "I'm afraid my concern for your dog caused me to act in haste without fully evaluating the situation, Mr. Blair. I hope you'll accept my apology too." There! She had reciprocated. It would be over and done. She waited for him to say good-bye.

Instead he smiled. "I can't fault a woman with a kind heart toward the beasties," he said. "And Rowdy can sound so pitiful when he howls."

"It sounded like he was dying," Kathryn admitted.

"I understand from my neighbor, Mrs. Sullivan, that you have a wonderful summer reading program for the Elementary and Middle Schools. Can you tell me about it? Do you give the kids an initial list of books to read? Or let them pick from a larger list? And what incentives do you offer, and how do you know they actually read the book that they checked out?"

Kathryn was impressed that after being in town for two days he knew about the summer reading program. And at that point she noticed that he had blue eyes. Startlingly bright blue eyes. She swallowed hard. What was the matter with her? "I start the children off with a list of six books," Kathryn told him. "They have to come and give me a verbal report. I hold a reporting session every Friday morning between eleven A.M. and twelve. I take each child individually into my office to report to me. That way they can't cheat. When those six books are read and reported properly, the students are given a total of sixty points. Their names and points are posted where everyone can see them on the bulletin board behind the checkout counter. After that they get to choose their own reading material, but they still have to report to me.

"For the first one hundred points they are awarded a

coupon for an ice-cream cone at Walt's. Reach two hundred points and you get a two-scoop sundae. Reach three hundred and you win a banana split with three scoops of ice cream, three sauces, whipped cream, and a cherry." Kathryn smiled. "We're going to have at least five three-hundred-point winners by summer's end this year. Three are in the Middle School, which is pretty good considering the distractions kids that age are bombarded with nowadays."

"Agreed," he said. "I think you've devised a great program, Miss St. John! Maybe next summer you'll allow me to offer a few suggestions for reading material?"

"Of course," Kathryn answered, surprised he would even be interested. His predecessor had never cared. She had been grateful for the program, and left it up to the library to do it. "I do try and challenge the children."

"Yes, that's a good thing. Make it too simple and they're bored," he said.

Suddenly they both heard Rowdy begin to howl.

"I never knew a clingy dog," Kathryn said, half irritated.

"He's not clingy." Tim defended his animal. "That's his *Help! I'm scared* howl." He turned and went back outside. Rowdy was hunkered down, attempting to make himself invisible behind the hitching post. He was shaking. Seeing Tim, he yelped and tried to leap at him, but his leash, still tied to the post, hindered him. "It's all right, boy," Tim assured him, kneeling down to put comforting arms about Rowdy.

"What on earth is the matter with him?" Kathryn, who had followed him outside, asked. "He's absolutely shaking all over. Is he sick? You did say he had had his shots."

Tim looked about, and then he spotted it. A large, fat ginger tabby cat was seated beneath a blue hydrangea bush, calmly washing its paws and staring directly at Rowdy. "That's the problem," Tim said, pointing to the feline.

"*The cat?* What on earth could Dickens have done to that dog of yours that's caused him to go all to pieces like that?" Kathryn asked him.

"Rowdy is afraid of cats," Tim told her with an apologetic grin.

"A dog afraid of cats?" she said disbelieving. "Nonsense!"

"Not at all," Tim replied. "I got Rowdy from friends who lived in the country. He was one of three puppies born to their dog after a casual encounter with a neighbor's male dog. When he was about six weeks old he found the family's litter of two-week-old kittens. He didn't hurt them. He was just curious. The mother cat attacked him, however. She scratched him up pretty badly, and he's been afraid of cats ever since."

"Good grief!" Kathryn exclaimed. Then she added, "Poor Rowdy."

Dickens the cat now stepped nonchalantly from beneath the bush, and while Rowdy practically clung to Tim the feline strolled down the brick walkway. Kathryn could have sworn it had a smug smile upon its face.

"I guess I've caused enough excitement for today," Tim Blair said with a smile.

She noticed that the smile extended all the way to his eyes, and that his teeth were even. What was the matter with her? Kathryn thought. She wasn't a woman to assess a man's good and bad points as if he were a race-horse. "Rowdy can't help it that cats scare him," Kathryn said. She reached out to pat the dog. "He's a good fellow. You've got a good house for a dog. I hear you rented the Torkelsen place. It has a lovely backyard. Martha was a sweet woman. She always returned her books on time, and brought us produce from her garden every summer."

"The garden's overgrown right now, but I'll start it up again next summer," he said. "I like fresh vegetables," Tim told her. He wondered what she would look like with that hair of hers loose and falling over her shoulders. And those breasts of hers were perfect. Just how old was she? "Rowdy and I had better get going," he finally said. "The week is half gone, and I've got to prepare to meet my staff next Monday morning. Can I get a library card for myself? I'm a reader when I have the time."

"What genre, or are you non-fiction?" she asked.

"Most fiction genres, and non-fiction," he told her.

"I'll have a card ready for you next time you come by the library," Kathryn said. She'd know soon enough what he liked to read, she thought, and then wondered why the hell she would possibly care. "Good-bye, Mr. Blair."

"Good day, Miss St. John," he responded, and untying the leash, he walked off, Rowdy bouncing along by his side.

Kathryn watched him go. *Nice butt,* she thought, and then chuckled. She had been assessing him the whole time he was with her. She couldn't recall the last time a man had interested her enough to look him over. And maybe it was just because he was new in town. Probably that was it. She walked back into the library where Mavis was waiting eagerly for Kathryn to tell all.

"Well?" her best friend asked.

"Well, what? He apologized for the other day in the IGA parking lot. I apologized in return. We talked about the summer reading program. He wants a library card."

"That's it?" Mavis said.

"He's got a nice butt," Kathryn replied.

Mavis laughed. "That's a rare commentary from you," she said. "Usually it's the men salivating over your butt."

Kathryn grinned. "Yeah. Go figure!"

"You like him," Mavis said.

"I hardly know him, but yes, I think he's a nice guy," Kathryn admitted. "Now let me go and eat my yogurt. I've got Rina Seligmann coming in to discuss a possible family program for the autumn at two." She turned without another word and went back to her office. Pulling the foil lid off of her boysenberry yogurt, she took a spoon from her desk and began to eat. To her surprise her mind wandered back to Timothy Blair. Well, he was cute. No, *cute* wasn't the right word, nor was *handsome*. His good looks, however, exuded the kind of masculinity she hadn't seen in a long while. Or maybe she hadn't been out of Egret Pointe in a while. Usually single women were left pretty much to their own devices in a small town, but she never had been. She had a lot of friends, her own age, older and younger. She actually had a social life when she chose to have one.

But the men in her life were all married with few exceptions. And until now she hadn't cared. And why did she suddenly care now?

Rina Seligmann arrived unannounced. "You're thinking," she said as she came into Kathryn's office and sat down in a chair. "Is that good?"

Kathryn laughed. "Dumb abstract thoughts," she said.

"Sam and I had a rather interesting idea," Rina began. "We thought it might be a good idea to do a family-oriented program during the Jewish holidays. Explain the different dates for the different new years worldwide. Show how they are similar, and how they are different, how some are tied in with the harvest and others not, and why."

"What a great idea!" Kathryn agreed. "Ignorance about other cultures and faiths is the basis of prejudice, I'm certain. A program such as you're suggesting shows how alike we actually are despite our differences. Yes! Tell me the date you want, and make it so, Rina. I love stuff that brings a light into the darkness."

"I heard the new Middle School principal was in the library today. I also heard you two had a dust-up in the IGA parking lot on Monday." Rina chuckled.

"It was a misunderstanding, more on my part actually. Here was this adorable shaggy dog howling its heart out in a locked car. Without checking out the situation, I barreled into the market and demanded to know who had left their dog in a locked car on a sunny August afternoon. Turns out the windows in the car were open, the dog had a water dish, and was just howling because he was scared. Mr. Blair put me quite firmly in my place." She smiled. "Then he came in this morning to apologize, so I apologized too, and we got to talking about the summer reading program."

"Mavis has high hopes," Rina teased as she stood up, preparing to leave.

"Mavis should stop trying to get me married off. I'm too young to get married," Kathryn said with a grin.

Rina chortled.

"Do you know how he ended up here in Egret Pointe?" Kathryn was curious.

"I think Joe Pietro d'Angelo had something to do with it. Ask him," Rina said. "I gotta run. I promised Emily I'd babysit Sean Michael while she runs to the obstetrician. Sam will be tickled you like the idea. Later!"

When Rina had left, Kathryn picked up the phone and dialed the law offices of Johnson and Pietro d'Angelo. "Tell me about Timothy Blair," she said to Joe Pietro d'Angelo when he came on the line.

"What do you want to know?"

"How did he end up in Egret Pointe?" Kathryn said.

"My cousin, Ray, in the city suggested him. They play squash together, and Ray knew he wasn't happy where he was."

"Why not?"

"No chance for advancement. The guy is forty-three, Kathy. He was the assistant headmaster. The head was your age, and he was going to hang in for a long time. So when Ray and Rose were here over the Memorial Day weekend, and Mrs. Riley dropped her bombshell, I knew we were going to need a new guy. Ray said his squash partner might be just the person for us. I asked Ray to have his friend get in touch with us if he was interested. He was. He came out and interviewed with the board just before the end of June. He's got degrees up the wazoo, including one in administration and management. He had the experience. We liked him, so we offered him the job."

"You offered him a job before you did a thorough background check?" Kathryn asked. "Was that wise, Joe?" She was surprised. Joe Pietro d'Angelo was usually a lot more careful than that. "I know the school board was hesitant to pick someone already in their employ for a lot of reasons, but to just hire a stranger seems chancy."

"We did our background check before he even interviewed," Joe told her. "We figured if we liked the guy and everything checked out, we had better hire him while we could get him. Timothy Blair is clean as a whistle. Never been arrested, not even for speeding. Never been married, but not gay. He was engaged once but she was killed in a hit-and-run accident. When his mother died, he came home to look after his father. That was his life for the last couple of years. Taking care of his old man, and working. Adopted the dog he has as a puppy from friends right after his dad died."

"What did his parents do?" Kathryn couldn't help herself. She wanted to know all she could about Timothy Blair, although she didn't really understand why she was so interested in the man.

"His father was the senior partner in Ray's firm until he retired. His mother remained at home. Did a lot of charity work. The family was very social," Joe said. His eyes twinkled. "How come you're so interested, Kathy?" He wished he could see her face right now.

"No particular reason," she lied, and knew he knew it.

"Well, that's all I can tell you, but I'll ask Ray for more

details if you want," he teased her, grinning to himself as he imagined her pale cheeks coloring with a blush. Redheads really glowed when they blushed.

"No, I was just curious. He seemed very nice, and liked my summer reading program," Kathryn said. "Thanks for filling me in on Mr. Blair, Joe. Say hi to Tiffany for me." Then without waiting for him to reply she hung up the phone. From what Joe had told her she suspected the Middle School was very fortunate in their new principal, but of course only time would tell.

The afternoon wore on. There was a library board meeting at six. Kathryn ate a sandwich, some salad, and iced tea before returning to the library. She then reported on the meeting her staff had had regarding the Christmas Book Fair. The board loved the idea of costumes and food, agreeing it would probably bring in more money than they would spend, especially if they could get some of the edibles donated, and the costumes were loaned for free. A committee was formed to handle that part of the event. The meeting broke up a little before eight P.M.

Kathryn fed Dickens, the library cat, before locking up. Dickens had his own cat door, and came and went at his leisure.

The cottage was stuffy, but Kathryn had turned the air conditioner on in her bedroom before she returned to the library for her meeting. She would open the windows downstairs in the morning. She considered which of the scenarios she had programmed into The Channel she would run tonight. Something simple. She just wanted some plain sex. Nothing involved. She showered first, and then climbed naked into her bed. Taking her remote, she

pressed the OPEN button, and the doors on the cabinet opposite her bed swung open, revealing her large flat-screen
television. Then she pressed the F button, smiling as she
did so.

She was a maiden in a sealed tower with a witch's-cap
slate roof. Sitting on an upholstered bench at her dressing
table, she brushed her long golden hair with a silver brush.
It was night, and outside her tower a nightingale began to
sing. The air was perfumed with the fragrant roses that
climbed the stone walls of her tower.

"Rapunzel, Rapunzel, let down your golden hair."

Surprised by the sound of a masculine voice, she rose
and went to the window. He stood in the shadows of the
forest that surrounded the small clearing in which her
tower was located. She could not yet see his face, but she
could see he was tall and sturdy of limb. He had come before, but she had ignored his pleas. Had not the old witch
who raised her warned her about the evil of men? Tonight,
however, she found she was lonely. And she was curious
too.

He called to her again. "Rapunzel, Rapunzel, let down
your golden hair."

"Why?" she asked him, leaning upon the window's
slate sill. "Why do you want me to let down my hair to
you?"

"There is no door to your tower, Rapunzel. If you let
down your hair I will use it to climb up to you," he said.

"Why do you want to climb up to me?" she asked in-
nocently.

"Why, so I may make love to you, Rapunzel. I will
kiss your lips, stroke your breasts, and then I will put my

cock in your sweet cunny so we may fly away to paradise," he told her. "I can make you happier than you have ever been."

Rapunzel considered his words, but before she could make her decision she had to know who he was. "Who are you?" she asked him.

"I am a king's son, a prince, Rapunzel. Only my cock is worthy of you," he told her. "I am called Everhard by name."

Prince Everhard. What a beautiful name it was, the maiden thought dreamily, and tempted by his sweet words and deep, sexy voice, Rapunzel lifted the great heavy length of her hair, which had never been cut in all her sixteen years, over the sill. It fell down the length of the tower, touching the grassy ground below. Her prince immediately sprang out of the shadows, and grasping the long tresses, began his climb to her chamber. Reaching her, he vaulted over the sill, taking her into his arms to kiss her.

Their clothing magically disappeared. They were both quite naked. She slid immediately to her knees before him, taking up his great long cock, licking the length of it slowly, slowly, finally taking it into her mouth to suckle upon it, her tongue rotating about it. When he was suitably hard he drew her up into his arms again, kissed her once, and then bent her over the sill of the window. She felt his cock sliding into her cunt, filling her full, and Rapunzel moaned with unadulterated pleasure.

He pushed her hair aside, revealing the delicate nape of her neck. "Ahh," he said softly, kissing it deeply, "you are so deliciously tight, my love."

"Go deep, and fuck me hard, my prince," she told him.

"That is what I want of you tonight. Good sex. Nothing more."

He obliged her and she was shortly weak with her delight as the large and long cock probed her, teased her, brought her to climax. The prince, however, true to his name, remained ever hard. He took her leaning over the sill. On the floor before the blazing hearth. On her back on her bed. He was tireless and masterful. He kissed her lips, her breasts, and every inch of bared skin on her body. He licked and sucked on her various parts until she squealed and begged for mercy.

Instead he spanked her until she was again begging for mercy. Setting her upright he lowered her onto his massive cock as he sat in a wing-backed chair. She gasped with the delicious sensation and for the first time that night she actually looked into the face of the man who was so magnificently servicing her. Her eyes grew wide with shock and surprise.

"No!" she said. "You cannot look like this, my prince."

"I look the way you want me to look," he replied. "Now ride me, Rapunzel, so we may both climax this time. Then you must sleep."

She felt the thick, long cock throbbing within her. She wanted to climax with him this one final time. She couldn't help it if he looked like someone she knew. She began to ride him, and very quickly, without warning they both reached a screaming climax.

"Good night, Rapunzel," Prince Everhard said.

Kathryn St. John felt her pleasure washing over her like a warm blanket as she fell into a deep sleep. Her last conscious thought was that she didn't understand why

Prince Everhard had looked like Timothy Blair. Certainly she hadn't done that deliberately.

And when she awoke in the morning she was still questioning herself. The prince in her Rapunzel fantasy had always just been a handsome generic man with large genitals. He had never before had the face of anyone she knew, and she didn't understand it at all.

She didn't put the faces of men she knew on her fantasy lovers. For one thing there were no men she desired enough to do so; and for another all the men she knew were taken. Besides, how the hell could she look any man in Egret Pointe in the eye under such circumstances? Well, the Rapunzel fantasy was out for the interim.

And to add to her discomfort Timothy Blair came to the library that day to borrow a few books. He popped his head into her office to say hello. "You've got a terrific popular commercial fiction section," he said, complimenting her.

"Best in the state," Mavis, who had tagged along behind him, said. "Kathy says all fiction has its uses even if it isn't a classic."

"You never know who'll be considered a classic one day," Timothy Blair agreed. "Why, Charles Dickens was considered a yellow journalist in his day, and not particularly respected."

"I didn't know that," Mavis said. "Did you know that, Kathy?"

There was nothing for it. She was going to have to look up. She felt her cheeks growing warm as she did. "Yes, I did know that, Mavis," she said in what she hoped passed for a cool and impartial voice. She tried very hard not to look directly at Timothy Blair as she spoke, but to her horror her eyes stared briefly at his crotch before she forced them away. Oh my God! Had he noticed?

"We have a bestselling romance author here in Egret Pointe. Emilie Shann," Mavis nattered on. "She's such a doll. She married her editor a few years ago. They have a cute little boy, and she's expecting again, twins!"

"I don't read romance," Timothy Blair said.

"Most men don't, although there are a few who do," Mavis told him chattily.

"Mavis, I have to get this budget straightened out," Kathryn St. John said. "I don't mean to be rude, Mr. Blair, but keeping us within our budget is important."

"Of course, Miss Kathy," he responded pleasantly. "I know all about budgets. I hope the next time we meet you'll call me Tim. Everyone does."

"Come on, and I'll check you out," Mavis said, and when she had she returned to her boss's office. "You hardly said a word, and practically tossed the man out physically. What's the matter, Kathy? Are you all right?"

She had to tell Mavis. Mavis was her one confidante, and had been since they were kids together. "Shut the door," Kathryn St. John said. "Then come sit down."

"This must be bad," Mavis replied, shutting the door and making herself comfortable in the chair opposite the librarian's desk.

"Last night I ordered up my Rapunzel fantasy," Kathryn began.

"The one that's just mindless sex, right?" Mavis wondered what would come next, and she leaned forward. "So, what happened?"

"That's the one, and what happened was, when I finally got around to looking at the prince's face, it was *his* face," Kathryn said.

"Whose face?" Mavis looked puzzled, and then she gasped. "Oh my God! Mr. Middle School Principal? Why, Kathy St. John, you slut!" And Mavis laughed.

"It's not funny, Mavis! I never put the faces of men I know on the fantasy men in The Channel, for a lot of reasons, but probably looking them in the eye is the best reason. And then just now I caught myself looking at his crotch! And I wondered if his dick was like the prince's in the Rapunzel fantasy."

Mavis couldn't help it. Her sides shook with laughter. "I knew you liked him the first time you met him," she finally said.

"I neither like nor dislike Mr. Blair," Kathryn St. John said.

"Poppycock, to use my dad's old expression," Mavis replied. "Whether you realize it or not, you're interested in the man. If you weren't, he wouldn't have been in the Rapunzel fantasy, Kathy. You've never put the face of any man you know or have known on a fantasy lover. I suspect most women don't, and for the same reasons you don't. Maybe this was a onetime thing, but if Tim Blair begins to show up in your other fantasies, then you're going to have to admit you're interested in him. It's the only reasonable explanation for it."

"Maybe my remote is broken," Kathryn St. John said hopefully.

Mavis snorted. "Those things don't break," she replied. Even the letters on the remote don't smudge away like they do on a regular remote. It's you, Kathy. Somewhere deep down this guy has caught your fancy."

"I don't want him to *catch my fancy*," Kathryn St. John said.

"Why not?" Mavis demanded. "You're not gay. You like sex, but your whole life you've avoided not just commitment to anything but the library, but to men in general.

"I know you grew up in a male-dominated household, but you knew just how to manipulate your grandfather and father. You're good at handling difficulty, and difficult people, Kathy. But I have never known you to let loose. Your dad and grandfather are gone now. Who the heck would care if you decided to dance naked in the rain?"

"My brother," Kathryn St. John said. "Hallock Kimborough St. John the bloody Fifth of that name. Mavis, you're right. When I realized how it was in my house, I learned to work around the 'Old Boy' network. I even had the houseman, Mr. Todd, eating out of my hand, but not my brother. He took his place as the St. John scion very seriously. I couldn't get around him like I could the others because we were siblings, and he *knew* what I was doing."

"But he never told on you," Mavis considered thoughtfully.

"No, he never did. As long as I behaved the way a proper St. John female was expected to behave, he wouldn't tell, because it gave him a certain power over me, and Hallock liked that. Why do you think it took him so long to marry? He had to wait until he could find a woman who could be precisely schooled into becoming the kind of wife he wanted. And he found her. In England.

"Debora is the daughter of distant cousins of ours in Devon. She had gone to an Anglican convent school, and then attended a school for nannies. She looked after the toddlers of a local marquis. Hallock met her when she was seventeen. And married her when she was twenty. I think when they married she had only been to London twice in all her life, and both had been class trips from convent school. She was unspoiled, and obedient. And she had been raised to believe that being some man's wife and the mother of his children was the pinnacle of achievement. She was perfect for him, and still is," Kathryn said. "I don't want to be like my sister-in-law."

"You're nothing like Debora," Mavis declared vehemently. "Not that she isn't a darling girl, because she is, but you're not her."

"But despite all of my achievements I feel my brother always looking over my shoulder, Mavis. I'm a grown woman pushing fifty, and no one, or nothing, intimidates me. But I can't stop being a proper St. John woman. Despite my quiet rebellion I turned out exactly the way they wanted me to turn out. At least publicly. Getting involved with a real-live man would only bring me difficulties that I really don't want. And as long as I have The Channel, I don't need to have a boyfriend, a gentleman friend, whatever they call it today."

"That's just plain crazy!" Mavis said. "Tim Blair is a nice man, and I think he's interested in you."

"He's five years younger than I am, Mavis. I don't need a boy toy," Kathryn answered her friend.

"How do you know how old he is?"

"I have my sources," Kathryn said with a little smile.

"You wouldn't be checking out those sources if you weren't interested," Mavis said with a grin. "I'm not going to give up on you, Kathy. I'm not! And I'll bet Tim Blair doesn't give up on you either."

"He's wasting his time, Mavis, and so are you," Kathryn St. John replied.

"We'll see," Mavis responded, chuckling. "We'll just see."

Labor Day came and went. The summer people went home. The school year began, and life in Egret Pointe took on a comfortable pattern of days just the way Kathryn St. John liked it. But every time Timothy Blair came to the library to return and borrow books he always stuck his head into her office for a quick hello. As long as it was nothing more than that, Kathryn St. John could manage.

Two weeks after Labor Day Joe Pietro d'Angelo came into her office. "I found some stuff out about the new principal I thought might interest you," he said, sitting down without an invitation. "You still interested?" When she hesitated he chuckled. "Yeah, you're still interested. Well the reason he isn't married is because his fiancée was killed in a hit-and-run by a drunk driver, crossing the street two days before their wedding. That was ten years ago. There hasn't been anyone since. He's dated occasionally, mainly for school charity functions where he was expected to put in an appearance."

"Who did he bring?" Kathryn said, and wondered why she had asked.

"He always went with one of the female teachers. Older women usually. Single women, widows. Ray says

the women teachers adored him. He's got the reputation
of being a real gentleman, and a nice guy."

"How would Ray know?" Again, why was she showing any interest?

"My cousin's on the board at Kensington Academy,"
Joe said. He grinned at her mischievously as he stood
up. "Nice to see you interested in a man for a change,
Kathy."

"I am not interested in him, Joe! I was just curious,"
Kathryn replied a little too vehemently, and her cheeks felt
warm.

"Yeah, okay, if you say so, but you should know the
girls on Ansley Court have been saying that he'd be a great
match for you," Joe told her.

"Wonderful! There's gossip about me now. I'm sure
my brother will be simply thrilled when he learns it,"
Kathryn St. John said irritably.

"For God's sake, Kathy, why do you care what Hallock thinks? He's a damned stuffed shirt, and you know
it. Besides, rumor has it that Debora is having twins again.
He's too busy digesting that news to be bothered with
you," Joe replied reassuringly.

"You don't know Hallock," Kathryn St. John said
grimly as she waved Joe Pietro d'Angelo from her office.

And sure enough, Hallock Kimborough St. John V
walked into his younger sibling's office that same afternoon. He was a man of medium height, a touch portly
although he worked out regularly at the gym. His hair was
a dark auburn, cut short, and he had light brown eyes.
Without asking, he closed her office door and sat down.

"What is this I am hearing about you and this new Middle School principal, Kathryn?"

She was ready for him. "I have no idea to what you are referring, Hallock," Kathryn St. John replied stiffly. "What is it you are hearing?"

"It has come to my ears that this man is interested in you, Kathryn. Please remember that you are a St. John, and have a reputation to consider," her brother said.

She laughed. "The town has obviously been without fodder for its gossip mill, Hallock, although now that the word is out about your wife, Mr. Blair's alleged interest in me will certainly be forgotten. Really, Hallock, twins? Again? A bit excessive and showy, considering that you already have five children, don't you think?"

To her absolute delight, her older brother flushed. But he was not so easily diverted from his original subject. "How do you know this man?" he demanded.

"I'm the town librarian, Hallock. He is the Middle School principal. Our paths will cross now and again. He is a library patron. He complimented my summer reading program for the children in his school, and when he did Mavis was present. Hardly a scandalous assignation, brother. And speaking of summer reading, my eldest nephew did not participate in the program. Why is that?"

"You know HK was away at camp for eight weeks," her brother answered.

"He had a week before he went, and two weeks after he came back. He could have read a minimum of three to five books in that time, Hallock. Being a St. John is no longer good enough in this fast-paced world. HK needs to be a well-read man."

"I wasn't," her brother responded.

"I should not brag about it if I were you," Kathryn said sharply.

"I continue to make money, sister. And my clients suffered only minor damage in the recession. St. John Investments is a sound company, just as grandfather and father left it to me," he said. "You have not seen a drop in your income, have you?"

"No, and I do thank you for that, Hallock," Kathryn told him. "But HK needs to read more. The twins come to the library regularly with Debora."

"My wife is an outstanding mother," he responded in pompous fashion.

"Are we through then, Hallock?" Kathryn asked.

"If you can assure me that there is nothing for me to be concerned about, Kathryn, we are through," Hallock said. "I have taken up enough of your time, and you have your work to complete." Her brother stood up, and leaning across her desk, placed a cold kiss upon her cheek. "Good afternoon, Kathryn," he said as he opened the door and left.

"What did old sourpuss want?" Mavis asked, sticking her head through the door.

"He wanted reassurance that the rumors about his dear sister and the Middle School principal had no basis in fact," Kathryn said.

"What rumors? There haven't been any rumors. I would have heard them if there had been," Mavis said.

"Well, he heard something from someone, and rushed to confront me. Do you understand now, Mavis? This is what I've been telling you. My brother has an inbred obligation to protect the family name from what he believes might be scandal. This is why I have lived my life the way I do. Do you know that he has control of the family trust? He can withhold my income. The library couldn't afford to pay me a salary, Mavis. We're a small facility in a little town. If they had to pay me, all of the staff would have to go, and I couldn't do it alone. You know I'm not a coward, but if I step out of line as far as my brother is concerned, he can ruin me. I have to toe the St. John line."

"That stinks!" Mavis said.

It did stink, Kathryn agreed. But it was what it was. She had no other choice but to behave as she had. Kathryn St. John knew there were some people who felt sorry for her, and the life she appeared to have chosen. But once, once there had been someone in her life, and she had planned to marry him no matter what her family said, because he didn't care if she was rich or poor. He loved her.

Jonathan Curtis had been Mavis's older brother. They had been friends forever until one day Jon kissed her and they were suddenly more than friends. No one knew, not even Mavis. And when his Guard unit got called up for active duty in the Gulf War, he had asked her to marry him, and she had said yes. He gave her his old fraternity pin in token of their pledge.

"I'll replace it with a ring when I get home," he told her. "It won't be a big diamond, Kathy, but it will come with all of my love."

But Jonathan Curtis never came home. He was the second of Egret Pointe's sons to be killed in the Gulf War. Ben Kimborough had been the other. And she had never dared to wear his fraternity pin, but Jon would have understood why. She mourned with Jon's family, but they never knew the true depth of her sorrow. And they never knew that Kathryn St. John might have been one of them. It was the only secret she had ever kept from Mavis, and to this day she didn't know why she had. The fraternity pin lay in the bottom of her jewelry drawer. She had never considered returning it. What would have been the point?

The library closed at five thirty after Labor Day. After the day she had just had, Kathryn St. John was in the mood for rough love tonight. She had deleted the Rapunzel fantasy, but not replaced it yet with anything. She was considering a barbarian-and-slave-girl fantasy. Maybe she would try it tonight. It sounded just right, considering her mood.

Mrs. Bills was still at the cottage when she came in. "Hope you don't mind me staying a bit late, Miss Kathy, but I had an extra something to do for Mr. Blair. I usually do him Tuesdays and Fridays, but he just unpacked his mama's china. Beautiful! But it all needed hand washing. Twelve of everything. So I went over early today to do it, and got half of it done before I had to come to you. Your dinner's in the oven, dear."

"I didn't know you worked for Mr. Blair," Kathryn replied.

"Oh yes. Doris Kirk put me in touch with him as soon as he rented the Torkelsen house. I was there to help him when his movers arrived from the city. Such a nice man. Lovely manners and how he loves that dog of his. But I have to admit I've become quite fond of Rowdy myself. As sweet-natured as his master, he is. I made you shepherd's pie. You had some leftover lamb from your Sunday roast. Had company, did you?"

"Mavis and her husband," Kathryn said.

Mrs. Bills took off the apron she had been wearing and put it in the kitchen cupboard where she had hung her jacket. Putting it on she pulled her car keys from the pocket. "Good night, Miss Kathy," she said, and was gone out the door. She would have to walk through the garden to the street where her car would be parked, but it was still light enough to see the path.

Kathryn St. John poured herself a glass of red wine, and taking her plate from the oven, went into her little dining room, where Mrs. Bills had set a place for her. There was a green salad in a small wooden bowl by the fork. She sat down, reaching for the tiny pitcher of mint sauce. Pouring a bit around the shepherd's pie, she began to eat. It was a perfect meal for an early-autumn night.

As she ate she thought about the barbarian-and-slave-girl fantasy she was considering. Yes, a rough barbarian with a great big dick who would force her to his will using a combination of his strength and his charm. Did barbarians have charm? Never having met one, she couldn't be certain, but her barbarian would. But she would not be able to get around him. He would punish her for her resistance, and then he would fuck her until she was weak and replete with satisfaction. Now that sounded like a great deal more fun than Rapunzel had been. She didn't know why she had put that silly fairy tale on her remote in the first place except at the time she wanted to fill up all six of her selections. In reality her life might be an orderly one. But in The Channel she wanted more danger and excitement.

She finished her supper, and discovered Mrs. Bills had

left her a dish of her favorite butterscotch pudding. Kathryn ate it and licked the spoon with satisfaction, thinking about what else she was going to lick before the night was through. Rinsing her dishes and setting them neatly in the dishwasher, she made certain the house was locked up, and then hurried upstairs to shower and brush her teeth. Finally she climbed into her bed, reached for the remote, and pressed OPEN. The doors to the painted cabinet opened.

"Barbarian and the Slave Girl, New, Section F," she said aloud as her finger pushed down on the little round pad. She was about to create a whole wonderful new fantasy, and that in itself was exciting.

Chapter Four

The tent in which she found herself was not particularly large, but neither was it small. It was heated by one small brazier. Outside she could hear the sound of music and laughter. She crept over to the tent's exit, lifting the flap cautiously, and peeked outside. There was a large fire blazing high. A large man sat upon a thronelike chair covered in animal skins with his back to the tent. He held an enormous goblet in one hand. From the other hand dangled a thick leather strap at least six inches in width and a foot and a half in length. Kathryn shivered, half with excitement and half with fear. Yes! This was going to be a perfect fantasy.

"Do you want to see everything that is going on, dearie?"

Kathryn turned startled to find a wizened old woman at her elbow.

"What?" she asked.

"We'll slip out and watch," the old woman said. "Your companion is giving the men a fine entertainment this evening. She's a real fighter, but don't worry. The master has saved you for himself alone." Grasping Kathryn's arm with her taloned fingers, she led her out of the tent to stand in the shadows half behind the throne.

Kathryn's eyes grew wide at the barbaric scene before her. There had been feasting and drinking. Now the leather-clad warriors were amusing themselves with a blond slave girl. They took turns mounting her, fucking her lustily, howling as they climaxed. The blonde fought them wildly, and sometimes they let her run a few feet before catching her and dragging her back into their clutches once again.

"Mina," the barbarian lord said. "Is that you behind me?"

"Yes, master. I have the other one with me," the wizened crone answered.

He dropped the strap in his hand, saying as he did so, "Give her to me."

Still holding Kathryn's arm, the hag half dragged her before the barbarian warrior. "Here she is, my lord Temur. Is she not a beauty?" Mina ripped the gauze gown from Kathryn's shoulders, baring her to the waist. "Look at those tits, my lord. Have you ever seen finer? She was the caliph's favorite slave girl."

The barbarian reached out and pulled Kathryn into his lap. One hand reached up to fondle and squeeze her bare breasts as she squirmed in his embrace. "I shall call you *Ember*," he told her, "because your hair is the red-gold of the embers in the fire." He squeezed a nipple hard, and she squealed. Temur laughed. "Tonight," he said, "you will be well fucked, Ember. I can make you scream with pleasure as your caliph never did. His head is now on a stake at the entrance to my encampment. He shrieked like a girl when we sliced off his cock. It was a puny thing hardly worthy of a beautiful slave like you."

Then suddenly he dumped her from his lap to the earth below, and stood up. "You are being too rough with her," he shouted at his men, striding over to where the blond slave girl lay cowering, curled up like a small animal.

Bending, the barbarian lord Temur gathered the girl up into his arms, soothing her, whispering in her ear softly, but Kathryn could not hear the words he spoke. He took the girl's face in his big hands, and said for them all to hear, "She will do what you ask now—won't you, my beauty? Behold." He demonstrated. "On your hands and knees, beauty." And when the girl had taken the position he instructed he knelt behind her, released his cock from his leather trousers, and grasping her by the hips, began to fuck her slowly at first, and then more quickly. His men gathered about him cheering him on as pure pleasure shone on the girl's face. When he had finished, the girl crawled to the throne where he had reseated himself with Kathryn, and kissed his feet.

"I will do whatever my lord commands," she said.

"Give my men the same pleasure you just gave me," he told her.

"Let me be yours alone!" the blond slave girl begged him.

"Do as you have been told, my beauty, or you will

be beaten," he threatened. "Take her away now," he said to his men, who came for the girl and carried her off to another tent across the encampment. His long, thick fingers kneaded Kathryn's breasts, marking her delicate skin. "Golden hair has but whetted my appetite," he murmured, low. "Now it is your turn to pleasure me, and be pleasured in return, my Ember." Temur stood, and as he did he lifted the woman in his grasp to toss her casually over his shoulder as he walked back into his tent. "Is all in readiness, Mina?" he asked the crone.

"Exactly as you wish it, my lord Temur," she replied.

"Then go to your pallet. Do not disturb us until dawn, old hag." He pushed through the flap into the tent, where he casually dropped Kathryn onto a bed of furs briefly while he pulled off his boots and leather trousers. "You will bathe me first," he said. "I stink from a day's battle, and the blond slave's sex. Come! Get up!"

She scrambled to her feet and saw a wood tub filled with water on the far side of the tent. He caught her by her long hair, and pulling her to him, kissed her hard. Then he yanked the rest of her ruined garment off of her. Stepping into the tub, he stood as she took up a sponge and a scrap of soap, and began washing him down. It was not an easy job, for he stood at least half a foot over six feet in height. Everything was long about him. His arms. His legs. His torso. His dangling cock now resting after its earlier exercises. He did not rush her, obviously enjoying the activity. The pouch behind his cock was the largest she had ever seen. She cleansed it gently, knowing a delicate touch was a better path to full arousal. When she had finished and thoroughly dried him, she murmured, low, "May I have the privilege of bathing too, my lord Temur?"

"Very well, but hurry. I am eager to ride you, Ember."

He sprawled upon the bed of furs, watching her through slitted eyes. Was there something familiar about him? There was, and yet there wasn't. She quickly bathed herself, and then coming to stand before him she dried herself.

"Spread your nether lips for me," he commanded her. "I want to see your treasures." And when she did he nodded, pleased. "Your pleasure button is large. Now come and squat down over my face and spread your lips for me so I may tongue you. You are to make no sound while I do, Ember. If you do I will punish you."

"But, my lord—" she began.

"You will not speak unless I permit it," he growled fiercely.

Ohh, she liked this fantasy. He was quite the brute, her barbarian lord. She crouched down over his head, pulled the flesh apart and closed her eyes. The tip of his tongue flicked delicately over her clitoris, sending a rush of delight through her. The skillful tongue swirled about the fleshy pink cavern, stroking, probing, teasing at her clit, which began to swell with the pleasure he was engendering in it. Then suddenly his lips closed over what he had called her pleasure button, and he sucked hard on it. Kathryn could not help herself. She screamed softly.

"Greedy bitch," he growled at her. "Now you will be punished for your disobedience!" He slid from beneath her, and jumped to his feet. His hand reached out for her long hair, and he wrapped a hank of it about his fist, forcing her up.

"Oh, forgive me, my lord Temur!" she begged him. The look in his eyes was positively and deliciously dangerous.

"I did not give you permission to speak, Ember," he told her. He half dragged her across the tent and put her between two tent poles. He pushed her hands through leather manacles attached to the poles, and commanded her to hold on to the poles tightly.

"What are you going to do to me?" she asked him.

"More disobedience, slave?" he roared angrily.

And then she felt the faint whoosh of air that preceded the leather strap as it hit her buttocks. The blow stung as did the blows that followed. Stung and burned, but did not really hurt her. Interesting, Kathryn thought, but then it was her fantasy, and she was not into painful pleasures like some women. She felt a tingle between her legs. His strap was arousing her lusts. Fascinating, she considered. Then suddenly he loosed her, and she fell to the tent floor.

"On your hands and knees, slave!" he told her, and she scrambled to obey him.

He was going to take her from the rear like he had taken the blond slave. But wait! What was he doing? She felt a finger rubbing her asshole and gasped with surprise. "No!" she almost shouted, and attempted to turn about.

He laughed. "So there is something you do not like," he said holding her in place.

His hand held her about the nape of her neck. "You will accept all I offer you, Ember, but your ass is tight, and needs several days of preparation before you can receive my cock there. We shall begin with a small dildo." And she felt him inserting something into her body.

"There," he told her. "'Tis no bigger than a man's thumb. 'Twill not hurt you." Yanking her up again by her hair, he dragged her across the tent to the bed of furs, where he pushed her onto her back. "Legs spread!" he commanded, and slid easily between her thighs.

Her eyes had fastened upon his cock. She had not been able to see much of it when he had taken the other slave girl but now she saw its full might. It was a massive thing, probably between nine and ten inches in length, and close to three inches around. Could such a penis fit in her vagina? She was obviously about to find that out as he rubbed the tip of it across her clitoris several times, and then touched the opening into her body, rubbing slowly, teasingly.

"Strapping you has made your juices flow copiously, Ember," he said.

"You are too big," she whispered. "You will kill me with that great cock."

"Nay," he said softly, brushing a finger across her lips, "you will take it in, and we will give each other much pleasure. It will take a moment or two to get used to my size, for your former master had a slender, delicate cock." Holding himself with a hand he rubbed against her, and she felt herself almost trying to suck him into her body. "You're eager for it," he said, "aren't you? You want to be impaled on this big rod of mine, don't you?"

He pushed himself in just enough so that the head of his penis was inside her.

Kathryn whimpered. He was so very big, and yet she wanted him. Still she was a little fearful, and only the knowledge that she could stop the fantasy if she chose kept her from panicking. It was only a dream fantasy, she kept reminding herself.

He was slow and deliberate in his actions, pressing his huge cock into her inch by inch by inch. To her surprise her body stretched to accommodate his length and bulk. And then he was fully sheathed. He smiled down into her eyes. He had blue eyes. He waited for her to grow used to his great size, but when her vaginal muscles squeezed him he took it to mean she was ready to be fucked. "Now, my fiery Ember," he said, "you shall learn what it is like to have a real man using you. Not some perfumed weakling!"

He began to ride her, his long, thick cock flashing back and forth within her heated body. Just having him inside of her gave her pleasure. She moaned with it, could hardly breathe with the thrill of it. She wrapped her legs about his torso and he roared with delight, going deeper and harder into her soft, compliant flesh.

Kathryn screamed with the pleasure he was giving her. "*More! More!*" she demanded of him. Her nails raked down his long back, digging deep, bloodying him.

She sank her teeth into his meaty shoulder and he howled with a mixture of pleasure and pain. "*More! More!*" she insisted. "Is this the best you can do? I want more!" But then Kathryn shrieked as his cock found her G-spot. The climax roared up, engulfing her, sending her spinning out of control. He shuddered above her, and she felt his cock releasing its tribute to her. "Nooo!" she sobbed. "I want more!"

The barbarian Temur fell away from her, panting. "By whatever gods exist, Ember, you are the first woman to ever defeat me in the battle of love. You are every bit as greedy for fucking as I am. I admit to you that I must rest a brief span, but then we shall begin again, and I will fuck you until you admit your defeat. Now get up and pour us two goblets of wine. The jug and goblets are on the table where Mina left them." He did not tell her the wine was heavily laced with aphrodisiacs. The night was young.

Kathryn did as she had been bid, returning with the goblets, handing him one, and keeping the other for herself. They lay sprawled on the fur bed in brief silence as they drank down the wine. When he had finished, he began to play with her breasts, stroking them, then kissing them—licking, sucking, and gently biting her nipples. At one point he reached beneath her to take the circular handle of the little dildo, rotating the instrument first, and then fucking her ass gently with it so that she was squirming.

"You are so deliciously carnal," he chuckled. "We will have many pleasant hours together. I do not think I shall sell you quite yet. I have not had my fill of you."

"You will never have your fill of me," she told him boldly.

"Do you want to be whipped again?" he demanded of her.

"You don't want to whip me, barbarian. You want to fuck me," Kathryn said softly. She reached out to caress his burgeoning cock, her hand slipping beneath to fondle his balls in her hand. The sack overflowed her palm. "Don't you?" she taunted.

He laughed. He had never had a woman who was so bold, so unafraid of him. He was Temur the Terrible. The mere sound of his name set strong men whimpering with fear. At the entrance to his camp right now, the head of a caliph, his genitals stuffed into his mouth, was displayed upon one pole. His vizier's head was upon a second pole, his headless body nailed upside down to another. It had been the vizier who had advised his caliph not to pay a tribute to Temur the Terrible. People quailed when they heard the sound of his army's horses on the wind.

But not this woman. She was strong and fierce. "Aye, bitch, I want to fuck you, and I will!" He thrust into her cruelly, and while she cried out, startled, she wrapped herself about him and urged him on until they were both satisfied for a brief time once again. After they had coupled four times he fell into a sleep. His features softened in his slumber, and Kathryn stared, shocked as she gazed closely at the barbarian for the first time. The handsome face beneath the rough stubble of his beard was that of Timothy Blair. No wonder the blue eyes had seemed so familiar.

"Fantasy end!" she cried out. What the hell was going on with her? She grabbed the remote and pressed B.

"I've brought a friend, Lady St. John," Porthos said as he drew another musketeer forward. "This is my friend, Timon, of the queen's personal guard."

Kathryn stared in horror. It was Timothy Blair again! "Fantasy end!" she shouted, sitting back up in her bed and throwing the remote into the drawer of her bedside table.

What was going on? Why was Timothy Blair showing up in her fantasies? She wasn't interested in the man. She barely knew him. She didn't want to know him. This was simply terrible. Every time he came to the library he stopped in to say hello. She even saw him in the village now and again. After tonight she could never look the man in the eye again. A barbarian? He wasn't a barbarian, but he certainly had been in her fantasy.

And God, she had loved every minute of it! But the barbarian Temur wasn't the real Timothy Blair. What was making her put him into her fantasies?

Kathryn tried to sleep, but she couldn't. She considered deleting this new fantasy from her remote, but she couldn't do that either. She hadn't had so much sexual excitement and fun in ages. Get ahold of yourself, old girl, she chided herself. You can put a different face on your barbarian. Who is the actor you like? The one who starred in *The Scorpion King*. The Rock. Dwayne something. Yes. He would be perfect. She closed her eyes and tried to sleep. Finally she dozed, but the next day was awful.

"You look like hell," Mavis said, bringing her in her morning cup of coffee.

"Thanks," Kathryn said. "I don't feel much better than I look."

"What's the matter?" Mavis sat down.

"New fantasy last night. I deleted Rapunzel. I decided a barbarian-and-slave-girl scenario would be a good one. And it was, until I realized the barbarian looked like you know who. So I ended the fantasy, and switched to my Three Musketeers, and guess what. Porthos had brought a friend he said was in the queen's guard. Guess who it was. I had to end that program too. How can this be happening, Mavis?"

"I've already told you how it's happening, sweetie," Mavis said. "Look, why don't you come to Sunday dinner at my house this week? I'll invite Mr. Blair too. Maybe if you actually get to know him you can get past your subconscious."

"What if Hallock finds out?" Kathryn St. John asked.

"You're having Sunday dinner at your best friend's house, Kathy. Even your stuffy brother can't object to that."

"I don't know if I can even look Mr. Blair in the face," Kathryn said. "The barbarian and I really went at it big-time."

Mavis giggled. "A St. John afraid?" she said mischievously.

"I am not afraid, but I'm going to be unable to stop wondering if his dick is as big as the barbarian's. The guy was massive, and I really enjoyed it. I couldn't delete the new program. But I'll try and put a different face on my barbarian next time."

"I can't help but wonder what Mr. Blair would think if he knew about The Channel, and what you're doing with him there," Mavis chuckled.

"Well, he doesn't know, and he'll never know," Kathryn St. John said. "I just have to get past knowing it if I'm not going to behave like a blithering idiot on Sunday."

"You'll do fine, sweetie. I'll do that stuffed loin of pork you like with apricots," Mavis said soothingly. "We're empty nesters. It will just be grown-ups. We'll eat, we'll drink good wine, and get to know Mr. Blair better. I'll bet no one has asked him to dinner yet either, although I hear that Michelle Baron has been making a fool of herself at the school of late. You would think two divorces by the time she was forty would be enough for her."

Kathryn giggled. She couldn't help herself. Michelle

Baron for all her two divorces was one of those very proper women who appeared to do everything just right.

Neither of her husbands had been able to live up to her exacting standards. If Michelle had seen the barbarian lord Temur with Timothy Blair's face, she would have been shocked. Or would she? "Does she have The Channel?" Kathryn asked Mavis.

"Who knows?" Mavis shrugged. "But if she does, you can bet her fantasies are all very Martha Stewart and Julia Child. I heard her last husband say she was like a dead woman in bed. So, you'll come to dinner on Sunday?"

"I'll come," Kathryn promised. "I need to get Mr. Blair out of my fantasies. Maybe becoming acquainted with the real man will help me with that."

On Sunday morning Kathryn went to the late service at St. Luke's. There was a vestry meeting scheduled afterward, and she was the Junior Warden on the vestry.

She had her own pew now, across from the St. John pew. She sat quietly before the service as Hallock strode down the aisle with the very pregnant Debora, and the other five children in his wake. Kathryn noticed he did hold the pew door open for his wife. Her brother nodded in her direction before stepping into the pew, and Kathryn nodded back.

Everything was exactly as it should be in Hallock Kimborough St. John's world, his sister thought, amused.

She walked home. It was a beautiful late-October day, and the maples lining the street were at peak color. The meeting had been blissfully short with no new business. Mavis had asked her to come at three. Kathryn would change into something more casual than her Sunday dress with its matching coat. Dinner at Mavis's house was never a formal affair, which was why she always enjoyed it. She stopped at the library to feed Dickens, who was hungry enough to give her a purr as he rubbed her ankles.

"You're a shameless beastie," she said scratching his ears. "But the library wouldn't be the same without you."

By ten to three she was ready to walk over to Mavis's house. Kathryn had changed into a pair of light wool slacks in the Gordon plaid, and a thick white cotton-and-silk turtleneck sweater. She clipped a pair of simple gold earrings shaped like leaves onto her ears. She had oxblood leather low walking boots on her feet, which were clad in dark green cashmere socks. Slipping her keys in her pants pocket she picked up the bottle of wine she was bringing and left the cottage.

It wasn't a long walk, and the sun was warm. Someone was burning leaves, and the pungent smell wafted around her as she walked. The houses were decorated for autumn with cornstalks, pumpkins, and gourds. There were children in the Sunday street playing touch football. They called to her as she walked by. "Hi, Miss Kathy!" And Kathryn waved back at them. In some of the houses Sunday dinner was being served, and she could see families at their tables.

She was expected for dinner at her brother's on the first Sunday of each month. Hallock considered it a familial obligation to host his sister, and although she could have done without his hospitality, she went. She liked her young sister-in-law and had to admit that her nephews and nieces were nice children. Hallock wouldn't have had it any other way, Kathryn thought with a smile. Having a family wasn't such a bad thing, even when one had a brother like hers.

Mavis's house was a big old colonial. As she reached the house's front path she saw Timothy Blair coming from the opposite direction. He was carrying a bottle of wine too. Kathryn chuckled. How would Mavis solve the problem of whose wine to drink? She stopped, watching him come. He was really a very big man, and then she blushed at her own thoughts. Was he big all over, like her barbarian? She hadn't played that fantasy again, and wasn't certain what she was going to do with it.

"Hello, Miss Kathy," Timothy Blair greeted her.

"Good afternoon, Mr. Blair," she answered, and they went up the path to the house together. "I see you brought wine too."

"What else do you bring for a dinner invitation?" he replied with a chuckle. "And if the meal is bad at least you know the wine is good."

"You'll get a good meal at Mavis's table, Mr. Blair," Kathryn assured him.

"Won't you call me Tim?" he asked her. "I call you Miss Kathy."

"Kathy will do just fine, Mr. . . . . Tim. It's a tradition to address the librarian here as Miss. It probably began with the first librarian, Miss Victoria St. John," Kathryn explained. "It was, after all, the 1890s. The tradition has remained. The previous librarian was my great-aunt Lucretia, who was known as Miss Lucy to the patrons." She lifted the door knocker and rapped.

Mavis opened the door smiling. "Ohh, good! You're both here. Let me see the wine you've brought. We'll

drink one bottle before dinner, and one bottle with it."
She looked at the labels. "Well, can you beat that? You've
both brought the same wine. Windmill Blush from the
Duck Walk Vineyard." Mavis chuckled. "Great minds,"
she said. "Jeremy, come and open one of these bottles,"
she called to her husband.

Jeremy Peabody taught High School English literature. He was straight out of central casting, with horn-
rimmed glasses, tweed jacket, and a pipe clutched between
his teeth. He was a quiet man with a dry wit. "Yes,
madam, at once," he said, his gray eyes twinkling at her.
"Where would madam have the wine served? At table or
elsewhere?"

"Living room, smart guy. We're going to be civilized
today. We'll sit and talk before dinner. Glasses are on the
table, darling."

"We're doing gracious?" Jeremy Peabody teased. "I
can do gracious."

"Come in and sit down. Don't mind the house fool."
Mavis invited her guests. "The fire is just perfect now. First
time this autumn I've burned a fire."

"I've got a fireplace at my place," Tim said. "I'll have
to get some wood."

"Jeremy will take you to where we get it. You'll want
to buy at least two cords for the winter now," Mavis
advised.

Jeremy Peabody had opened one of the bottles of wine.
He poured four glasses and passed them around. Then,
raising his glass, he said, "Good friends, good times!"

"Well, how are you settling in at the school?" Mavis
wanted to know.

"Actually, quite well," Tim answered. "I've got a really great bunch of teachers. I think one or two of them were a bit put out that they weren't considered for my position, but I think I've got it all smoothed over. Gloria Sullivan has been a godsend for me. She gave me a complete update just before school opened, and so I knew who was going to need a little extra care and feeding. And the kids are terrific. I understand I missed out on the Miller twins, however, but I'll have their little brother in a few more years. They say he's quite a handful."

"Rose and Lily Miller are enormously bright girls," Kathryn said. "They're social activists." She chuckled. "Do you all remember the time they released all the animals from the science lab? A couple of guinea pigs, and rabbits, and two white rats, along with some mice. The mice found their way to the lunchroom, and chaos ensued."

Her audience laughed.

"The poor creatures were completely relieved to be caught and brought back to their cages, where they were fed and petted constantly," Kathryn concluded.

"They didn't believe in incarcerating animals," Mavis explained. "They said it was inhumane."

"Sorry I missed all the fun," Tim said with a grin.

"I have them in my ninth-grade English class this year," Jeremy remarked. "They wanted to know why *Beowulf* wasn't on the syllabus for the year. I was astounded. Usually I get complaints about having to read so many books."

"What did you tell them?" Tim wanted to know.

"I told them if they wanted to read *Beowulf* and render me their reports on it I would give them extra credit,"

Jeremy replied. "Hell, it's a pleasure to teach kids who are actually interested and not looking for the CliffsNotes or an old Classic Comics version of the book."

"Amen to that," Tim agreed. "When I was assistant head at Kensington I also taught a couple of English lit classes. I discovered the only way to get some of the kids to read the book was to hold an open discussion on the book's contents. I always knew the kids who didn't read because they were the ones who didn't take an active part. You got marked down in my class for that. One kid's father actually called me out for it. He said the kid was going to work on Wall Street eventually, so what did Shakespeare matter?"

"The Philistines are at the gates," Mavis said.

Kathryn was unusually quiet as they spoke. She needed to concentrate on Timothy Blair so that when she finally had to get involved in conversation with him, she wouldn't be thinking of Temur the barbarian lord. But she had to admit that he looked pretty fit beneath those beige slacks and white Irish sweater. He had broad shoulders and a broad chest that eased into a narrow waist. If the top half of him was any indication, the bottom half would certainly match, and Kathryn blushed a little at the thought. She had to get her mind off of his male attributes. She was behaving like a teenager who had never seen a set of genitals. She was a St. John for God's sakes! With a pompous brother who was about to father another set of twins. Still waters obviously ran deep in the St. John clan, although one would certainly never discuss such things.

"Kathy, come and help me in the kitchen," Mavis said, standing up. "Dinner in about five minutes, guys." She left the living room, going into the center hall and back to the kitchen, Kathryn behind her. When the swinging door from the hall swung shut, Mavis turned around and said, "You've hardly uttered a word, Kathy."

"I'm trying to get used to his being civilized and dressed," came the reply. Kathryn was grinning. "If I can make light of the naked, then maybe I can look him in the eyes and make polite conversation. You know," she considered. "I'll bet that if he stripped down right now, he'd look just like my barbarian."

Mavis giggled. "Okay, if that's settled, then talk."

"But he doesn't talk like my barbarian. I look into that handsome, smooth-shaven face, and I can't imagine him saying, 'Spread your legs for me, slave!'"

"Oh my God, does he say that?" Mavis actually grew pink cheeked.

"Yep, and even worse," Kathryn replied.

"Being raised in an all-male household has really affected your libido, sweetie. You have got to separate the two, Kathy. I know you say you don't want to marry, and he may not want to either. But wouldn't it be nice to have one male friend you could depend on? And I'll bet he would like one female friend he knew wasn't going to have expectations. Oh, at first people will gossip. But when they see it's just an adult friendship they'll stop talking. Why shouldn't you have a male friend?"

"My brother will have a fit, and make a big deal out of it," Kathryn said.

"Kathy, a long time ago when you chose to walk down the side aisle of the church you declared your independence from the St. John men. You don't owe Hallock a damned thing, and if he says anything to you, you have got to tell him so. I don't know why he's so set with his only sister remaining an old maid." She opened the oven door and pulled out the roasting pan, setting it on the butcher block section of her counter. Then, opening the second oven, she drew out a casserole of sweet potatoes and a platter of local fresh broccoli. "Take these out to the table while I slice the pork loin," Mavis said.

Kathryn took some oven mitts and picked up the first dish. Pushing through the kitchen door into the dining room, she set it on a hot mat. Then she went back for the broccoli. "Shall I tell the men that dinner is served?" she asked Mavis.

"Come back for the bread basket, and then yes, go tell them," her best friend replied as she carefully sliced the loin into perfect chops and set them on a large platter.

The broccoli and rolls on the table, Kathryn went back to the living room. "Mavis says dinner is ready," she said.

"Smells terrific," Timothy Blair said as he unfolded his length from the couch. "Where do I sit?" he asked when he had reached the dining room.

"To my right," Mavis said as she came in with the pork and set it and herself down. "Kathy is always on Jeremy's right. I hope you like roast pork, Tim. I stuffed it with apricots. It's one of Kathy's favorites."

"I am a man with large appetites, Mavis," he replied. "And roast loin of pork is one of my favorites too." He sat down, and immediately served himself two of the chops.

"I think this fellow is going to be my new best friend," Jeremy Peabody said as he passed the sweet potatoes. "He likes to eat and drink, and he's literate."

"He's such a snob." Mavis teased her husband. "All these old Egret Pointe families are, you know."

"I'm not a snob!" Kathryn protested.

"No, you aren't, but your brother sure is. Have you met Hallock Kimborough St. John the Fifth?" Mavis asked. "He's on the school board."

"Wasn't in favor of you at all," Jeremy said mischievously. "Wanted that old poop, Bob Wright. You'll end up dealing with him sooner or later."

"Why?"

"He has several kids in the school system and more to come. Who would have thought Hallock the Fifth was a baby factory, but then his very young wife is quite hot. Right now there are five little St. Johns and Debora is expecting twins again. The oldest son, Hallock the Sixth, is in seventh grade this year. And there are twin girls in fifth."

Timothy Blair looked to Kathryn. "What does your brother do?" he asked her.

"Brokerage firm," she said. "And he recently told me that my nephew didn't need a summer reading program since he was going to follow Daddy into the family business."

Tim burst out laughing. "You're not very alike, you and your brother, are you?" he said. "He sounds like something from the nineteenth century."

"He is," Kathryn agreed with a small smile. "Did you ever see that play—it was a movie too—*Life with Father*. Hallock the Fifth is very much like Clarence Day."

"But as I remember the play, Mrs. Day managed Mr. Day quite well," Tim replied.

"Debora manages the house, and the children," Kathryn said. "But no one manages Hallock the Fifth. He, like all the St. John men before him, is obdurate and convinced that he is always in the right." She turned to Mavis. "Dinner is delicious, as always."

"I second that!" Tim said enthusiastically.

Mavis had made fresh pear tarts for dessert. They had coffee in the living room. Outside it had grown dark.

"When you're ready," Timothy Blair said, "I'll walk you home, Kathy."

"No need," she responded a bit too quickly.

"Perhaps not, but I'd like to nonetheless," he told her.

Mavis shot her a look that said *If you refuse I'll kill you right now.*

"Thank you," Kathryn said meekly and Mavis smiled, satisfied.

After a few more minutes of chatter the two guests decided it was time to go.

"You did pretty good," Mavis whispered to Kathryn as they hugged.

"Thanks for dinner," Kathryn responded.

Outside the air was crisp with the sun gone down. The sky was clear, and Venus was bright in the evening firmament. There was the scent of burning fireplaces as they walked along the lamplit streets.

"You really don't have to walk me home," Kathryn said.

"I want to," he replied.

"Why?" she said directly.

"Because I'd like to get to know you better," he told her candidly.

"Why?" she queried him again.

He laughed. "You sound like one of the schoolkids, Kathy. Okay, I'd like to get to know you because you're intelligent and pretty as all get-out. You remind me of someone, but I'll be damned if I can put a name to your face."

"Suzy Parker, the model and actress from the fifties and sixties," Kathryn told him.

"Of course! Do you remember that terrific movie she made? *The Best of Everything*? She played the actress who got mixed up with the Louis Jourdan Broadway producer who dumped her. She went crazy then, and fell off of a fire escape to her death."

"The Rona Jaffe novel," Kathryn said. "It was one of my favorites."

"I never read the book, but my mother loved the movie. She had a tape of it," he said. "We watched it together a lot when she was dying."

"You were an only child?"

"Yep."

"Lucky you!" Kathryn said.

He laughed. "A lot of only children will tell you how they missed having a sibling. I never did. And frankly my folks never had a lot of time for kids, but I had so many advantages being the only one."

"What did your family do?" She was frankly curious.

"My dad was a partner in a high-powered law firm. My mom very socially active. Junior League, Episcopal Churchwomen, a charity for orphans among other things," he said. "I had a nanny until I was ten. I went to private school, and after the nanny left I went to camp each summer. The summer I was seventeen my folks began taking me abroad with them in the summers. I think I love Italy best of all in Europe."

"I love Italy too," Kathryn said. "Venice in particular."

"God yes! And it's best in the non-tourist season. I don't stay at one of the big hotels though. I have a little *pensione* on a small canal off the Grand Canal. There's a room on the top floor with an iron balcony and a view of the city that's spectacular," he said. "On a clear day you can see all the way to the Lido."

"I love to travel," Kathryn admitted. "Whenever I feel I can take some time away from my library duties I go. My last trip was to Hong Kong. What an exciting city."

"I was there last year," he said. "I needed to get away after Dad died. I taught all day, and then helped out with my father in the evening. He got very frail, although he was as sharp as a tack mentally until he died. But when he died, our old housekeeper retired. She only stayed on after my mother died because of Dad. So as soon as I took care of what needed to be taken care of and summer vacation came, I took off."

"You lived with your parents?"

"Only after my mother died. Dad was retired, and I didn't like the idea of him being all alone in the house at night. He was fine during the day with Helga, and Rowdy for company. I don't have much of a social life, so I figured why waste money on my condo when there were four bedrooms in the co-op," Tim explained. "Dad was glad for the company. We played a lot of chess and Monopoly in the evenings. And with a portable wheelchair I could get him to a couple of concerts. My dad loved Mozart. And we went to the park a lot. My dad loved the lake and the fountains there."

Kathryn was surprised by the love she heard in his voice as he spoke. "You really loved your dad, didn't you? I guess I loved mine, but he didn't have a great deal of time for a daughter. St. Johns want sons. Even my mother was disappointed when I was born. She had had Hallock six years before, then miscarried a second boy two years after that, and then I was born. I think if that second son had lived, it might have been better for me. Then she died, and I was left to raise myself."

"No nanny, or someone like an aunt?" he asked.

"Nope. Just Hallock the Third, my grandfather; Hallock the Fourth, my dad; and my brother. And we had a houseman, Mr. Todd. He taught me to do my laundry when I turned thirteen. He said it wasn't proper for a gentleman to be laundering a young lady's personal undergarments now that I was a teenager."

"Let me guess," Tim said. "You had just gotten your first bra."

Kathryn laughed, surprised he had figured it out. "Yes," she said. "If it hadn't been for Mavis's mother, I would have been in great trouble. She was always filling in the gaps for me. The men in my family assumed I came by all my feminine knowledge naturally, for after all, I was a St. John."

"It must have been difficult for you," he said sympathetically, picturing a little girl with pigtails all alone in a house of men.

"It was when I was small, but then when I was about eight I figured it out, and did what I had to do to survive the male-dominated world in which I lived," Kathryn said.

They had reached the library now and he walked through the back garden with her to her cottage. She had left a light burning and he waited while she pulled her keys from her pocket, and opened the door. "I won't ask you in," she said. "I think you understand why. Thank you for walking me home. It was unnecessary but very nice of you."

"The cinema at the mall is having a festival of old movies," he said. "*The Best of Everything* is on the schedule. Would you like to go with me on Friday night? I've discovered a great little Italian restaurant there too."

Dinner and a movie. God, how long had it been since she had had dinner and a movie with a man? And now that she had spent an evening with Timothy Blair, she was a little more comfortable with him. Temur the barbarian was not quite as vivid in her memory right now. Of course Hallock would have a conniption fit when he learned she had been seen out with a man at a movie, but to hell with her brother. Mavis was right. It was time for her to have some fun. If not now, then when? "I'd love to go out to the movies Friday night. I haven't been out in ages. You realize, however, we'll start the gossip mill turning, because sure as hell, someone is going to see us."

"I think I'd enjoy being the subject of a little gossip with you," Tim told her, smiling down into her green eyes.

"Good night, Mr. Blair," Kathryn said, stepping into her cottage and closing the door as she did.

"Good night, Miss St. John," he replied. Then he turned and went off down her walk, whistling.

Gracious, what had she done? She had made a date with a man five years her junior. Well, she didn't care! Mavis was right, and there was nothing wrong with the town librarian and the Middle School principal being friends. She was entitled to friends, wasn't she? Everyone was entitled to have friends, even Kathryn St. John, damn it!

A call from her brother the next morning before she left for her office infuriated her.

"Good morning, Kathryn. Hallock here. Someone saw you bringing a man into your cottage last night. Really, sister, at your age? You have to remember who you are. Who was this man, and why was he in your home?"

"He was not in my home, Hallock. I had Sunday dinner at Mavis and Jeremy's yesterday. They had invited Mr. Blair, the Middle School principal. He was kind enough to walk me home. And he did not come past the front door stoop. Your informant was incorrect. And just so you are aware of it in advance, Mr. Blair and I are going to a movie on Friday night. And we will have dinner prior."

"Kathryn, I really don't think this behavior is very wise on your part," he said.

"Excuse me? Hallock, I celebrated my forty-eighth birthday in August. What gives you the right to speak to me in such a fashion? You are absolutely insulting!"

"You mustn't forget who you are, Kathryn," her brother said coldly.

"I am well aware of who I am, Hallock, but being the town librarian doesn't mean I have to cloister myself off."

"You had best remember who holds the purse strings, sister."

"And you had best remember that I know where you

go, and what you do every Thursday afternoon at three
P.M. precisely, Hallock." She heard him swallow hard.

"I don't know what you think you know, Kathryn,"
he began.

"My information is very reliable, Hallock," Kathryn
told him. "Don't test me. You will regret it if you do. And
don't ever call me again about my behavior."

"You are such a bitch," he snarled at her, slamming
down the phone.

Chapter Five

K athryn laughed, and then heaved a sigh of relief. She
should have done this years ago, right after she found
out about Hallock's little assignation with Mistress Betsy.

It was common knowledge that Betsy Travers was the
local dominatrix. She lived on the edge of the village in
a neat little house with a picket fence. Mavis, who knew
everything, had told Kathryn who she was after Betsy
Travers became a regular library patron. She adored romance novels, and was always first on the list for the new-
est Emilie Shann or Shirlee Busbee or Thea Divine novel.
Her taste in romance ran to sexy and historical. She was
not at all into contemporary.

One day, after Betsy Travers had departed the library
with three new novels, Mavis chuckled and said, "Considering what she does for a living, her taste in literature is
funny to say the least."

"What does she do?" Kathryn asked.

Mavis had told her.

Kathryn was astounded. "And the police haven't arrested her?"

"Why? She's not doing anything illegal," Mavis said matter-of-factly.

"How on earth do you know?"

"She buys stuff at *Lacy Nothings*. They order it special for her. I was in the changing room one afternoon and heard her talking to Nina. She's very discreet, but at least a dozen guys in town go to her regularly. Nina didn't know I was there, and believe me, I didn't come out until Betsy had gone. I didn't want her to know I'd overheard. Nina was upset, but I promised not to say anything. I never told anyone except Jeremy, until now. It's too good not to share with my best friend. Jeremy knew, of course. He says your brother goes there every Thursday at three P.M."

"Hallock? No! How does he know?" Kathryn asked.

"He wouldn't tell me, but because he didn't believe whoever told him he drove past the Travers house a couple of Thursdays right after three o'clock. And there was your brother's car."

"Hallock would never park his car in such a place where it could be seen," Kathryn said. "If he's going to this woman, he wouldn't want anyone to know."

"She's got a back drive where her clients go. They put their cars in an open shed. Jeremy took down the license plate number, and then went by your brother's office later. Same car. Same license. He was so fascinated by the whole thing he went every Thursday for a couple of weeks and your brother's car was there at Betsy's place."

Kathryn had been amazed by this revelation. She had looked up what a dominatrix did and was even more astounded. Her brother wanting to be spanked and otherwise humiliated? It was difficult to believe. After she had learned of her brother's predilection she had done what Jeremy Peabody had done. She had checked out Betsy Travers's back shed for a couple of Thursdays, and sure enough, it was her brother's car.

And this morning she had used her knowledge to make her brother back off. She was too old to answer to him, and why she hadn't done this years ago, she didn't know. *You like him,* a little voice in her head said. *You want to go out with him, not just this Friday, but after that.* Do I? Kathryn wondered. A male friend. Someone other than Mavis. Mavis, who had a husband and family and couldn't be the kind of friend she had been when they were younger and there was no Jeremy. She didn't blame Mavis. Mavis had moved on with her life. Kathryn St. John had not.

As the week progressed she thought more and more about what it would be like to actually go out on a date again. She hadn't been on one in years. She went with friends to concerts in the city. But they went in groups, and more often than not Rina Seligmann's brother and his life partner met them in town. She and Mavis went to the movies together as Jeremy wasn't a particular movie fan. No one really noticed that Kathryn St. John didn't date. She was past the age where people cared. She was the town's old maid librarian. Would she even know how to behave on a real date anymore? So much had changed for dating couples. Good grief! Kathryn thought. When had life become so damned complicated?

"What should I wear?" she asked Mavis, and she felt like a fool having to ask.

"It's dinner and a movie. Be comfortable," Mavis said.

"Slacks and a sweater?"

"Fine," Mavis replied. "Why are you so darned nervous?"

"Tell me the last time I went out with a real-live man," Kathryn said.

Mavis thought. And she thought. And she thought. "I give up," she finally said.

"Precisely!"

Mavis couldn't help laughing. "He's probably just as nervous. You're pretty formidable, you know. I'm surprised he got up the nerve to ask you, Kathy."

"I am too. I'm more surprised I accepted, but you were right. Hallock's silent influence has been coloring everything I do, to the point where I have no real life outside of the Egret Pointe library."

"Is Tim still showing up in The Channel?" Mavis wanted to know.

"I don't know," Kathryn said.

"What?"

"I haven't had the nerve to go back to The Channel since the episode with the barbarian," she admitted.

"Kathy St. John, I don't believe it!" Mavis exclaimed. "You're afraid!"

"Mavis, don't you dare judge me," Kathryn said. "If he had shown up in my Tom Jones fantasy, or in my Roman fantasy, or even the Highwayman fantasy, it wouldn't have been so bad. Even as Rapunzel's prince again. But he showed up as a leather-clad barbarian with the most spectacular dick I had ever seen. He fucked the ears off of me when he wasn't smacking my butt with a leather tawse or pulling me around by my hair. It was all I could do not to cut and run at dinner the other night."

"But Tim Blair is a nice guy," Mavis said. "He isn't your barbarian."

"I know," Kathryn answered. "That was why I didn't run. Walking home we really got talking, and it was dark except for the streetlamps, which don't throw a lot of light. That made it easy. I didn't have to look at him, which helped. He is a nice guy, but he's big, and I can't help but wonder if the fantasy matches the reality."

"Maybe you'll find out eventually," Mavis said softly.

Kathryn smiled. "You're really a terrible person, Mavis Peabody."

Mavis chuckled. "Let's go over to your cottage on our lunch break, and go over your wardrobe. We can pick out something together like we used to do as girls."

In for a penny, in for a pound. "Why not?" Kathryn replied. Mavis was obviously enjoying this whole situation, but then what were best friends for, if not times like this?

"Ohhh, this is yummy," Mavis said, pulling a fluffy pink sweater with a wide cowl neck collar from a drawer. "Wear it with those light gray wool slacks."

"It's too girly," Kathryn protested.

"You bought it, Kathy," Mavis said. "Must have been a moment of weakness."

"No, I did not. Debora gave it to me a couple of

Christmases ago. I've never even worn it. Baby pink? On me?"

Mavis held the sweater up in front of Kathryn. "It's absolutely gorgeous with your hair and eyes. It's a perfect pink for someone with red-gold hair. Debora has a very good eye, Kathy. Lord, it's soft." She looked at the label. "Angora and cashmere."

"You don't think it's too . . . too . . . Oh, hell, Mavis, you know what I mean."

"No, I don't think it's too-too, Kathy. You shouldn't look like the town librarian when you go out on a date."

"A date. At my age," Kathryn St. John said, shaking her head.

"Hey, you look like thirty-five, and besides, forty-eight isn't the end of the world nowadays. They say fifty is the new thirty."

"Terrific, and I look like thirty-five," Kathryn said gloomily.

"You still look fuckable, sweetie," Mavis said cheerfully.

Kathryn St. John laughed. She knew Mavis was right. She didn't look her age.

"I'll expect a full report Saturday morning before eleven," Mavis told her.

"There'll be nothing to report on," Kathryn said. "We're eating, and seeing an old movie. Nothing more."

"You don't think he'll try to kiss you?" Mavis asked.

"Mavis, for God's sake, we're grown-ups, not teenagers!" Her cheeks were hot.

"I'll bet he at least tries," Mavis said with certainly.

"You're scaring me to death," Kathryn told her.

"Now I'll be watching his every move the whole damned evening."

"Once you kids start going steady, maybe you can double with Jeremy and me," Mavis teased wickedly.

"Keep it up and I'm wearing a plaid suit and oxfords," Kathryn threatened.

Mavis collapsed with laugher on her friend's bed.

"And horn-rimmed glasses!" Kathryn said.

Mavis said nothing more, because she knew from long experience that if she dared Kathryn, her friend would show up for her date in the plaid suit, the oxfords, and the glasses. Kathryn St. John had never refused a dare in all her life.

"What's the matter with Miss Kathy?" Caroline asked mid-morning Friday.

"Why should there be anything the matter?" Mavis asked.

"I don't know. She just snapped at me. She never snaps," Caroline said.

"Hey, even the perfect Miss Kathy has a bad day every few years," Mavis replied. She controlled the grin that was threatening to break out on her face.

At four thirty Kathryn called Mavis into her office. "I'm going to leave in a few minutes. I have to shower and dress. You lock up for me, okay?"

"Wear the short black boots," Mavis said. "They go with the pink sweater and the gray slacks, sweetie."

"How about a nice white Irish sweater?" Kathryn said.

"Pink!" Mavis responded sternly. "It's a date, not dinner at my house."

"But I'm not a pink person," Kathryn said.

"Tonight you're a pink person, and wear your hair down," Mavis told her.

"I'll pull it back," came the answer.

"No! Just leave it down," Mavis said. "Get ahold of yourself, Kathy. Now get out of here. You said he's picking you up at five thirty. Go!"

Kathryn St. John hurried from the library and across the garden, letting herself into the cottage with her key. She turned a light on in the living room, and saw the front-door light was lit. It would be dark or almost dark by the time he came. Running up the stairs, she peeled her working clothes off, hung them up, and pulled out her gray slacks and black boots from the walk-in closet. Opening a drawer, she lifted the pink sweater out.

God, it was so feminine! She wasn't used to soft and pink.

Undoing her hair, then tucking it up, she showered, slowly lathering the soap generously, stepping into the water jets to rinse. She was going on a date. Kathryn St. John was going out with a man tonight. She stepped from the shower and dried herself off. Opening her lingerie drawer, she pulled out a pair of white silk panties, a lacy bra and a pair of cashmere socks. She stepped into the briefs and hooked the bra. Next came the pale gray slacks, and finally the pink sweater.

She looked at herself in the mirror. It wasn't too bad. The wide rolled cowlneck fell in a graceful drape. She wore pink in The Channel as Lady St. John, and it was flattering, she considered. And Lady St. John wore ringlets, Kathryn thought, as she let her hair down and brushed it out. It fell in thick waves about her shoulders. My God!

She was drop-dead sexy, and she couldn't recall the last time she had thought that about herself. Forty-eight years old, and sexysexysexy tonight. She slipped her feet into her low black suede boots, put her cell and her reading glasses into a matching clutch. Then she went downstairs. Her foot had barely touched the floor when there was a knock on the door. She hurried to open it.

His jaw dropped. He gulped, and grinned foolishly.

"Are you all right?" she asked him as he stepped into the cottage.

"I came to pick up the mousey little town librarian and I get the ghost of Suzy Parker," Timothy Blair said.

"I have never qualified as mousey," Kathryn said, taken aback by his reaction.

"It's a rule. All town librarians are mousey," Tim told her. "When did you get so gorgeous? That sweater is delicious. You look terrific, and I love your hair down."

"Before you declare your undying devotion to me," Kathryn said caustically, "I'll get my cape, and we'll go. Your car parked out front of the library?"

He laughed. "Okay, you're not mousey, even in the library, but you really do look terrific tonight, Kathy. Better than I deserve." He took the pale gray cape from her and draped it around her shoulders. "Yeah, I'm out front."

She slipped her keys into the cape pocket as she turned the front door to lock and pulled it shut.

"Question?" he said.

"As long as it's not about my choice of clothing," she said.

"Why is the town all decorated? The trees have corn-stalks tied to them with orange ribbon. There are pump-kins, gourds, baskets of apples. Is this some weird country thing?" Timothy Blair said.

"Didn't you see the banner across the main street?" Kathryn replied. "It's our annual fall festival. We have it at the end of October every year. It's a benefit for the hos-pital. It's tomorrow and Sunday. Didn't you hear about it at school? Then before Christmas we have a fair to benefit the library. It's small-town America, Tim."

"I've been too busy implementing some new ideas to listen to gossip," he answered her.

"Mavis can tell you that in a small town, gossip is how we know what's happening," Kathryn said, and she smiled. He really was a city kid. Would he ever get used to living in Egret Pointe?

He helped her into his car, and they headed for the mall outside of the village.

"Italian okay with you?" he asked. "The movie starts at seven thirty."

"Fine with me. I'll eat almost anything except fish," she told him.

The front of the restaurant was a pizzeria. The dining room was in the rear. It was early, and so they got a table almost immediately. He ordered spaghetti with meat sauce and meatballs with a salad. She ordered meat ravioli and a salad. The waiter brought a basket of hot garlic bread and a tub of sweet butter, along with two glasses of the house red wine.

"Hey, don't eat all the bread," he complained as she reached for her third piece.

"I can't help it," Kathryn said. "It's too yummy." Oh God! Did she just say *yummy*? It was the damned pink sweater. It was enchanted, and it was making her say silly, cutesy things.

But he just grinned. "I like a woman with a good appetite. My fiancée liked to eat too, and she was a little thing, but she never gained a pound."

"You were engaged?" she pretended ignorance.

"Yeah. She was killed before the wedding. Accident. Funny. I haven't spoken about it in years," Tim remarked.

"I'm sorry," Kathryn replied. What else did you say to something like that?

"Look," Tim said, "if I'm a bit awkward tonight, put it down to the fact I haven't been out on a real date since Phoebe died a couple of years ago."

"You've been out on not-real dates? What's a not-real date?" she asked, humorously attempting to alleviate the situation.

He laughed now. "A not-real date is the assistant headmaster escorting one of the widowed or single older teachers to school functions," Tim told her.

"Ahhh," she said, enlightened. "Well, I haven't been out on a real date in so long I can't even remember the last time. There aren't too many gentlemen callers for the town librarian. Actually there aren't too many single men in my age group available."

"I'm forty-three," he said. "Last February."

"I'm older," she told him.

"Yeah, I know. You're five years older than I am. I guess that qualifies you as a cougar," he teased.

"A cougar?" Kathryn St. John looked puzzled. "Obviously I've missed something. This has got to be a new colloquialism, right?"

"Right. A cougar is an older woman who dates a younger man," he told her.

"Ohh, I actually like that," she replied. "Much nicer than 'cradle robber.' And how the hell did you know how old I was?"

"Gossip, m'dear." He grinned wickedly.

She laughed, suddenly realizing she wasn't uncomfortable with him any longer. He was funny, and he was fun. And Kathryn St. John was a cougar on the prowl tonight.

Their meal came and they both ate with gusto, enjoying the well-cooked, well-seasoned food on their plates.

"Tiramisu?" their waiter asked when they had finished.

"We have time," Tim said. "Make it two!"

He put his arm around her in the movie, and while startled at first, she found she felt comfortable enough with him now to let it be. She cried when the Suzy Parker character, Gregg, was killed falling off of a firescape. She always cried at that part of the movie. She reached for her handkerchief and discovered she had forgotten to put it in her clutch. Tim handed her his. It was big and smelled of sandalwood.

"Thank you." She sniffled. "I'll have Mrs. Bills wash it and return it to you."

"That's okay," he said. "Force of habit. I always carry two. Phoebe used to cry in movies also."

Later, as they left the movie, she told him, "I always thought Suzy Parker was underrated as an actress by Hollywood. That was a pretty meaty role, and she nailed it.

But all they ever saw was the first of the beautiful super-models. Pity."

"Is she still alive?" he asked her.

"No. She died a few years back."

"Want to stop for ice cream?" he tempted her. "Walt's is open late on Friday and Saturday nights, I'm told."

"We've already had dessert," Kathryn said.

"Is there a law in Egret Pointe that says you can only have one dessert a day?" Tim teased. "I'm hungry again." He pulled into a space in front of Walt's ice-cream parlor. "If you're watching your figure, I'll get something to go."

"Get two to go, and we'll eat it back at my place," Kathryn invited him. "Strawberry with hot fudge, please."

"Don't want to be seen with me?" he teased her.

"We've already been seen, Tim. There were at least three couples in the restaurant I recognized, and who recognized me. And the movie was full of Jeremy's Books into Movies class. Let's keep the town guessing for a while, okay?"

He grinned at her. "Do your friends know what a really bad girl you are?" Tim asked. "I like you, Kathy St. John. I think we could be friends." Then he exited the car, and went into Walt's for their ice cream.

Well, that was interesting, Kathryn thought to herself. Did she want to be friends with Timothy Blair? And what kind of friends would they be? Movie buddies? Friends with benefits? Boyfriend/girlfriend? There was a host of possibilities available to her.

He liked her. The truth was that she liked him too.

If only he would stop showing up in her fantasies. That was the only thing making her uncomfortable about him. She missed The Channel, but having all the men she had sex with there look like Timothy Blair was more than disconcerting.

On the other hand there could be an advantage to it, Kathryn thought for the first time. She could fuck Tim all she wanted in The Channel, and no one would ever know it.

He would never know it. She would remain the town's chaste St. John librarian, and Hallock wouldn't be on her case once he realized her friendship with the Middle School principal was just that. A simple and innocent friendship. Why hadn't she thought of this before? The men in The Channel didn't really exist. So what did it matter what they looked like? She knew Tim Blair enough now not to be embarrassed when she saw him or dealt with him. No matter his appearance, he wasn't the man in The Channel. Obviously she had a little crush on him. It would pass.

"You're deep in thought," Tim said, climbing back into the car and handing her the bag. "Two sundaes. One strawberry with hot fudge, and the other dulce de leche with caramel sauce. Let's get them back to your place before they melt."

Five minutes later they were in the living room of the cottage. Kathryn walked over to the fireplace, and suddenly a cheerful blaze sprang up. "Gas," she said. "I'm not a purist like Mavis and Jeremy. And I never have to clean the fireplace out of ash and soot. Or rather Mrs. Bills doesn't."

He chuckled as they settled down on the couch opposite the fire to eat their sundaes. "She's a marvel, isn't she? I owe Doris Kirk big-time for putting us in touch."

Her cheeks were pink, and her green eyes sparkled as she ate her sundae. He didn't think.

Kathy didn't look forty-eight at all. She was one sexy lady. He would love to pull her into his arms and kiss her. He hadn't kissed a woman since Phoebe, and wondered if he still knew how to kiss. But Kathryn St. John had given him no indication that she was interested in kissing him, and he wasn't a man to push the issue. He wanted to get to know her better, and if it was right then the time would come.

"I had fun tonight," Kathryn said.

"Enough fun to do it again?" he asked softly.

She was startled by the request, and blushed. "Sure," she finally said. "Call me anytime, Tim."

"How about tomorrow?" he asked. "I get the feeling the new Middle School principal should show up sometime at the Harvest Festival. I don't want to look unfriendly, after all."

"Actually, that would be a very smart thing to do. You want to look like you're making an effort to blend into the town and town life. You know my brother is on the school board, and he can be very influential. If you really plan to make your home here, then that would really be a good start for you. If you like, I'll take you to the festival and introduce you around."

"I've met your brother," he told her.

"You have? When on earth did you meet Hallock?"

"Your nephew is being a disciplinary problem this year. I had to call his parents in to speak with them. Your sister-in-law did not come. Indisposed, your brother said, and then he went on to tell me how the teachers were all handling Hallock the Sixth badly."

"Of course," Kathryn said. "St. Johns are never wrong. It's everyone else who is wrong. I'm sorry you got your baptism of fire so soon."

"I've met men like your brother before, Kathy. Rich men from old families are either the salt of the earth or they are a pain in the ass. Your brother falls into the latter category. However, I appealed to his ego. I told him I had complete faith in my teaching staff; but neither did I believe that his son was incorrigible. The problem lay in the fact that Hallock the Sixth didn't fully understand that he has a vast responsibility, coming from a family with such an esteemed background. Like most boys his age he is rambunctious. I told your brother that as a busy man, he probably hadn't realized the lad had reached the age where he needed to be taught that as a St. John he not only had privileges, but a duty to be an example to others as well."

Kathryn choked on her ice cream. "Oh my God, you really do know how to reach people like my brother. You sandbagged him, and I'll bet he sat there nodding in agreement with you because he didn't know it. What was the upshot?"

"He said he hadn't thought the boy was old enough for those lessons, but then children did mature more quickly today. Then he said Hallock would mend his ways immediately if not forthwith. Finally he shook my hand, and said that while he hadn't been in favor of hiring me, he thought I was proving to be quite satisfactory. That he would look forward to working with me," Tim concluded.

"And my *rambunctious* nephew?"

"Has toned down his behavior," Tim said.

Kathryn laughed. "Well played, grasshopper," she said.

Tim stood up. "I think I had better get going while there is someone still up to verify that I didn't spend the night."

"Ah, you're catching on." She chuckled.

"What time tomorrow?" he asked her.

"I'm not working tomorrow, so how about noon? That way I get to sleep in."

"You don't get to sleep in when you have a dog," Tim told her. "Would you mind if I brought Rowdy?"

"No, not at all," Kathryn replied as she escorted him to the door. "It was lovely, Tim. Thanks so much."

"Back atcha, Kathy. See you tomorrow." The door shut behind him, and he heard her turn the bolt. It had been a surprising evening. The first time he had seen her he had been smitten. Tall, lean, and that red-gold hair. The pink sweater she had worn tonight fascinated him. He hadn't figured Kathy St. John for a woman with a soft pink sweater. It had certainly shown off her round breasts to perfection. He had wanted to touch those breasts, and thinking about them now made him hard. Since Phoebe's death he hadn't had such a reaction to a woman.

Some of the younger and prettier single teachers at Kensington had, after what they believed was a suitable period, tried to attract him. He just wasn't interested. It was after the twenty-five-year-old French teacher had attempted to cajole him into taking her to a school function when one of the widowed teachers in the English department had stepped in to to save him. "Sorry, dear, but he's mine. Mr. Blair has kindly offered to escort me." The French teacher had gone away defeated, and he had thanked his savior. After that, he always asked one of the older women to accompany him to these functions.

And then he had come to Egret Pointe and met the town librarian. And he wanted to date her. Hell! He wanted to kiss her, and caress her, and fuck her. It wasn't natural for anyone, man or woman, to remain celibate. It had to be unhealthy. But would he eventually be able to cajole Kathy into bed? Judging from Hallock St. John V's large brood, St. Johns obviously appreciated sex. Hallock V was a married man, however. His sister was a different matter. God, was she a virgin? A real spinster? Mavis Peabody would know, and damn, he was going to find out before he made the wrong move.

Kathryn peeped through the window in her front door, watching him go off across the garden. She hadn't lied when she told him that she had had a good time. She had. It had been nice to get out for an evening. And she was going out with him tomorrow. In broad daylight. To a town function. Oh, there was going to be talk. She chuckled. Yes, by Saturday night she and Timothy Blair would be the talk of Egret Pointe.

But first she was going to enjoy an adventure with her barbarian in The Channel. She made certain the cottage was locked up, then hurried upstairs to bathe and get into bed. Now that she had decided the barbarian with Tim's face wasn't going to bother her, let the games begin. Picking up the remote, she pressed the F button and found herself, not in Temur's tent, but in an elevator, the interior of which was polished pecan wood. There was a mirror in the rear of the elevator, and beneath it was a small red leather bench. A little crystal chandelier hung from the elevator's ceiling.

"Going down," said a voice she recognized as The Channel's.

Oh my God! She had gotten into bed naked. But then she realized she was wearing her pale gray slacks and a white cashmere-and-wool turtleneck. Her pink suede slippers, which were lined in lamb's wool, were on her feet. She heaved a sigh of relief. She couldn't feel any motion until the elevator stopped with a gentle bump. The bronze doors opened without a sound, and Kathryn St. John found herself facing a pretty young girl with short blond hair wearing a neat light blue wool suit.

"Miss Kathy? Hi, I'm Carol, Mr. Nicholas's second assistant. Please come with me. He wants to see you." She turned and Kathryn followed, stepping into a big room with pale, creamy carpet so deep she sank into it. She took a quick look about her. The lower halves of the walls were paneled. The upper halves were papered in a large elegant floral, mostly in greens, cream, and coral. Gazing up, she saw the room had a coffered oak ceiling. One side of the room was a seating reception area with a couch upholstered in gold silk brocade, a row of matching chairs, and a mahogany coffee table.

On the other side of the room there were two beautiful mahogany desks with matching workstations and chairs. On the opposite side of the room was a third desk. Seeing them approaching, another woman got up from the single desk. She was a motherly, elegant woman with a young face and snow-white hair. She was dressed in a violet-colored wrap dress. "Miss Kathy, I'm Elizabeth, Mr. Nicholas's personal assistant. Thank you, Carol. Please come this way, Miss Kathy. He's looking forward to seeing you." She led Kathryn through a pair of carved and paneled mahogany doors. "Mr. Nicholas, Miss Kathy is here," she said, and then withdrew.

He came forward, both hands outstretched in greeting. "Kathy, my dear, how delightful to see you. Do come and sit down." His voice held just the hint of a cultured British accent. He gestured her toward a mulberry-colored velvet brocade couch.

"Don't you ever change?" Kathryn asked him. He was exactly as she remembered him. A man of middle years, medium height with dark eyes, and wavy silver-gray hair.

He chuckled. "My dear, you are one of the few people who know who I really am," he told her. "I remain as always."

She shook her head. "As charming as ever, Nicholas. Tell me, why did you seduce me all those years ago? I have always wondered, and of course then I didn't have the courage to ask you. Besides, I was flattered that you even noticed me."

"You were young and delicious, and someone had to take your virginity, Kathy. I could not bear the thought it would be some awkward boy," he told her. "You were too fine for that. But I have not asked you here today to discuss old times, as pleasant as it is for me to do so, for you have matured like a fine wine into a beautiful woman of a certain age, who is even more irresistible today than you were as a dewy girl."

"You were not programmed into my remote, Nicholas," Kathryn said. "I was looking forward to an evening with my barbarian."

"There will be no more evenings with Temur, or your musketeers, your highwayman, Tom Jones or Senator Flavian, or Consul Tiberius. I am revoking your privileges in The Channel, Kathy," Mr. Nicholas said quietly. Then, reaching toward her, he proffered a goblet of red wine.

She took it, and drank half of it down. She was in shock. "What have I done, Nicholas?" she said. Her voice was trembling.

He took her other hand in his and patted it comfortingly. "You have done nothing wrong, Kathy," Mr. Nicholas said. "But allow me to explain."

"Please do!" she said sharply.

Mr. Nicholas laughed. "Ah, there is that quick burst of temper you usually control so well. I'm glad to see it's still there. Kathy, you know what The Channel is. It is a lure, a trap if you will, to entice certain souls into my control. My nephew, Fyfe MacKay, thinks it is a waste of resources, but it isn't. Women are a very valuable commodity, and have been ever since time as you know it began. If I cull one useful soul out of every hundred thousand subscribers, I consider it a victory. And I have harvested two souls here in Egret Pointe alone, which I think is amazing. I had hoped to have your soul, my dear, but I realize now I will not gain it. What is weakness in the moral structure of the St. John men is not apparent in the females of that family.

"When you helped me introduce The Channel to the ladies of Egret Pointe, I rewarded you with a special remote that could program six fantasies, unlike the average remote that can only contain two. Most women have a tendency to grow bored with The Channel after a time and leave it. But you have remained for years. I do not have another subscriber who has been with me as long. You have made a life that contains but two elements: your work, and the fantasies you play out in The Channel.

"Fyfe says I have a weakness where you are concerned, and perhaps he is right. My nature, as you know, is very warm, and creatures of your kind do not usually retain my affections, but you have. There is more to life, Kathy, than what you have made of it. It is past time that you faced the reality of passion. The charming Mr. Blair quite lusts after you, my dear, and while you have not admitted it yet, you lust after him."

"I don't!" Kathryn St. John denied. "I most certainly do not!"

"Then why do your lovers in The Channel suddenly all bear his face?" Mr. Nicholas asked her.

"I thought there was a short in my remote," Kathryn said. She drank the rest of her wine down, and the goblet automatically refilled itself.

"Come now, my dear, you didn't really believe such a thing for a single moment." Mr. Nicholas chuckled. "You have always been a terrible liar, Kathy."

"And you have always been an excellent one," she replied. "I remember how you lied to my grandfather and father that first time you brought me home late. Your car had had a flat tire, and your chauffeur backed you up."

"Your grandfather and your father both knew what I was about," he said, shocking her. "I had their permission to take your virginity and briefly make you my mistress.

The St. John patriarchs have always been willing to deal with me in exchange for their good fortune, my dear."

"Well, I'll be damned," Kathryn St. John said candidly.

Mr. Nicholas laughed and shook his head. "Alas, my dear, you won't be, although *they* were. And I shall have your brother too, in exchange for finding him the perfect wife; and your nephew shows great possibilities, Kathy."

"Please, Nicholas, don't take The Channel away from me," she said. "It's all I really have, except for the library."

"You could have Timothy Blair if you chose, Kathy, and you should choose. I understand that you don't want to be controlled by men the way your grandfather and your father controlled you, the way your brother attempts to interfere in your life. You want to be an independent woman. It is not impossible for you to be one, and still love a man. Your life is not a normal one, although it may appear so to those around you who think of you as this St. John generation's old maid librarian."

"I am not a girl, Nicholas," Kathryn said softly.

"No, you are not, but neither do you look your age—nor will you ever. You will age slowly and quite well, Kathy. I did not realize that by giving you the six-button remote you would enjoy The Channel so very much. The idea was to tempt you to the dark side, but I'm afraid you are just too nice a woman," Mr. Nicholas said, his tone almost disapproving. "Everyone likes you. Your staff, your family and friends. Indeed, everyone with whom you come in contact. You serve your church"—and here he shuddered slightly—"and the charity your family founded for single mothers quite, quite well. You are generous to a fault with your own money. You forgive library fines when you think it expedient. You are simply too good, Kathy, and you have reached a point where you are unlikely to change. You can be of no further use to me."

"You are being cruel!" Kathryn cried.

He smiled. "Yes, I am, aren't I?" he said.

"Please," she pleaded, ashamed to be doing so.

"If you want to be fucked from now on, my dear, you shall have to succumb to your schoolmaster's charms, Kathy. I can tell you you won't be disappointed. Your imagination with Temur is more truth than fiction." He chuckled. "And if it will make you feel any better about this situation, I can tell you that he enjoys games, or at least he did with his late fiancée," Mr. Nicholas said.

"I don't know how to behave with a real man," Kathryn said.

"Of course you do," he told her. "If I may use a human expression, it's like riding a bicycle. You may not have done it for years, but once you get back on it, it all comes back naturally, Kathy. It's not like you to be afraid, my dear."

"I am not afraid!" she insisted.

"Yes, you are," he responded. "You are afraid of not being in control of the situation, and indeed there will be some times when you are not in control; but the reverse will be true for him. There will be times when you have the upper hand, and times when he does. That is nothing to be frightened of, Kathy. Passion is both give and take."

"What if I can't be like other people, Nicholas? After

all, I've had The Channel to rely on all these years," Kathryn said.

"Then you are doomed to a long, dull, and sexless life, I fear," he answered her.

"You would wish that on me?" she said despairingly.

"Strange to say, my dear, I wish you nothing but happiness. It is all up to you now, Kathy," Mr. Nicholas told her.

"Will I ever see you again?" she asked him.

He looked surprised. "Most people do not wish to see me ever," he said.

"Religion makes everything either black or white. Good or evil," Kathryn replied. "But I believe there are a myriad of colors in between the black and the white. And nothing is all good, or all evil. Even you, Nicholas." She reached up and stroked his smooth cheek. "Will I ever be allowed The Channel again?"

"It is unlikely, my dear, but of course not impossible," Mr. Nicholas told her. Then he took the hand caressing his face and kissed first the palm, and then the wrist of it.

Kathryn was surprised when a frisson of excitement raced through her. He was still a most fascinating creature. "Good-bye, Nicholas," she said.

"Good-bye, Kathy, my dear girl," he returned as he swept his hand gently down her face, and her eyes closed.

When she opened her eyes, she was naked and in her bed. The remote for The Channel was missing, and in its place was an ordinary television remote. She began to cry, and she continued until she cried herself into a restless sleep. She awoke early, when the dawn was just staining the eastern skies. Her head hurt, and she was thirsty. She got up and gulped two Excedrin and two Tums. Dr. Sam always told her to take the Tums with the Excedrin or aspirin. Then she fell back asleep for several more hours.

When she awoke again it was just before eleven in the morning. Kathryn lay in her bed, waking slowly. She clearly remembered what had happened last night. It was so unfair! But no one could thwart Mr. Nicholas. He had made his mind up, and she was stuck with it. Have a sex life in the real world. Was such a thing possible for her? It was going to have to be, because Kathryn St. John knew she absolutely, positively could not live without an active sex life, and Mr. Nicholas had said Timothy Blair was interested.

Of course he was, she told herself. The arm casually tossed about her in the movies yesterday. The way he had looked at her across the candlelit table when they had dinner out. She could tell too that he had wanted to kiss her good night, but had refrained because he didn't want to offend her. She had seen the question in those blue eyes of his, and she had neatly avoided it.

Kathryn swung her legs out of the bed. She had an hour before Timothy Blair came to pick her up for the Harvest Festival. She came downstairs into her kitchen, toasted an English muffin, buttered it, and ate it with a cup of blueberry yogurt, along with some blueberry-pomegranate juice and her vitamins. Back upstairs, she showered quickly, brushed her teeth, and smeared moisturizer and sunblock on her face.

Checking the thermometer on one of her bedroom windows, she pulled on a pair of white silk panties and pale gray slacks. Taking the white wool and cashmere sweater she had been dressed in last evening in Nicholas's office, she fitted her boobs into a underwire lace bra before donning the sweater. Thank God she wasn't sagging noticeably yet. Socks and the low black suede boots finished the ensemble.

Brushing her hair, she pulled it back into a horse's tail and fastened a band about it to hold it. She slipped on a pair of silver-and-turquoise clip-on earrings, a silver bangle on one arm, and her watch on the other. A little bit of green eye shadow for her green eyes, a touch of bronze lipstick, and she was presentable. Kathryn pulled a small shoulder bag from a drawer and put in her cell, her keys, and her lipstick. She was ready.

But for what? Reality, Egret Pointe style? It was going to be her life, now that she had been banned from The Channel. She still couldn't believe Nicholas had done such a thing to her, but her special remote was gone. And so now were her fantasies. Unless she decided to make some real ones. Did she dare? She heard the door knocker fall on her front door, and taking a deep breath Kathryn St. John, went downstairs to answer it.

CHAPTER SIX

H e was wearing jeans, a striped rugby shirt, a bomber jacket. "Hi," he said.

Briefly she felt breathless. "Hi," she said back.

"Ready to go?"

"Where's Rowdy?"

"In the car, since I was only going to be a few moments. Window is open," he said.

She laughed. "I know you don't mistreat your dog now," she said. "I've got tickets for the Harvest Supper tonight. Come on, Tim, and see small-town America at its absolute best." She stepped through her door, reaching back to pull it shut.

They walked through the library garden. It was a sunny day.

"Who did this garden?" he asked. "It's gorgeous, just like an English cottage garden. You've still got dahlias."

"We haven't had a hard frost yet," Kathryn said. "The garden was begun by Miss Victoria, and added to by Miss Lucretia. I just pay the gardener to come in and keep it. I'm afraid I have a black thumb. Not at all like a proper St. John. My sister-in-law is English, and she comes now and again to do a bit of gardening and make suggestions."

"Your cottage, the library garden. It's like something out of a fairy tale," he said.

He opened the passenger door of the Contour, and helped her in. Rowdy was waiting.

"How old is this car?" she asked him as the dog wagged himself in welcome.

"Twelve years old, but I keep it in good running order," he said. "If you take proper care of your car, you don't need to replace it for twenty or more years."

"You're a frugal man," she noted as he slid behind the wheel, fastened his safety belt, and they got under way. "I like frugal."

"No necessity to waste money," he said.

"But you have money," she replied casually.

He was a bit startled, but then he remembered it was a small town. "Yeah, I inherited a little from my folks." He had actually inherited a lot from his parents. "Makes it easier for me on an educator's salary. Where are we going?"

"It's a field outside of town that belongs to a local farmer. He loans it to us every autumn for the festival," Kathryn told him. "You drive, and I'll navigate."

"Sounds like a plan to me," he said, and following her directions, they quickly reached the site of Egret Pointe's Harvest Festival.

The field was obviously a meadow the rest of the year. It had been mowed short to accommodate the fund-raiser. Men from the local volunteer fire department were directing the festival goers to the designated parking area on one side of the field. It was crowded, and parking was already at a premium.

"There! There!" Kathryn pointed to a vacant space.

Tim quickly pulled in, just beating out another car.

"Tourists," Kathryn said. "Too bad."

He chuckled.

They got out. Tim took Rowdy's lead, and they walked back to where the little pavilions and booths were set up. The afternoon seemed to speed by. There was a livestock exhibit with sheep, goats, and poultry. Tim was fascinated by a cage of green-legged hens from Poland. There was a dog show with prizes for prettiest, ugliest, biggest, smallest, hairiest, and most obedient, among other silly categories. Every kid in Egret Pointe had brought his dog, and everyone got a ribbon to take home. The entry fee for each dog was one dollar. The money had to be honestly earned, and could not be given by a parent.

It went to the hospital as part of the fund-raiser.

"What a terrific idea," Tim said as Kathryn explained it to him. "It teaches the kids the the act of giving of oneself. Whoever thought this up was a genius."

"Thank you," Kathryn said. "It was my idea. If you don't teach children how to give of themselves, how will they learn?"

"I know," he said. "I thought next year we would direct all of our school fund-raisers to Heifer International. The kids can decide how they want the money distributed, whether it be for a cow, a flock of ducks, whatever. I want them to see how money can be used for the good, to really help less fortunate people."

"Now that is real genius," Kathryn told him.

In mid-afternoon he admitted to hunger as they approached a stand selling food.

She cautioned him not to eat too much as they had the Harvest Supper at six. He gobbled two hot dogs smothered in chili and cheese while she ate a corn dog. They shared a drink, passing it back and forth, laughing together. And Kathryn realized she was having fun. Real fun. They ran into her brother, his very pregnant wife, and their children.

Hallock was positively jovial. "Have supper with us!" he invited.

"We'd be delighted," Tim replied before she could refuse.

"Excellent! We'll send the kids home so we can have a little grown-up time," Hallock St. John said. "See you in the tent at six. No more cotton candy, Coralyn!"

He moved off with his family.

"You really are kissing up to my brother, aren't you?" Kathryn teased.

"I figure if I'm going to do some old-fashioned courting of his little sister I had better be on his good side," Tim replied. "Isn't that what you do in small-town America when you decide to court a lady? Make friends of her family?"

She laughed. "You're kidding, of course." But her heart was beating a little faster than it usually did.

"Nope, I'm not kidding. Since Phoebe died, there hasn't

been a woman who attracted me enough that I wanted to see more of her, get involved with her. Until now," Tim told her. "The moment I laid eyes on you I knew you were someone I wanted to know better, spend time with. You've been pretty standoffish, Kathy, until recently."

"It didn't seem to discourage you," Kathryn said softly.

"No, it didn't. Maybe I'm a bit old-fashioned, but I'm still a man who, when he sees something he wants, goes after it full bore," Tim answered. "I think that you like me, and if you like me, then unless there is some other reason for avoiding me, I'd like to see you on a regular basis, for dinner, a movie, a walk in the woods, or along the beach, and maybe more if we decide we want more. Any thoughts on this?"

She realized they hadn't moved from the spot where her brother had greeted them. And he was looking down at her. Kathryn St. John raised her head to look at him. "Yes," she said. "I would very much like to have some kind of a relationship with you. Relationship? Is that the word they use today? Dinner, a movie, walks. Yes. Let's see where it takes us, Tim. And now, before everyone in town wonders why we continue to stand here looking at each other, let's go say hi to Emilie Shann, the novelist. She signs books for us to raise money for the hospital."

They walked down a row of booths selling homemade jams, preserves, and fudge.

Ashley Kimborough Mulcahy, owner of *Lacy Nothings,* had a booth selling edible underpants in a variety of flavors—pumpkin, cinnamon, and chocolate being favorites—along with some cute flannel nightgowns for both men and women, with matching nightcaps. She waved at Kathryn and raised an eyebrow and cocked her head, noting her escort.

"We're distant cousins," Kathryn said. "She's married to the famous restorer."

"Sit with us at supper, Kathy," Ashley called.

"Can't. We're with Hallock and Debora," she said back.

"Save two places for Ryan and me," Ashley replied.

"Okay," Kathryn agreed. At least she'd have someone interesting to talk with at the table.

"R and R? Yes, they did some work for my parents," Tim said. "She's cute, and obviously preggers."

"They have one little boy, Benjamin, after her brother. He was killed in Desert Storm, along with my . . ." Kathryn stopped, unable to say his name. "Mavis's brother," she finally got out.

Tim noticed, and saw the sudden sadness in her eyes. He didn't ask. One day he would, but not today. "Hey," he said, "look at the long line of women up ahead. Must be your friend the romance author." His eyes lit on Emily Shanski Devlin, known to her public as Emilie Shann. "She's cute, and she's pregnant too. Is there something in the water that I should be warned about, Kathy?"

She had recovered from her momentary sorrow, and laughed. "They both married in their thirties to men who love them madly," Kathryn explained.

"And obviously often," he responded drolly.

She giggled. She couldn't help it. He saw the funny side of life, and she liked that about him. "Wait till you see

Mick Devlin and Ryan Mulcahy," she told him. "They are both hunkish. Is that a word, Tim? *Hunkish?*"

"Hunk, hunkish, hunkley," he replied. "Yes, I believe it's a word group." Then he grinned at her. "Modern colloquialisms. Don't know if it's made the *Oxford Dictionary* yet, however."

Emily saw them. She waved, and they waved back. The readers waiting for autographs turned eagerly to see who the wave was for, but seeing Kathryn St. John and Tim Blair they turned away. "It's just the town librarian and the Middle School principal," they heard a woman say quite distinctly.

"Well, that certainly puts us in our place," Kathryn murmured.

The farmer who owned the field was giving hayrides in a big wagon through his apple orchard.

"Come on," Tim said to her. "I've never been on a hayride." Pulling her over to the half-filled wagon, he pulled out ten dollars and put it in the contributions jar being held up by the farmer's wife, boosted Kathryn into the wagon, and then climbed up to join her. "Look!" he remarked as they started off. "The moon is coming up over the bay."

The sun was setting in a blaze of fiery colors to the west, and a round moon was rising over the water. It was a real autumn moon, large, symmetrical, and deep gold in color because of the reflecting rays of the setting sun opposite it in the deep blue darkening sky. The planet Venus twinkled large and bright mid-heaven.

"It's perfect," Kathryn said. "Oh, I'm so glad, Tim!

Your first Harvest Festival, and everything has been ideal for you. You'll always remember it that way. Warm sun, cool breeze, big old butter yellow moon."

"And the prettiest woman in Egret Pointe sitting next to me," he said softly.

Kathryn felt her cheeks warm.

The hay wagon rumbled across the meadow and amid the trees of an apple orchard. There were still some leaves on the trees, and unharvested apples that were bruised or otherwise slightly damaged left on the ground, the farmer told them, for the deer and other animals. On the other side of the orchard was another small field that rolled down to the bay. The moon was now shining a beam of gold across the gently rippling waters. They traveled a short distance along the beach, and then turned back.

Tim's arm was now about Kathryn's shoulders, and she had her head on his shoulder. They spoke little, simply enjoying the beauty of the early evening. The few other passengers in the wagon weren't local.

Returning to the festival again, they saw it was almost six o'clock, and people were beginning to stream into the big tent for supper. Hallock had already commandeered a table, and waved to them to join him. To Kathryn's delight, Dr. Sam and his wife, Rina, were there, along with the Mulcahys, the Devlins, the Pietro d'Angelos, and the Johnsons. Everyone shouted a welcome as Tim and Kathryn joined them.

"Where were you?" her brother asked, but his tone was pleasant. "I thought you might have forgotten us."

"Tim had never been on a hayride," Kathryn said. "We took one."

"I couldn't resist the harvest moon," Tim said.

"Not the harvest moon," Emily Devlin said. "That's the September full moon. The October one is called the hunter's moon."

"Oh," Tim remarked, "I didn't know that."

"The romance author knows her moons," Mick Devlin said with a grin. "I hear you taught English in the city."

"I did," Tim replied. "Next year I plan to introduce and teach a literature class for the seventh and eighth grades."

He fit in, Kathryn thought. He spoke to Mick about editing, Ryan about restoration, her brother about education in general.

"A nice man," Dr. Sam remarked quietly.

"Yes, he is," Kathryn agreed.

Rina Seligmann looked knowingly toward Carla Johnson and Tiffy Pietro d'Angelo and nodded. They grinned back. Rina had a matchmaker's heart, and she had always wanted to see Kathryn St. John married happily.

"You didn't come to the Dr. Sam Dunk today," Dr. Sam said.

"I can never dunk you," Kathryn replied.

"I know," he chuckled, "but you always spend a great deal of money trying to, Kathy. Still, you had other things to do with your young man."

"We're not so young, either of us," she remarked with a smile.

"To me you're young," he said.

"I'm just ten years younger than you, Sam Seligmann," Kathryn responded. "But since you missed me I'll come back tomorrow, and spend a lot of money trying to get you off your perch and into the Jell-O."

The traditional Harvest Festival supper was being served. Rowdy lay quietly by Tim's feet. There was country ham, sweet-potato casserole, creamed corn, cut green beans, rolls and butter. For dessert, dishes of baked apples were brought to each place by the servers, who were all volunteers from the local churches, and teenagers from the High School. The meal had been cooked by the local volunteer fire department and the ladies auxiliary. The apples were large. They swam in heavy cream and were rich with brown sugar and cinnamon. Coffee and tea were offered the diners. The gathering began to break up as everyone got ready to go home.

Tim and Kathryn carefully picked their way across the field to where Tim's car was parked, bidding farewell to their friends as they went. Rowdy bounded along on his lead.

"Don't stay out any longer," Hallock V said to his sister. "You don't want people to talk, sister."

"Since I have appeared two nights in a row in Tim's company I think the talk has already begun, Hallock," Kathryn teased her elder brother gently.

He was silent a moment, and then he said, "Do you like him, Kathy?"

"Yes, I do," she answered simply.

He nodded. "No scandal," he said. "Remember that you are a St. John."

"I never forget it, Hallock," Kathryn said. Then she kissed his cheek. "Good night now, big brother."

"Good night," he replied, returning the kiss. "Come, Debora," he addressed his very pregnant wife, taking her by the arm.

Debora turned and winked mischievously at her sister-in-law. "Have fun," she mouthed at Kathryn.

"What was that about?" Tim asked. He had gone to open the car and turn on the lights so she might see more easily.

"Hallock warning me to cause no scandal with you," she told him wickedly.

Timothy Blair reached out and pulled her into his arms. "What we do together is our business, and I mean no disrespect to your brother when I say it." Then he kissed her, a long slow kiss, his mouth playing across hers softly. Releasing her, he opened the car door for her. The kiss had been pure heaven, he thought. She tasted of autumn.

Kathryn was astounded. "Oh my!" she said softly as she got into the car. It had been the first real kiss she had had in years. Her heart had hammered. Her stomach had roiled. It was just as if she were a girl once again, being kissed for the first time.

"Make that a double *oh my*," Tim said getting into the driver's side of the car.

"You liked it?"

"Didn't you?" he countered as he settled Rowdy in the backseat.

"Uh-huh, but it's been a while, Tim," she admitted to him.

"Me too," he said. "Not since Phoebe," he told her. "Can we try it again to see if we really like it?" He reached out for her, but Kathryn held up her hand.

"Not in public, please."

"My place? Your place?" he asked.

"Mine," she said softly. "I'll turn on the fire."

"And we'll sit in front of it talking, and necking," he said.

"Uh-huh," she responded. She felt absolutely giddy with excitement, and surprised by her own reaction. *Hold on, Kathryn,* she said to herself. It was a kiss. A simple kiss. But he wanted more kisses, didn't he? And kisses could lead to . . . Oh God! She wasn't ready for this. Not yet. Not ready? The woman who had programmed six wild fantasies with Romans, barbarians, a fairy-tale prince, and a couple of eighteenth-century rapscallions? That woman wasn't ready for some kissing games?

But the men in her life had all been fantasy creations. The man sitting next to her driving back to her cottage was flesh-and-blood real. Some women might have been fearful of the fantasies in The Channel, but Kathryn St. John wasn't. It was real-life men, and the thought of sex with them, that scared her to death.

Was her body good enough? Could she reach orgasm? Would she have to fake it, and what if it turned out she didn't really like him? She no longer had a fall-back position. *Nicholas! Nicholas! What have you done to me?* she asked him silently.

"Did you have fun today?" he asked her. "I did."

Startled out of her reverie she said, "Yes, yes, I did have fun. I love the Harvest Festival. It seems to be more fun each year."

"How long has it been going on?" he queried.

"Ever since the town was founded in the 1700s there has been a Harvest Festival at the end of October," Kathryn said. "It became a fund-raiser for the hospital in 1902, when the hospital had been here for a couple of years and the need to raise money to keep it going became apparent," she explained. "The hospital began in a large Victorian house donated by two widowed sisters who had lost their only sons in the Spanish-American war. They died within a year of each other and both wills had stipulated that their house and their monies go to giving Egret Pointe a hospital of its own. The current building was built after World War Two, and it gets updated as we get the cash to do it. Little town like ours needs a hospital. The county seat with its big medical facility is forty miles away."

"You forget about the importance of community when you live in a big city," Tim said as he pulled up into the library's small parking lot. He loved how earnest she was when she spoke of all things Egret Pointe.

"Do you think you'll like living here, Tim?" she asked. "I know you've only been here two and a half months, but it must be a big change for you. You've lived all your life in the city, haven't you?"

"Yeah," he said as he came around to open the door and help her out. "Stay, Rowdy. I like what I've seen so far, and I really love the school. The staff is great, and most of them are open to new ideas. Gloria Sullivan has really paved the way for me." He took her hand firmly in his, and they began to walk through the library garden to her cottage. "Have you any idea how cute you are when you talk about this town, Kathy?"

She laughed. "It's been a long time since anyone has called me cute," she told him. "Isn't there a cutoff age for cute? I must be way past it."

He grinned. "You look sexy and sophisticated, I'll admit, but there are certain times when you speak about the town when you are so enthusiastic and damned cute it tickles the dickens out of me." Then he stopped and pulled her into his arms, looking down into her face from his six-foot-four height. "Kathy St. John, I really, really like you. And if you really, really like me, then eventually we are going to need to take this a whole lot further. I know we haven't known each other a long time, but I feel as if I've known you forever." Then, kissing her lips softly, he continued walking toward her front door.

Kathryn stopped him by standing stock still after they had moved just a few steps forward. "Hey," she said, "you can't expect me to wait to get into the house before I answer you, Timothy Blair. I haven't wanted to get involved with anyone for a lot of reasons you may or may not understand. But something is different about you, and maybe we ought to get to know one another better. If it doesn't work out, then I hope we can stay friends at least. That okay with you?"

"Yep," he said quietly. "Now can we go inside, so I can kiss you a whole lot more without the town being in on our secret?"

"Yep," she agreed, and pulling out her keys, opened the front door.

He practically pushed her through it, pulling her back into his embrace, his mouth fusing onto to her mouth in a hot, passionate kiss that seemed to go on and on and on.

Wow, Kathryn thought, matching him kiss for kiss for kiss. He's every bit as good as the boys in The Channel. Maybe even better, she considered, as she pushed off his jacket. "Mmmmmm!" she murmured as he released her lips briefly before kissing her again. Ohhh, way better than the boys in The Channel. Finally she pulled away. "Don't you want a fire for atmosphere?" she teased, drawing him into her living room. They fell onto her comfortable couch together, and Kathryn grabbed at the remote that would start the fireplace and pushed the button. "There," she said, "isn't that more romantic?"

"You are not going to be an easy woman, Kathy, are you?" he said, smiling at her. His blue eyes got crinkly at the corners when he smiled. A big finger ran down her nose.

"Probably not," she agreed.

"Want to tell me some of the reasons you haven't wanted to be involved?" he asked her gently. He picked up her hand and kissed it.

"You first," she said. "I'm not the only one who's been avoiding the opposite sex." She looked directly at him.

"My folks loved each other. Really loved each other. I want the same thing. Women say they have to kiss a lot of frogs before they find a prince. Well, the same thing holds true for men. We kiss a lot of lady frogs before we find the princess. Phoebe was my princess. I was thirty-one, and she was twenty-six when we met. It was love at first sight for both of us. We dated six months, and set a wedding date. And then she was killed in that hit-and-run accident.

"Then my mother got sick. She wasn't a woman for doctors, and it took us a while to convince her she needed to see the family doctor. He diagnosed her with osteoporosis, and prescribed calcium in large doses. She continued to feel lousy, and her pain got worse. My dad was suddenly helpless. This tough lawyer went to pieces. I finally stepped in and insisted on some serious testing. The first thing they found was that she had bone cancer. And the second thing they found was that all the calcium had virtually killed her kidney function. She went on dialysis, but it was too much for her. She died a few months after her diagnosis. Dad went to pieces for a while, and I moved back in to look after him. When you're taking care of your father there isn't too much time for wine, women and song." He grew quiet a moment, and then said, "Now, what's your story, Kathy?"

"Everyone in town thinks I'm the usual St. John spinster," she began.

"But you're not?"

Kathryn shook her head. "A long time ago I was in love with Jonathan Curtis, Mavis's older brother. We kept it a secret because the St. Johns wouldn't have thought the Curtises good enough for one of their women. The family 'were in trade,' as my grandfather would have said. They owned what had been the General Store in Egret Pointe. The IGA now sits on the property. Like a lot of men in this town, Jonathan belonged to the local National Guard unit. We're a patriotic bunch here. He asked me to marry him just before he went off to the Gulf War. We were going to brave my family when he came back."

"But he didn't," Tim said, seeing the sadness in her eyes.

"No, he didn't. He and Ben Kimborough were the two men from here killed in that war. No one knew that we had been serious about each other. I never even told Mavis, who has been my best friend since we were five," she said. "So I just kept my secret. And then I became what was expected of me. It hasn't been so awful. I have my cottage, an income from the family trust, a job I love."

"All that's missing for you is a cat," he joked.

"Hey, we have a library cat," she shot back.

"I think I need to kiss you again," Tim said.

"Hey, no pity kisses," she told him.

"The only one who is going to be pitied is me, if you don't kiss me," he replied.

"Well," Kathryn said, "you do have a certain charm, Principal Blair."

"Flattery will get you a helluva long way with me, Kathy." He chuckled, and pulled her close again, his lips meeting hers.

She felt dizzy with pleasure and murmured approval as his tongue met her tongue, stroking it slowly, languidly. She couldn't believe how new and exciting this all felt, considering her years of adventures in The Channel, yet it did. His fingers spread themselves into her soft red-gold hair as he held her face in his hands. She met him kiss for kiss for kiss. And after the surprise of the initial invasion of his tongue had dissipated, her own tongue grew active.

When she began to actively participate in their love play Tim's heart jumped, and suddenly he was getting very hard, very fast. It was like being eighteen again, and that was quite a shock to him. He realized if they kept this up they were both going to want more than either of them was really willing to give at this moment. And come morning, they wouldn't be real friends any longer. He didn't want that. He wanted her, but he wanted her when she was ready to commit to more than a casual "friends with benefits" relationship with him. But this wasn't the time. And where did all these thoughts come from? Was he even ready to begin another relationship? And with a woman who was years older than he was? And a member of a prominent local family?

He gently released his hold on her. "I don't want to go too fast," he said.

For a moment she looked a little bemused, but then she laughed. "You're right, but I was really enjoying myself, Timothy Blair. You are one terrific kisser."

"I'm pretty out of practice, Kathy," he told her.

"Kissing, sex, it's like riding a bicycle," she heard herself quoting Nicholas. "Once you start again it all comes back to you."

Now he laughed. "I suppose you're right," he agreed. "But if I continue to kiss you, Kathy, I'm going to want to put you on your back, and move on to other delights."

"I think we need to wait a little bit for that," Kathryn said. "Besides, if you stay much longer Rowdy will start to howl and waken the entire neighborhood. You'll have to leave him home next time, Tim."

"Or we could go to my place," he suggested. His dick was beginning to retreat. He stood up. "I'd better go before I compromise you. Hallock would never forgive me."

"No," she agreed reluctantly, "he wouldn't." She stood up too. "I'll walk you to the door, Principal Blair," Kathryn said demurely, and she did.

"Good night, Miss St. John," he said, and he gave her a quick final kiss.

"Good night," Kathryn replied.

A dog barked somewhere in the night.

"Oh Lord!" Tim Blair said, and turning, raced for his car.

Kathryn burst out laughing. She didn't know if it was Rowdy who had barked, but it was funny nonetheless.

The next day was Halloween, and Kathryn went back to the Harvest Festival. There was a costume competition for the younger children that year that the library was sponsoring, and she had agreed to be a judge. To everyone's delight she spent over twenty dollars trying to hit the target that would dump Dr. Sam into a vat of lime green Jell-O. Three tries for two dollars. But Kathryn never even came near to putting the beloved town doctor into the green goop. He teased her as he sat upon his perch.

"No wonder you never made the High School girls' softball team. You pitch like a girl, Kathy St. John."

"I *am* a girl!" she shouted back, tossing a ball, which fell short of the target and landed in the Jell-O.

"Nah, you're an old lady. That's it! You pitch like an old lady!" he taunted.

"I am not an old lady," Kathy said indignantly. But despite the trash talk, she could not get him off his perch until Ashley Mulcahy came up behind her and murmured to her to pitch her ball a little lower and to the left. Kathryn did, and hit the target dead center.

A bell rang, and the look on Dr. Sam's face was priceless as he was pitched into the Jell-O, but he came up laughing. "You had help, you library vixen!" he shouted.

Kathryn danced a very undignified victory dance. "Thanks, cousin," she said to Ashley, who laughed.

"He's sat up there all day, and no one got him," Ashley said. "Doctor won't let me do stuff like that since I'm so far along. He was feeling pretty smug and safe without me this year." She chuckled.

As it was near time for the Harvest Festival to end, Dr. Sam peeled off his jumpsuit and came around to greet both women. "Couldn't resist the chance, Mrs. Mulcahy, could you?" He chortled. "I almost got through the whole day."

"Hey, Dr. Sam, Kathy is my cousin. I had to help her," Ashley said, grinning.

"I'll never be able to do it again," Kathryn told him.

"Probably not," Dr. Sam agreed gleefully as she swatted at him.

November was upon them now. The trees were almost stripped bare of their leaves, the glorious October color now gone. The days grew shorter. And everyone in town suddenly knew that Principal Timothy Blair was courting Miss Kathy. Mostly they went out on Friday and Saturday nights, just like dating kids. From kissing they had progressed to old-fashioned petting, and Kathryn looked forward to each and every date.

She invited him to Sunday dinner one week. He reciprocated the following week.

And then one morning in his office he received a surprising call.

"Mr. Blair, this is Debora St. John, Hallock's wife. How are you?"

"Quite well, Mrs. St. John. How may I help you?" he replied, curious.

"Oh no, this isn't about the children," Debora quickly said. "I was wondering if you would come to Thanksgiving dinner. Kathy is coming, and we would be so pleased if you would join us too. Nothing fancy, of course. Just an ordinary Thanksgiving."

Tim doubted Thanksgiving at the St. Johns was ordinary. *Ordinary* was not a word he would associate with either Kathy or her brother. "I would be absolutely delighted to come for Thanksgiving dinner," he heard himself say. "What time would you like me?"

"Four o'clock would be lovely," she answered. "I'm so glad you're coming!"

And she did sound glad, which touched him. "See you then, Mr. Blair." She rang off.

It was an excuse to call Kathy. He punched in her number.

"Egret Pointe Public Library, Mavis speaking."

"Mavis, Tim Blair. Is Kathy there?"

"Hey, handsome," Mavis cooed. "Sure, I'll put you through."

Two rings.

"Kathryn St. John speaking."

"Hey," he said. "Your sister-in-law just invited me to Thanksgiving dinner."

"Good grief," she replied. "It would appear you have been accepted, and in record time, I might say. Debora would not have invited you without Hallock's okay."

"How fancy?" he asked her.

"Jacket and tie," she told him. "But it doesn't have to be a suit."

"Why don't I pick you up?" he suggested. "No need for us to take two cars, is there? What's the parking situation at your brother's house like?"

"Minimal," she said. "Yes, pick me up. What time did Debora say?"

"Four," he replied.

"Pick me up at four then. It's just five minutes to the St. John manse," Kathryn told him. "We'll be considered right on time."

"How's the Christmas Book Fair coming along?"

"Pretty good actually. We've got several committees of very dedicated people this year. Making it Dickensy to fit in with the merchants' shop décor this year has met with a great deal of enthusiasm from everyone," Kathryn said. She paused. "Could I get you to participate, Tim?"

"How?" He had actually wanted to be part of her event, but he hadn't known how to ask her, or if asking her would have been considered forward.

"I don't want to have a Santa Claus. It's not in keeping with the fair's theme. But I would love it if you would be the ghost of Christmas Present. We would set you up on a large throne surrounded by Christmas décor. You would appear several times during the fair, seat yourself, and read a Christmas story to the children. Then you would hand out sugar plums to each child when you were finished. We need a big man for the part, and you're a big man."

"I'll do it!" he said enthusiastically. "It's a wonderful idea, Kathy."

"Thanks," she said. "For the compliment, and for helping out."

"Want to go for ice cream after dinner tonight?" he asked her.

"Only if you come and share supper with me. Mrs. Bills is making her mac and cheese, which is wonderful."

"I'd love it," he said. "What time?"

"Six, Principal Blair," she teased him. "It's a school night."

"See you at six then," he said, ringing off.

Kathryn called her house. Mrs. Bills answered. "Is the mac and cheese enough for two?" she asked. "Mr. Blair is going to have supper with me."

"Of course it's big enough for two, but don't expect any leftovers. That man has a grand appetite. I'll make a bigger salad, and get a bit of ham, dear. Shall I do baked apples for dessert?"

"He's taking me to Walt's," Kathryn said.

Mrs. Bills chuckled. "I thought the man was courting you. My goodness, dear, he's every bit as discreet as you are."

"It's just ice cream, Mrs. Bills," Kathryn said, glad the woman couldn't see her pink cheeks. "Frankly I'd rather have your baked apples."

"I'll do some, and you can have them for breakfast," Mrs. Bills said. "If that's all, I'll ring off, Miss Kathy."

"Bye," Kathryn said. Then she smiled to herself. Oh hell, why not admit it? He was courting her. But to what end? Just to get into her pants? Or did the man have marriage in mind? And did she want to get married at age forty-eight? She was used to her cottage, and doing things the way she wanted to do them, and when she wanted to do them. She was too old for children now, so what was the point of marriage? Companionship in her fast-approaching old age? Ewwww! That sounded terrible.

Sex. That seemed to be the only reason to let Timothy Blair court her. She hadn't screwed around with a real man in years. Fyfe MacKay might look human, but he wasn't, so she didn't count him. But maybe she should. And at The Channel Corporation's island spa, she wasn't in danger of being discovered being a very wanton woman. Fyfe had been like all her lovers in The Channel, and she knew why he had seduced her. He wanted what his Uncle Nicholas had had at one time. And she had so enjoyed letting him have it.

She had always loved being in charge in The Channel, but she knew in real life it was unlikely she was going to be in charge. Or could she be? She wasn't going to know until she tried it again for real. And right now reality was all she had left, because Nicholas had revoked her Channel privileges. Had he ever done that to anyone else? But even if she saw him again and asked him, it wouldn't change things for her.

She had to stop obsessing over this. What was going to happen was going to happen. She was the town librarian, who was dating the Middle School principal. Everyone seemed to think it was a terrific thing. Even her older brother approved. But of course it would never occur to Hallock that his sister might want to get her brains fucked out, and that the Middle School principal was giving all indications of being more than willing to oblige her. Hallock saw a proper St. John woman, and a most respectable man who socialized in an accepted manner.

Kathryn was actually quite surprised that her brother was being so amenable about Timothy Blair. She wondered exactly what Hallock's motive was. There would be a motive, she knew. Debora would know something. Kathryn picked up the phone and called her brother's house.

Debora answered. "The St. John residence. This is Mrs. St. John speaking."

"Hey, Deb," Kathryn said. "I just got a phone call from Tim Blair. He's tickled to death you invited him to Thanksgiving dinner. Now tell me why."

Debora St. John didn't mince words. "Hallock checked him out, Kathy."

"My brother did what?" Kathryn was a bit taken aback.

"Hallock has friends in the city. He wanted to know personal stuff, not just all the résumé stuff. Did you know your boyfriend is a rich man?"

"No," Kathryn said slowly. "I know he's a nice man."

"Well, he's also rich. His father was one of the founding partners in his law firm. When he retired they bought him out for five million dollars with the proviso that they got to keep his name on the masthead. And the co-op Tim's selling," Debora said. "Another five million, and only because the real estate market is still down, and he was decent enough to agree to a price now instead of just renting and waiting for the market to go up again. And his family is very well thought of in certain circles. They go back to 1634 on both sides. They came to the section of the Massachusetts Bay Colony that's now Maine. Hallock is very impressed by all of this knowledge, but please don't tell him I told you. He says any man that you ever dated that he liked you dropped like the guy was on fire."

Kathryn laughed. "Well, that's a truth for certain, Deb. Somehow getting Hallock's seal of approval always had the effect of turning me off," she admitted.

"Do you think you might be interested in marrying him one day?" Debora asked.

"I don't know," Kathryn replied. Then she added wickedly, "I haven't slept with him yet, Deb. And maybe at my age I just want a friend with benefits."

Debora giggled. She was well used to her sister-in-law's pithy remarks after almost fifteen years of marriage. "I'm glad Hallock wants him at Thanksgiving," she said. "And I'm glad you aren't being put off. You know, Hallock just wants his sister happy, Kathy."

"What Hallock wants is to run my life like he runs yours, Deb. However, since I actually like Timothy Blair, I will let my brother believe he is succeeding in doing just that," she told the younger woman. "Kids all okay?"

"As always, disgustingly healthy," came the reply.

"And you? You okay?"

"I can't see my feet at this point," Debora said.

"What can I do for Thanksgiving?" Kathryn asked.

"Would you do the stuffing for me?" Debora asked.

"How many guests?"

"Eight, and the children's table," Debora said. "The bird will be twenty-five pounds."

"Done!" Kathryn promised. "The housekeeper's working full out?"

"She's a blessing," Debora said.

"Then as always, you have everything in hand," Kathryn said. "I hope to God that brother of mine knows how damned lucky he is in you."

"Thanks," Debora said. "Coralyn, what are you eating? Gotta go!" And she hung up.

Kathryn smiled. Okay, so she had no sex life right

now, but she was suddenly beginning to appreciate what she did have. A loving family. A home she loved. A job she loved. And a younger man eager to get into her pants. And sooner or later he was going to get up his courage and try. And she was going to let him succeed.

CHAPTER SEVEN

"Hot fudge and strawberry?" He laughed. "You're crazy—you know that, don't you?"

"Hot fudge and vanilla?" she countered. "Booooring!"

"It's traditional," he said.

"It's booooring," she said. "It's something Hallock would order."

He fell back, hand clutching at his heart. "Your brother? You are comparing me to your brother, woman? Eat up! We obviously have some serious talking to do."

"I don't want to talk," Kathryn said mischievously.

He saw what he thought was a wicked light in her green eyes, but he didn't want to make a mistake with her at this point. "What do you want to do?" he asked her slowly.

Suddenly she was the proper Miss St. John again. "Finish your sundae, Tim. Then I'll tell you what I want to do."

"Hi, Mr. Blair, Miss Kathy." Two preteen girls passed their table, giggling.

"Girls," he said back.

"It's going to be all over your Middle School now," she teased him.

"What?" He actually looked confused.

"That we're dating." She laughed. "They're already Twittering on their cells. One of them took a picture of us just before they spoke too. So tomorrow, when you get arch looks from a lot of your students, that's going to be why."

"Can anything be kept secret in this town?" he asked her, chagrined.

"Uh-huh," she said. "Now finish your ice cream. Then you can take me home, and we'll *talk*." She dipped her spoon into the glass sundae dish, and demurely continued consuming her strawberry ice cream with the hot fudge sauce.

"What will we talk about?" he said with a wicked grin.

"Let me surprise you, Timothy Blair," she answered.

"You constantly surprise me."

Kathryn laughed. They had known each other three months now. They had been kissing for two while dancing around the fact that each time they saw each other they were more sexually attracted. Nicholas had cut her off from The Channel. She hadn't had sex in weeks, and she wanted it. She wanted it badly. And Nicholas had said it was past time for her to live in the real world. But if she was going to be in charge of the situation, she was obviously going to have to make the first move.

They finished their ice-cream sundaes, and leaving

Walt's, walked home to Kathryn's cottage behind the library. He had taken of late to parking his car a street or two away for the sake of discretion. They got to her door, and opening it up, Kathryn stepped into the little center hall, pulling him behind her. She took off her jacket, then helped him off with his coat and hung them in the hall closet. Then she surprised him.

Instead of turning the gas fire on, Kathryn took hold of his tie, and drew him after her up the narrow staircase. He followed without hesitation, but suddenly he was wondering if he was really ready for this kind of a relationship. There had been no one since Phoebe's death. No one. He hadn't had sex with a woman in years, but then she claimed the same disadvantage. Was this a wise thing they were doing?

I'm acting like a slut, Kathryn thought, as she brought him down the small upstairs hall and led him into her bedroom. *But I don't care! He's been hinting at this for a month now. Let him put his money where his mouth is. I want to be fucked all night long. But this isn't The Channel, and he's forty-three. I'll be lucky to get one good poke out of him. God, I hope he's good at it. What if he's a "wham, bam, thank you, ma'am" guy? I'd have to kill him then. Nicholas, I hate you for this!*

The bedroom was dark but for a small lamp on her bureau that she had left on earlier. Kathryn turned in his arms and began pulling his jacket off. Her fingers skillfully undid the buttons on his shirt. She whisked the tie from about his neck. Her hands went to his belt buckle, and he stopped her then and there. *Oh God! I've made a fool of myself,* she thought, feeling her face getting hot.

"Easy, love," Tim's voice crooned in her ear. "We're going to get there, but not so fast. Let's enjoy the ride. I like the way you *talk*." His voice was filled with laughter.

"I thought it was time we moved to the next level," she said. "But if you don't want to, you can leave now. I should be over feeling like a complete idiot by the time we meet for Thanksgiving dinner at my brother's house."

He chuckled. "Oh no, Kathy, you don't get away so easily. I can't believe you're a woman to start something and not finish it." His big hand cupped her face, and he kissed her mouth softly. "I don't know what kind of men you were with before, but I'm a guy who likes to take it slowly. Passion shouldn't be rushed, even after a drought."

"It's been so long for both of us. . . ." she began. Well, at least it had been for him.

The Channel might not be reality in the strictest sense, but it sure left a girl satisfied. Who needed real men? She did. She sighed.

He kissed her lips again. "Don't talk, Kathy. Let's just see what happens," he said, low. Then he pulled her sweater over her head and laid it on a chair. Pressing her back into the wing chair by the bedroom fireplace, he knelt and slipped off her boots and soft socks, setting them neatly beneath the side chair. He stood her up again, unzipped her slacks, and slid them off, adding them to the sweater. Then he sat her back down again in the chair, clad only in her briefs and bra.

Standing directly in front of her, Tim drew off his unbuttoned shirt and his undershirt, laying them on the chest at the foot of her bed. He sat on the chest to take off his shoes and socks. Then standing, he unzipped his slacks and stepped out of them, putting them with the rest of his garments. Holding out his hand to her he pulled Kathryn to her feet and reached around her to unhook her bra, letting the scrap of silk and lace fall to the floor. Then, stepping back, he viewed her breasts.

She felt her face growing warm again, but the look in his eyes was admiring. When he pulled her against him the sensation of warm flesh on warm flesh was exciting.

Kathryn had round breasts with nipples the size of pansies. Tim pulled her closer and her breasts flattened against him. His chest was broad and smooth. That was good. She didn't like hairy men.

"Put your arms about my neck," he told her softly, and when she did he pushed off her panties, his hands going around to cup her buttocks. "You're round in all the right places," he said, smiling down at her. "Do you have any idea of how badly I want to fuck you, Kathy? I haven't had wet dreams since I was fifteen."

The rough words coming from him startled her. But what had she expected him to say? *Copulate? Have sex? Engage in sexual intercourse with you?*

"I will admit to thinking about what it would be like to fuck with you," she said.

"Phoebe and I used to do what is referred to as talking dirty to each other," Tim told her. "I liked it. Proper schoolmaster on the outside. Fucking barbarian on the inside."

Barbarian! He had said *barbarian.* Kathryn swayed against him. "I want to see your cock," she said. Then she pushed his boxers off and reached for him. Nicholas had said she wouldn't be disappointed. She wasn't. He was long, already thickening and hard in her hand. She reached beneath to cup his balls. Oh God! His sack was heavy. She didn't need to look. Her touch told her that he was every bit as large as her fantasy barbarian, Temur. She wanted to suck him. But what would he think of her if she did without an invitation? God! She was letting him run the show, and she didn't want to lose control of what was happening between them. "Let me suck you," she said.

"No," he replied. "I'm already hard, Kathy. I want to give you some pleasure before we come. And I want us to come together. I've got a big dick, and you need to be nice and wet, or I could hurt you. But another night, love, and you can have it any way you want. Tonight, however, I just want us to have a good, long fuck."

She kissed him to let him know she liked what he said. And she did. They kissed and kissed until her lips felt bruised. He put her on the bed, and put a few pillows beneath her hips to elevate her. Then he slid between her thighs, peeling her nether lips apart, and began to lick her cunt with the most skillful tongue she had ever experienced. He was amazing. None of her lovers in The Channel had tongued and sucked her like he was doing. He nibbled on her clit, which was now swollen to double its size. Kathryn moaned, unable to help herself. "Oh God, that is so good!" His lips fastened about her clit and sucked hard. Kathryn screamed softly. "Oh yes, Tim! More, please!"

He laughed softly. "Later," he promised, "but right now you are very wet, and I'm very hot to fill your cunt up with my cock." He positioned himself above her, drawing her slowly onto his massive penis. He moved carefully at first, but when he realized that she could take him in easily, he sheathed himself as deeply as he could go.

"Oh God, yes!" Kathryn half sobbed. She was impaled on his big dick, and she had to fight with herself not to come right then and there.

He saw her difficulty, and murmured soothingly, "Easy, easy, Kathy. Breathe a slow, deep breath. That's it. Now again. Better?"

She nodded. It was better. She was amazed by his gentleness and his skill as he began to move on her. Closing her eyes, she let herself be swept up in the pure pleasure as sensation after sensation washed over her. His cock moved rhythmically in and out, in and out. Kathryn wrapped her legs about his torso and moaned as he pressed deeper into her.

She was practically floating, and then he found her G-spot. She screamed softly, and the pleasure began to build quickly as he pumped her, pumped her, pumped her.

"I can't hang on much longer," he finally groaned.

"I'm ready!" she gasped and then climaxed, the walls of her vagina convulsing around his throbbing cock as its juices erupted like a volcano. "Oh God!" She sighed gustily. "That was wonderful, Principal Blair. Can I come to your office again soon?"

He laughed weakly. *Wonderful* didn't begin to describe what had just happened.

Then he groaned. "Damn! I forgot the condom." He rolled away from her.

"We should be okay," she said. "I don't have any diseases, and I get a gyno yearly. I haven't had any lovers in years."

"But what if . . ." he began.

Kathryn laughed. "Not a snowball's chance in hell," she said. "I'm too old."

"I'll take your word for it," he said. Reaching out, he took her hand in his. "This was nice, Kathy. I guess this makes us friends with benefits now."

"I guess," she answered. Her hand felt small in his, and when he put his arms about her and drew her close, Kathryn almost cried. She suddenly felt protected, and as if no one or nothing in the world could hurt her. Now where the hell had that come from? She wasn't one of those women who needed a man. All she needed was a good fuck on a regular basis. Sex was all she wanted. Nothing more. The Channel had been perfect for that, but now Nicholas had her screwing around with a real-live man, actually enjoying it, and getting sappy feelings about it.

Tim could sense her confusion. She was a woman who didn't play at the game of love any more than he did. She was probably wondering where this was going. So was he. Friends with benefits. It was okay for thirty-somethings, he supposed, but was it all right for the very proper Miss St. John and the Middle School principal? But having had a taste he knew without a doubt that he wanted more. Eventually they would have to decide what this relationship was all about. But not right away.

They lay hand and hand in the dim silence for some time. But suddenly Kathryn heard the grandfather clock in the downstairs hall strike once. Was it twelve thirty? One?

Half after something. "What time is it?" she said softly turning to look at her bed's clock. The lighted dial read twelve thirty.

"I had better get going," he said. "We both have reputations to consider." He got up and dressed quickly. Then bending, he kissed her lips gently. "This has not been a one-night stand, Kathy, has it?"

"No," she said, "it's not a one-night stand, Tim. I wish you could stay the night so we could do this again."

"Thanksgiving night," he said. "Come home with me after dinner. No one has to know you're there. We're using my car for transport. It will be dark. I'll put the car in the garage, and we'll go into the house through the breezeway. No one will see us. And I'll cook breakfast the next morning," he promised. "I do a pretty mean breakfast. We could have a whole weekend together if you want."

"I should say I'll think about it," Kathryn said, "but after tonight I don't believe I want to think a whole lot. What is that old saying? For once in your life do something bad, and you'll survive. Yes! And that's my final answer."

Tim grinned, and leaning over the bed gave her a quick kiss. "Good night, love," he said. "I'll let myself out."

"Good night," she responded. She listened as his footsteps echoed down the hall. She heard the faint creak of the front door as it opened and closed. When she was certain he was gone she got out of bed, and slipping downstairs, turned the deadbolt lock before hurrying back upstairs. *Sex!* She had just had some very satisfying sex, and she felt wonderful. It hadn't been a bad first time. A little careful, a little cautious, but it had been good. She wondered if Tim could be, would be a bit more adventurous? Time would tell. The fact he had suggested coming to his house after Thanksgiving dinner was pretty daring. And they were going to have to be very careful, or all of

Egret Pointe would know. There was probably a morals clause in his contract.

Oh God! What was she getting herself into? Maybe she shouldn't have been so quick to say yes to his very delicious suggestion, but she wanted more of that big dick of his, and neither one of them could qualify as a kid. They were two consenting adults, and if they wanted to have sex they should be able to without anyone else getting involved. Or so conventional wisdom would dictate, but this was Egret Pointe, and more often than not conventional wisdom didn't apply.

In the morning she found a single crimson dahlia in a bud vase on her desk. "Mavis," she called, "where did this come from?"

"Tim dropped it off at my house on his way to work," she said. "Told me to put it on your desk." Mavis cocked her head to one side. "So? What's happening?"

"Nothing," Kathryn replied.

"Honestly, Kathy, you have never been able to lie to me," Mavis reminded her best friend. "Now I want all the juicy details. What happened?"

"Nothing," Kathryn repeated.

Mavis's eyes suddenly grew wide. "*You did it with him, didn't you?* Oh my God! And don't say you didn't, because you're as red as that dahlia."

"Stop babbling, Mavis," Kathryn said. "I will neither confirm or deny, but I would just as soon Egret Pointe didn't explode with unfounded rumors by sundown."

"Okay, okay," Mavis responded. "But . . ."

"No questions!" Kathryn said sternly. "Do I ask you about Jeremy?"

"Jeremy is my darling, dull husband. You know who is hot hot hot, and every single teacher in the Middle School has been dangling their bait for him," Mavis said.

"Well, I am not dangling my bait," Kathryn replied.

"You don't have to," Mavis chuckled. "You had him hooked at first sight."

"Mavis! Please! The next thing I know, my brother will be demanding to know if his intentions are honorable," Kathryn said.

Mavis laughed aloud at this.

"And I have to sit through Thanksgiving dinner with Hallock. Right now he actually likes Tim. I want to keep it that way. Hallock assumes I'm still a virgin. He never knew about . . ." She stopped.

"Never knew about my brother?" Mavis said softly.

"How did you . . ." Kathryn began, astounded. It was Nicholas she had considered.

"Jonathan was my big brother, Kathy. You're my best friend. How could I not know, when I loved you both so much? And when he was killed I saw the light go out of your eyes. It was gone for several years."

"He had asked me to marry him, Mavis, and I had said yes. We were going to announce it when his Guard unit got back from Kuwait. If my family objected, we were going to elope. If they came around, we would have let them do a grand St. John wedding. It didn't matter to us which. We just wanted to be married. And then he was killed. What would have been the point in telling everyone at that point?"

Mavis nodded. "I figured you'd say something one day. I would have liked to have you as a sister-in-law,

Kathy, and my mother would have loved being able to claim you for real. She always said you were her other daughter."

"Water under the bridge," Kathryn said softly. "After that I didn't want any more reality in my love life."

"What made you change your mind?" Mavis wanted to know.

Kathryn St. John knew she couldn't tell her best friend the truth. That her virginity had been taken by someone known as Mr. Nicholas, who was the CEO of The Channel Corporation. Someone who had been close friends with her grandfather and father. That Nicholas was the devil himself, and the devil wasn't a creature in a red suit with a pitchfork and horns. He was a charming older man with custom-made suits and shoes, perfectly manicured hands, a stylish haircut, and elegant manners, who knew just how to seduce and use women.

No. She couldn't say that. Of course if she had, Mavis wouldn't have believed her, but still she couldn't bring herself to tell her friend the truth. That Nicholas had let her have a taste of The Channel. That she had been the one to introduce it to the women of Egret Pointe. That as a reward for her aid, her remote had allowed her to program six delicious and decadent sexual fantasies. That now in an act of supreme cruelty, Nicholas had banned her from The Channel because he said she could no longer be of use to him, as she was too good a person. That it was time she experienced reality.

"I guess I finally got bored with The Channel," she said. "I thought it might be fun to screw around with a real man for a change."

Mavis nodded. "Maybe you might even like something more," she suggested.

Kathryn smiled. "Let's not get ahead of ourselves, girlfriend. Now let's set up a meeting tomorrow morning to finalize everything for the Christmas Book Fair. We've got just two weeks left."

"Will do," Mavis said, and then turning, she left Kathryn's office.

Kathryn stared at the perfect dahlia on her desk. What a sweet gesture. It had been a long time since anyone had sent her flowers. And he had been so discreet. He had obviously picked it from his garden. It must have been something from old Mrs. Torkelson's plantings. She had been well known for her dahlia garden. This flower must have come from some tubers she had forgotten to take up last year that had grown and bloomed this year. The crimson color was so bright it almost glowed.

The phone rang and she picked it up. "Kathryn St. John here."

"Do you like it?" Tim asked her.

"Yes, the color is spectacular," she told him.

"You're spectacular," he replied. "Now tell me, what is it? I found it blooming in the backyard this morning, and it didn't look like a weed."

Kathryn laughed. "It's a dinner plate dahlia. Mrs. Torkelson grew them."

"Ahh," he said. "Then I did good."

"You did good."

"I wanted to say thank you, but I didn't want everyone in town wondering why I was sending you flowers."

"Hmmm, yes, your discretion is appreciated," she

teased him. "That single crimson dahlia was far more thoughtful than a big bouquet with a card reading, 'Baby, you were great!'" Kathryn said mischievously.

He burst out laughing. "Glad to be of service, ma'am," he told her.

"I like your service plan," she responded.

"Are we on for the movies this Friday night?" he asked.

"Same time and place," she agreed.

"Gotta go, love," he said. "I'm on lunch duty today."

"Bye," Kathryn answered, and hung up the phone. He was comfortable with her, and she found she was comfortable with him. Sex had entered the equation, but it hadn't made things between them awkward. But as a woman who liked everything orderly, she had to admit that not knowing exactly where this relationship—she supposed now that they had had sex it was a relationship—was headed. Reality sometimes sucked.

The next morning, Friday, Kathryn sat down with her staff. "Are we ready?" she asked them. "We've only got two more weeks until the Christmas Book Fair. Let's have your reports. Caroline? Books?"

"Everything promised has come: hardcover, trade and mass-market paper," Caroline Collines said. "We've got a terrific selection of this year's best sellers, from practically every publishing house in the city. Rina Seligmann's brother, Aaron Fischer, the agent, was a tremendous help, Miss Kathy."

"Wonderful! Peter?"

"Well, between our historical society and my friends in

the city, we just about have all the costumes needed. You should all get your fittings next week so everything fits comfortably. And some theater contacts of mine are going to help with the décor," Peter reported with a pleased grin. "They're setting up faux shop fronts to give us the feel of Dickens's London."

"Peter, that's wonderful. Thank you so much," Kathryn said. "Susan?"

"St. Ann's is loaning us their card tables and chairs. I've got red and green paper clothes and napkins and Christmasy paper plates and hot cups. I corralled a group of my friends to do the baking. We'll have tea, hot chocolate, hot mulled cider. It's not entirely Dickens, but I think people will like the menu. We're doing two chowders, corn and New England clam. Debora has volunteered to show us how to make little meat pasties, which are very English. She did a taste testing for us last week, and they were delicious. There will be scones, crumpets, jam, lemon curd, and tiny individual pies: mince and apple. We're going to have a table selling all the foods we're featuring. When we first decided to do this, I put up notices in all the churches asking for home-baked goods, jams, jellies, pickles, and relishes. The response has been wonderful, Miss Kathy."

"Sounds like we've got a real money maker, Susan. Thanks for all the hard work," Kathryn said. "Marcia, what do we have for the children?"

"I researched all sorts of old-fashioned games. Considering most of these kids are 'computer babies,' it should be quite an eye opener for them. We're doing a treasure hunt, and the Ghost of Christmas Present, to be played by our new Middle School principal, Mr. Blair, will be reading

Christmas stories of all kinds to the children. Peter's buddies in the city are supplying a gold-and-red velvet throne for him to sit on," Marcia Merryman, the children's librarian, reported.

Kathryn shook her head. "You all have been just wonderful. This is going to be a really successful Christmas Book Fair this year. What are we selling in the booths beside books, Caroline?"

"Handmade children's dresses with matching dresses for girl and doll. One lady is bringing a small stock of handmade christening gowns. We've got knitted goods, sweaters, gloves, mittens, scarves, and hats. Ashley Kimborough—whoops—Mulcahy is bringing some adorable flannel night wear for kids and adults."

"We'd make more money with her X-rated stuff," Mavis said dryly.

The library staff laughed.

"Agreed," Kathryn said, "but this is a family event."

"We've also got a candle maker and a potter joining us," Caroline finished.

"It sounds like we're ready to have a Christmas fair, and I think branching out from just books and games is a wonderful idea. We'll make it an almost one-stop-shopping experience for Egret Pointe," Kathryn said. She was very pleased.

"If they don't spend all their money at the mall next Friday," Peter Potter said.

As the meeting broke up Mavis said to Kathryn, "We're going to be at Hallock's for Thanksgiving too."

"Aren't the boys coming home?" Kathryn asked.

"No. This is the year they both go to the in-laws, and

besides, Andrea and Pam are pregnant this year. New grandkids coming. One in late spring, the other in mid-summer," Mavis said. They just told us. So now we'll have three."

"Congratulations," Kathryn said.

"Don't congratulate me," Mavis replied. "I didn't do anything except have two sons who seem to enjoy making babies. I really have to ask them if they know what's causing those pregnancies."

"And have them realize you know all about sex?" Kathryn laughed.

"True," Mavis agreed. "I think they still believe the stork brought them, and it's their generation that discovered sex." Then she changed the subject entirely. "Movie night again, Kathy?"

"Yes. They're running *The African Queen* tonight, along with an old World War Two newsreel, and five cartoons," she replied. "Tim and I really like those old movies."

"Dinner first?" Mavis probed.

"Yes."

"Dessert after the movie?" Mavis teased.

"Maybe," Kathryn replied with a wink. "You know me. I love dessert!"

"Don't we all." Mavis cackled.

But when she was alone in her office again, Kathryn began to consider. What if he wanted sex tonight? The first time had been good. Not great, but a good start. She couldn't remember sex with Jonathan, it had been so long ago. But she had been young then, and very much in love.

After his death she hadn't wanted to be involved again.

Being involved meant getting hurt. And she wasn't much into dominant males in reality. Or was she? Jonathan had been very laid back, like his sister. *I guess I'm just going to have to play it by ear,* Kathryn decided.

They met for dinner and talked. They saw the movie and talked. As they were driving out of the mall Tim said, "Want to come home with me tonight?"

"I thought you said next week," Kathryn answered. Oh God! Was she ready for this? But the other night had been . . . had been . . . what? Exciting? Yes, it had been. And now the added element of jeopardy in going home with him was even more thrilling. No one would know Egret Pointe's staid and proper Miss Kathy was fucking Mr. Blair. People would stroll by in the morning or even late tonight walking their dogs, and they wouldn't know. And the possibility of getting caught by someone just added the right *soupçon* of danger.

"I find I'm a greedy man," he answered. "I don't want to wait till next week."

"Good," she replied. "I'm a greedy woman. I don't want to wait till next week either. Are you into games, Tim?"

"The kind where I tie you up, and have my way with you?" he asked. "I think we could arrange something amusing for our personal delectation, m'dear."

She laughed. "How nice to know that under that tweed sports jacket there beats the heart of a proper villian. I like bad boys, Tim."

"I like bad girls," he countered, "and bringing the town's proper librarian to a screaming climax is so enticing, love."

"Then I guess we had better go to your place, sir," she told him.

He chuckled. "Let's set some ground rules first. Can I spank you?"

"Oh yes!"

"Tie your arms to my bedposts?"

"You have bedposts? Oh yes, tie me up, Principal Blair," she said.

"Will you suck my cock tonight?"

"With pleasure, sir."

"Ass-fuck?"

"Not into that, I'm afraid."

"No ass fucking then," he agreed. "But I might put a finger there."

"Never had a finger there, but it doesn't sound too awful," Kathryn replied. "Can I do it to you too?"

"Never had a finger there but it doesn't sound too awful," he parroted her.

Kathryn laughed. "Okay, we have enough dos and don'ts. Let just take off our clothes and see what happens."

"You are without a doubt one of the most reasonable women I've ever met," he told her as he pulled into his drive. The garage door opened automatically before them, and then closed behind them. He turned off the car engine. "Ready for an adventure, Kathy?" he asked her.

"As ready as I'll ever be," she responded, smiling as she undid her seat belt and climbed out of the car.

They exited the garage, hurrying through the darkened breezeway. Rowdy greeted them at the door, delighted to have company. Tim let him out.

"He won't be gone long," he said, shoving her into

the kitchen, pulling her leather jacket off, and pulling her slacks and panties down as he maneuvered her against the kitchen table. "First," he said, "we're going to do it here."

My God! He *was* going to be adventurous. He wasn't all just dirty talk. She wiggled her feet from her shoes, kicking off her slacks and briefs as she did. "Fuck me!" she husked in his ear, her hands going to his zipper, pulling it down, reaching in to draw out his cock.

"Until you beg for mercy, love," he promised her, and as her legs wrapped around his torso he thrust into her, and began to move rhythmically against her. He drove deep and hard. What was it about this woman that made him so damned hot? He had loved and adored his late fianceé, but he had never wanted her with such a passion as he wanted Kathy St. John. Given the opportunity, he could fuck her forever.

Her eyes closed tightly, her arms and legs clutching at him, Kathryn concentrated on the pure pleasure he was giving her. His hard, thick cock was wonderful. It filled her, and her vaginal muscles tightened about him eagerly. Every time his penis propelled itself forward inside of her, she wanted to scream with delight. The table beneath her was uncomfortable, but she didn't care. She just wanted more cock. "Do it to me! Do it to me! Yes! Yes!" she hissed at him. "Don't you dare stop. I want every bit of you."

He laughed softly. "What a greedy girl you are, love," he said. Finding her G-spot, he forced her to her first climax.

"No!" she protested, but she couldn't hold back. She shuddered hard several times. Then her legs fell away from him. "There'd better be more where that came from," Kathryn said in dark tones. She moved to pull up her slacks and panties.

"No," he said. "Let's keep your pretty butt just like it is."

It was then she noticed that his penis was still rigid. Reaching out she caressed it with delicate, teasing fingers. "That is so fine, Principal Blair."

He grinned a slow grin, and turning her around, gently bent her over the table.

"And again," he whispered against her ear as he pushed into her again. "You have the most deliciously tight cunt, love," he told her. "I want to stay in it forever." His big hands fastened about her hips to steady her. "Do you like it when I fuck you, love? Do you like my big dick inside your hot cunt?" His lips brushed against the nape of her neck.

Kathryn shivered. God! Who knew the respectable Principal Blair was such a delicious animal?

"Tell me!" he hissed at her. "Do you like being fucked?"

"Yes! Yes! I want you to do it all night, Tim. *All night!*" she half sobbed.

He pulled out of her just as she was getting close again.

"No, damn it!" she cried.

"You are going to do exactly what I tell you to do, Kathy," he said in a suddenly hard voice. "From this moment on I am the master, and you are the slave. You are going to go to the end of the hall outside of the kitchen. My bedroom is the last room on the left. You're going to strip off the rest of your clothes, and then you will wait for me, submissively kneeling before the bedroom door. If you don't want to play this game I'll take you home now. Decide!"

"I'll play," she told him, and picking up her slacks and panties, left the kitchen and walked slowly down the hall to his bedroom. She quickly stripped off her sweater and bra, and lay her clothing carefully on a side chair. Then she knelt, head bowed, and waited for him to come to her. It had never occurred to her that a real man would or could play such a fantasy game. It was exciting. He was exciting. She was so wet with her own lust that the insides of her thighs were moist. Her heart was beating rapidly, but she waited patiently for him to join her.

When he walked into the bedroom he was naked. Without a word he stood before her and pushed his cock between her lips. "Suck!" he said, and she did until he came in her mouth, sucking the thick gobs of cum down as if it were the finest wine. He sighed with pleasure. "Nicely done, love," he complimented her. "Now onto the bed with you."

She arose, noting as she did that her knees ached a lit-tle, reminding her she was no longer the twenty-five-year-old girl in The Channel. "How shall I arrange myself for your delight, master?" she asked him.

He smiled at her form of address. "On your back, slave," he commanded. Kathryn obeyed, and immedi-ately he was fastening her arms to the tall bedposts, slid-ing thick silk ropes about her wrists. "Open your legs for me," he said. Then he shoved a thick, hard pillow beneath her hips so her cunt was well displayed to him. He got up from the bed, and going to his closet, drew out a tray that he brought over to the bed, setting it on one of the two nightstands.

She was impressed as she quickly looked over the tray. There were all kinds of toys, jars, and small boxes on it. She recognized some of the items.

He opened one of the boxes and pulled out a little square of flannel, which he moistened with a clear liquid from a glass bottle. Then he wiped her vagina and labia free of her juices. The cloth was cool, but the dampness made her flesh tingle.

"What is it?" she asked softly.

"A little something special to make you more acutely aware," he said. Then, reaching for a jar, he scooped up a handful of cream and began to massage her with it, beginning with her legs and her feet. As he worked with each foot he rubbed each of her toes between his thumb and his forefinger, drawing them out as he finished with each digit. His fingers were surprisingly skillful. They moved up each leg, and then to her belly. The cream smelled like apricots, and bending his head he used his tongue to smooth the cream across her torso. "It's edible," he murmured.

"It feels wonderful," she said, low. Her cunt had begun to tingle, the effects of the flannel wipe, she was certain.

"You have such wonderful round breasts," Tim told her, rubbing the cream between his hands, taking her breasts between his palms, and rolling each of them about in turn. Then he crowned first one nipple, and then another with a dollop of cream, sucking them one at a time while he pushed three fingers into her vagina, frigging her slowly until she was moaning, her lower body wiggling with her rising need to be fucked.

"You sure know how to torture a girl," Kathryn told him, squirming.

"We're just starting, love," he told her, his fingers pushing as deep as they could go. "You have surprisingly sophisticated tastes in sex, Kathy. I would have thought you far more repressed." He withdrew his fingers.

She whimpered a little protest, then said, "I'm a librarian. I read a lot, and frankly I've been curious. Not that I ever expected to experience any of this. You're pretty sophisticated yourself, for a school principal. All that waspy front hides a deliciously dirty old man." *And am I one lucky lady,* she thought. *Okay, Nicholas, maybe I did need a touch of reality, and Tim is certainly real.*

His mouth covered hers in a hard and burning kiss that seemed to move between one kiss and another and another. His tongue thrust into her mouth to do battle with her tongue. They sucked on each other, stroked wetly, licked. She could feel his hard penis against her thigh as they played. She wanted to touch it, stroke it, but she was his prisoner, bound by her arms to the bedposts.

Suddenly Tim drew away from her and reached over to the tray, picking up a long feather that came to a point. He smiled down at her wickedly.

Then, spreading her open with one hand, he began to apply the feather to her helpless flesh. He stroked the walls of her cunt slowly, the tickling sensation strangely arousing.

The feather gently worked its way about her cunt, and then he brought the pointed tip of the feather to her clit. Their eyes met. Tim flicked the point across it. Her eyes widened.

He smiled again, and began to work the feather back and forth against the sensitive nub. Unable to help herself, Kathryn squirmed and made a little sound. The feather persisted. Her clit began to swell with its excitement. And then just when it was getting truly exciting, he stopped. "You're too eager," he cautioned her, then bending forward, he licked her cunt with long strokes of his tongue, which was oddly soothing. Her excitement level dropped.

"You're mean," she told him.

"I'm going to loose you," he said. "There are things I want you to do." He reached up, and drew the silk loops open so she could slide her hands free.

"What?" she wanted to know.

In response he reached for a small flask of thick oil and poured some between her breasts. "Hold them together now," he told her, and when she did, he slipped his dick between the two breasts and slowly fucked.

By bending and leaning forward as the head of his cock pushed high, Kathryn was able to give the tip a little lick with her tongue. When he was ready to come again she took him into her mouth, sucking him dry a second time.

He groaned with pleasure.

"Next time let's do it with that big beautiful cock of yours shoved as far up my cunt as you can," she said. "Games are fun, but I want to be fucked by you."

Lying with his head on her breasts now he nodded slightly. "We're going to take a little break now, love slave," he said.

He dozed. She felt him relax against her. Now here was the difference between reality and fantasy. In The

Channel her lovers never grew tired. Kathryn sighed. *At least let me have a little access to that fun machine, Nicholas,* she thought. *Tim is a good lover, but he's real, he's human, and humans get tired in this world.* But there was no answer. She had been cut off, and it was obvious she was going to remain cut off. There was nothing for it but to doze too.

When she awakened it was to the touch of his tongue foraging around her clit.

"Nice," she murmured, and the tongue continued until she experienced a little clitoral climax and sighed.

He swung himself over her and his big cock drove into her. Slowly, slowly he moved himself inside of her, rousing her lusts carefully.

"Faster!" she demanded.

"Not yet," he responded. "You're in too much of a hurry. You want to take your time, and enjoy every inch of me."

In response she tightened her muscles around him feeling him swell and throb within her. One hand played with the back of his neck, feeling the tiny hairs rising at her touch. "Faster!" she repeated.

And this time he did begin to increase his tempo slightly, pushing her legs up and back so he could penetrate her deeper.

"Oh yes!" Kathryn hissed, working her vaginal muscles more to encourage him.

Tim chuckled. "Easy, love, I'm close enough to coming as it is. If you want to come with me, then stop teasing my poor cock." And immediately she ceased. When she did he began to pump her faster and faster until she was whimpering with her need. "Baby, want to come?" he teased, slowing himself.

In response she sank her teeth into his shoulder and bit down hard.

"Okay, love," he half groaned in her ear. "Let's take a ride to heaven."

And with several hard thrusts he brought them home.

Kathryn soared, eyes closed, heart racing, her juices flowing copiously. Okay, for now she could live with reality. Oh yes! This reality she liked. And maybe, just maybe, it was better than her fantasies. Tim Blair was a man who really knew how to fuck.

"You are something else, Kathy St. John," he groaned. "I'm going to have to start eating my spinach if I'm going to keep up with you. But I will, 'cause I love fucking you!"

CHAPTER EIGHT

He loved fucking her. She loved fucking him. Suddenly she wondered if he liked her too. But he must. They were suddenly becoming a couple. Dinner, movies, and even lunch now and again in her office. If all he wanted to do was get in her pants he wouldn't bother with all the rest, would he? God! She sounded like a teenager in one of those YA novels. But then why did she care? She wasn't looking for anything more than a discreet sex partner. Or was she? Why this confusion? She wasn't one of those wishy-washy females who couldn't live without a man.

They both fell asleep, and she realized he was holding her hand as she drifted off.

When she awoke in the morning, Tim was gone, and Rowdy was lying on the bed next to her. She could have sworn the dog grinned at her.

Then Tim stepped from what was obviously the bathroom, clad only in a towel. "Morning, love," he greeted her. "I've put towels out for you, and I'm off to make us breakfast. Rowdy, down!"

The dog reluctantly jumped off the bed, looking up at Tim with accusing eyes.

"Fixing breakfast like that?" Kathryn teased him.

He dropped the towel mischievously and leered at her.

She laughed. "Get dressed, big boy," she told him. God! What a hunk. He looked so tame in his clothes, but without them he was six feet four inches of well-toned body. His butt was so tight she could have probably bounced a quarter off of it. His smooth chest and muscled arms brought back memories of last night. And that big cock of his hanging long and lean now between his thighs. Kathryn sighed. She needed a cold shower for sure. Getting out of the bed, she walked naked to the bathroom. She might be forty-eight, but she still had a good body.

What breasts! he thought to himself as he watched her go. And that ass of hers was perfect. He'd love to get his dick between those perfectly symmetrical cheeks. She'd be hot and tight. It would feel really good. Jesus, what the hell was the matter with him? He was acting like some kid who just had his first fuck. But Kathy St. John was one hot woman. It was difficult to believe she was five years older than he was. Still, what did age matter, when they were so compatible?

He stopped, surprised. They *were* compatible, and not just in the sack either. She was as well educated as he was. She was clever, quick, and funny. And they seemed to like a lot of the same things. Was this woman going to mean more to him than just a sex partner? It suddenly dawned on him that maybe he would like that. His family was gone, and he had no one but Rowdy who cared if he lived or he died. There was nothing left for him in the city. Egret Pointe, it seemed, was a whole new beginning. Pulling on a pair of sweats he walked barefooted to the kitchen to begin preparing them breakfast.

When Kathryn had showered and dressed, she joined him to discover homemade cinnamon French toast, little sausage links, juice, and freshly brewed coffee. "Oh yum!" she said, delighted. "French toast is my favorite. How did you know?"

"It's my favorite too," he told her. "Sit! Three syrups too," Tim said.

"What kind?" she asked.

"Raspberry, blueberry, and maple," he replied.

"I'm a traditionalist," Kathryn answered. "Pass the maple!"

"Maple is good," he agreed, "but blueberry ain't bad, love."

"This is such a treat," Kathryn told him. "I rarely eat breakfast."

"Why not?" he wanted to know. "It's the most important meal of the day."

"Oh, I have a yogurt, but I don't cook except Sunday dinner now and again. But I do love to eat," Kathryn admitted to him. "Sometimes one of the library staff brings something unsuitably sweet and gooey in, and we all share."

"I love to cook," he said. "My folks had a housekeeper who did it all. She was a terrific cook, and taught me how. I started collecting cookbooks. Fanny Farmer, *Good Housekeeping*, Julia Child, Paula Deen. Cooking is relaxing and creative for me."

"I never knew a man who cooked," Kathryn remarked. She cut a piece of her French toast and ate it. "Oh God! This is delicious," she said excitedly. "What is in it, Tim?" Swallowing, she popped another piece in her mouth.

"The usual," he answered. "Egg, half-and-half, a little bit of sugar, a smidge of vanilla, ounce of Jack Daniel's. And I cook only with butter."

"That must be it, along with the bourbon," Kathryn said chuckling. "I never thought about putting whiskey in French toast."

"It's not even a tablespoon, Kathy, but it flavors it perfectly," he said.

"Uh-huh!" she agreed. Then she proceeded to eat five pieces along with four links of sausage. She was stuffed, but it was a good stuffed.

When they had finished they carried their plates to the sink, where Tim rinsed them and put them in the dishwasher. Then, taking mugs of coffee, he led them to the living room, where a bright fire was burning.

"I've got some paperwork from school in my study," he said. "Do you mind if I get it done? It won't take long."

"Go ahead," Kathryn told him. "I'll take a book from your bookcase and read. This is such a cozy room with the fire, and a cup of coffee." She pulled the book she wanted from the shelf and curled up on the couch. To her surprise Rowdy came and put his head on the cushion next to her.

"You've made a friend," Tim said with a smile. Then he went off to do his paperwork.

Kathryn opened the book and read a few pages, but then she set the book aside and sipped her coffee, her other hand absently scratching Rowdy's silky head. She couldn't remember the last time she had been so relaxed and content. A night of wild sex, a good breakfast, and a quiet house. It was absolutely perfect. She glanced out the living room's bay window, and saw it was raining a gentle rain. Now it was beyond perfect, she decided. Then the cell in her pocket rang. Instinctively she picked it up without looking and answered. "Kathryn St. John."

"I stopped at the library with the children, Kathryn," her brother's voice said. "I wasn't aware you weren't working today. Shouldn't you take another day other than a Saturday when the library is so busy?"

Oh God! "We alternate Saturdays, Hallock. I would have thought after all these years you knew that. You brought the children to the library?"

"Debora is a bit under the weather. You aren't home either," he noted.

Oh God! Think! Think! "No, I'm not," she admitted. Where was she? He probably checked her little garage at the far edge of the library grounds. Once it had been a barn housing her predecessor's horse and buggy. "I'm shopping in the village, Hallock. I see no reason to take the car, waste gas, and contribute to the ozone layer when I shop in the village, brother. God gave me two good legs. I utilize them."

"I'm pleased to see that you are so responsible, Kathryn. Sorry we missed you. I'll see you on Thursday next then. Good-bye."

She closed her phone. Note to self. Check to see who's calling before answering.

"Did I hear you talking to someone?" Tim asked, coming into the room.

"My brother. I didn't look before I picked it up. He knows I'm not in the library, or at home," she said. "I told him I was shopping on foot in the village."

"Will he attempt to find you there?" Tim wondered.

"No, but I'll speak with Ashley Mulcahy of *Lacy Nothings,* so if he asks she'll swear I was in the dressing room of her shop trying on naughty underwear. Hallock will back off immediately."

"Do you have naughty underwear?" he asked mischievously.

"No gentleman would ever ask a lady if she had naughty underwear," Kathryn replied, pretending outrage.

"You haven't answered the question," he said.

"No, I haven't, have I?" she responded. "Have you finished your paperwork?"

"Almost," he said.

"Up for a ride afterwards? It's raining a little, but it's not bad out."

"A ride on a rainy day? It actually sounds nice," he agreed. "I'll finish my work."

"I'll treat you to lunch at the old inn on the bay," Kathryn said.

"I like an equal-opportunity woman," he replied.

Kathryn picked up her cell and called Ashley Kimborough Mulcahy, her cousin.

Ashley's assistant, Nina, answered the shop phone. "*Lacy Nothings*. How may I help you?"

"Nina, is Ashley there? It's Kathy St. John."

"Hang on," Nina said.

"Kathy? What can I do for you?" Ashley asked.

"Lie," Kathryn responded. "Look, if Hallock asks, say I was in your shop this morning, okay? And make sure Nina says it too."

"Why Kathy," Ashley said softly, "are you being a bad girl?"

"Yep," Kathryn admitted, "I am, and at my age too. I'm being discreet, but you know my brother. Mr. Glass-half-empty."

"It's the new Middle School principal, isn't it?" Ashley whispered.

"I'm not going into details, Cousin Ashley," Kathryn said firmly.

"It has to be," Ashley continued. "You've been seen out with him a lot in the last month. You go, girl! He's cute. Is he good in the sack?"

"How would I possibly know such a thing?" Kathryn tried to sound offended.

"Because you've got Kimborough genes, Cousin Kathy, and Kimborough women always have active libidos. Whoops, gotta go. The Carstairs bride has just arrived. Bye, Cousin Kathy."

Kathryn smiled. Ashley was right. Kimborough women had always been hot to trot. And St. Johns and Kimboroughs had been intermarrying since they helped found the town in the 1700s. Her paternal grandmother had been a Kimborough. In Egret Pointe many of the old families were related.

"I've gotten my work done," Tim said, coming back into the living room.

"And I've set up an alibi should Hallock check up on me," Kathryn said. "Ridiculous but necessary."

"Actually, I like your brother, but I know it would upset him no end to learn I had spent last night fucking his sister to a standstill," Tim responded. "Getting him to accept us as a couple will ease his mind somewhat."

"We're a couple now?" Kathryn said softly.

"I told you the first time that this wasn't a one-night stand, Kathy. I'd like us to be a couple unless you don't want to be," Tim answered her.

"I've never been in a couple's relationship. Not publicly. Jonathan Curtis and I had to be ultra discreet," Kathryn replied.

"You were kids," Tim said. "We're not kids. I really like you, Kathy, and I want to be able to go out with you without your brother worrying."

"I don't know why he persists in worrying at this point in time," Kathryn said.

"He will always worry about how his family appears to all and sundry. It's in his gene structure," Tim told her. "It's rather charming of him to be so old-fashioned."

Genes again, Kathryn thought. "I suppose you're right," she agreed.

"So let's make Hallock happy about our relationship.

He doesn't have to know any more than we're a couple, and are dating."

"I would hope not," Kathryn responded. "My brother has to fuck like a rabbit to have sired all those kids, but the thought of me having sex gives him an attack of the vapors. It's like dealing with your Victorian auntie."

Tim laughed. "Don't be so hard on him, Kathy. He's a guy raised with a sense of great self-importance by his family, and he's scared to death he doesn't measure up. Attempting to be controlling is a defense mechanism for him."

"I don't know how Debora stands it," Kathryn said.

"She has to love him very much," Tim replied.

Kathryn was silent for a long moment, and then she said, "I guess she does."

He went to the garage first, and then seeing no one on the street, beckoned to her.

There was no one out in the rain to see them drive down Wood's End Way. Then Kathryn directed him to the coast road. They drove the winding highway for about an hour while Kathryn explained that it was first a dirt path, and then at last, in the 1930s, it was paved. They finally stopped at an overlook, and sat briefly looking out over the bay. The sky was gray and the water dark.

"See that big flat-topped boulder offshore? That's called Seals Rest. On a sunny February day you'll see the harbor seals sunning themselves on it. And in the summer there are lots of boats. And if Easter is in late April, we have a sunrise service on the beach near the village."

"You love it here, don't you?" he said.

"I've lived here my whole life," Kathryn told him. "Oh, I've traveled all over the world, Tim. I love to travel, but Egret Pointe is home. I couldn't, wouldn't, live anyplace else but here."

"I thought I couldn't live anyplace but the city. I was born and grew up there. But after Dad died, well, it just didn't seem like I belonged," he said. "I could have remained in the family apartment, and Kensington Academy would have been happy to have me until I was ready to retire. But it just wasn't right anymore. When the opportunity came for this job, I was skeptical at first, but I've been here a little over three months now, and I love it," Tim said.

"I'm glad!" Kathryn responded.

They left the overlook and headed back toward the village, stopping at the East Harbor Inn for a late lunch. Then, with the lowering skies growing darker, Tim took her back to her library cottage. She made him tea and gave him a slice of Mrs. Bills's sponge cake. They sat before her gas fire, talking until they both realized it was almost eight.

"I'm not going to ask you to stay," Kathryn said softly. "Last night was wonderful, but maybe we should both practice a little self-control."

He stood up. "Let's go back to the East Harbor Inn for an early dinner tomorrow after church. It's time I went back to church. I haven't been since I moved here."

"I can tell you all the churches in town," Kathryn volunteered.

"I'm Episcopalian," he said.

"So am I, and it's St. Luke's." How perfect was this? "The late service is at ten o'clock. Rite Two."

"I like Rite One better," he admitted.

"So do I," Kathryn said as she walked him to the door, taking his leather jacket from her hall closet and helping him on with it.

He pulled her close, kissing her softly, gently at first, then hard and fiercely. "I'll see you in church tomorrow, Kathy," he told her, letting her go.

Kathryn watched him walk down the path toward the street. Wow! For the first time in thirty years she had a boyfriend. They were a couple. He had said it. *A couple.*

The next morning Hallock St. John V lifted a bushy eyebrow when he saw Tim Blair come into church. Then his sister waved to Blair, and the man joined her in her pew. What was happening here? But then a man who joined a woman for church services certainly qualified as respectable in Hallock V's world. And when the services were over Kathryn and Tim joined him and his family, greeting them warmly.

"I couldn't help but notice," Hallock remarked none too subtly, "that you seemed to know the hymns."

"I'm a cradle Episcopalian," Tim said. "We belonged to the Church of the Resurrection in the city. The Blair family helped found it. I've been so busy settling in that I haven't had the opportunity to get back to church."

"Ahhh," Hallock V said in pleased tones. "St. Luke's welcomes you, Tim."

"I've asked Kathryn to dinner at East Harbor Inn today. Would you, Debora, and the children like to join us, Hallock? With Thanksgiving coming up on Thursday and Mrs. St. John's delicate condition, it might be a welcome treat for her."

"Why, that's very generous of you," Hallock V replied. "Debora?"

"I would love it!" Debora St. John said. "But we will leave our brood at home with the housekeeper. An adult dinner would be wonderful." She was beaming, and gave Kathryn a quick arch look.

"Two o'clock then, at the inn," Tim said. "I'll see you then." And he hurried off.

"Well, well," Hallock V said, but his tone was actually benign. "Can it be that the gentleman is courting you, Kathryn?"

"Would you disapprove if he was?" she questioned him.

"On the contrary, I highly approve, and I hope my blessing will not put you off the fellow. You can be so contrary that way, Kathryn, and at your age you really can't be too fussy. Does he know you're five years older than he is?"

"Yes," she responded.

"Yet he's not put off. Excellent! If I hadn't checked out his background and his bank account, I should think he was a fortune hunter."

"We're not getting married, Hallock!" Kathryn snapped at her older brother.

"Of course you aren't. It's too soon for him to have asked, but it's not impossible," Hallock said. "If he does, for God's sake say yes."

"I didn't think you wanted me to marry," she snapped at him.

"I don't care if you do or you don't, sister," he told her.

"Stay out of my business, Hallock!" Kathryn said in a tight voice.

"We'll see you later, Kathy," her sister-in-law said sweetly. "Come along, darling, I think you've caused enough trouble for today." And she led her husband off.

Watching them go, Kathryn could see how well Debora had Hallock under control. Her brother might think he was lord of the manor, but he really wasn't. She felt her irritation easing. Tim was obviously right about her brother, and Hallock meant no harm.

He picked her up at one forty-five and they drove out to the East Harbor Inn, arriving at the same time as her brother and his wife. Kathryn saw her brother nod approvingly to his wife. Hallock was a firm believer in punctuality. Score another point for Timothy Blair, but then she smiled to herself. If Hallock liked Tim, then he was going to be less inquisitive, which was all to the good.

They were given one of the best tables by the hostess in the dining room. They sat in a big bay window with a perfect view of the harbor. Hallock ordered his usual Glenfiddich with water. Kathryn had a glass of red wine, and Debora an iced tea.

"I've never had Glenfiddich," Tim said. "Do you like it?"

"Best Scotch whiskey as far as I'm concerned," Hallock said.

"Make it two then," Tim decided.

"Kiss-up," Kathryn murmured softly.

He pretended not to hear her.

"Our special today is Prime Rib with Yorkshire pudding," the waitress said. "We also have salmon done on a cedar plank. Shall I give you time to decide?"

"You had me with the Prime Rib," Tim said. "And I like it very rare."

"Me too!" Kathryn echoed.

"Medium rare for us," Hallock said and looked at his wife, who nodded.

The drinks came along with a basket of warm breads. There were tiny muffins, blueberry and cranberry, small crusty dinner rolls and the inn's famous corn bread. The salads came. There was never a choice of salads at East Harbor. You took what they were serving that day. This Sunday, it was spears of endive with a raspberry vinegrette. To Kathryn's amazement, Tim fell into easy conversation with Hallock.

"He's a lovely man," Debora said quietly to her sister-in-law. "And he obviously likes you or he wouldn't be going to such trouble to put your brother at ease." Debora still maintained her English accent after almost sixteen years in her adopted country.

"You just like him because he has a dog," Kathryn teased Debora.

"Does the dog like you?"

"Oddly, he seems to," Kathryn replied.

"You're doing my stuffing for me, aren't you?" Debora asked.

"I'll bring it over Wednesday afternoon. I'm going to try cranberries in it this year along with the onion and celery. Let me do the sweet-potato casserole for you."

"Rina Seligmann is doing it for us," Debora said. "And Mavis is baking. The housekeeper will set the table, and all I'll have to do are the veggies. It's really an easy Thanksgiving for me, Kathy. Everyone has been so kind. I don't know why, but this pregnancy has been a bit difficult. It seems the others were easier."

"Well, it is your fifth pregnancy, Debora," Kathryn remarked. "The Seligmanns are coming?"

"Rina is having her whole family for Hanukkah. She said she was tired of doing both Thanksgiving and Hanukkah because they're so close, so she told her kids they could do their own Thanksgivings from now on," Debora explained. "So I asked her and Dr. Sam to come and share the day with us."

"I like Rina Seligmann. She's a smart woman, and a funny lady," Kathryn said.

The meal came, the large dinner plates filled with juicy prime rib and slabs of Yorkshire pudding. Two covered vegetable dishes were set on the table. There were carrots in one and tiny brussels sprouts in the other. About them the inn's dining room was beginning to fill up with other families and couples. When they had finished the meal, their waitress brought them a dessert menu. The men chose apple crisp with homemade vanilla ice cream. Kathryn and Debora picked the inn's homemade lemon sherbet, which was served with lemon bars.

"I prefer something light after such a gorgeous meal," Kathryn said.

"And I have a sudden desire for all things lemon." Debora laughed.

The desserts were brought, along with three coffees and a cup of chamomile tea for Debora, who could never drink coffee when she was pregnant. When the check came, Tim was ready with his credit card but he left the waitress her tip in cash.

"That was nice," Debora said to him, smiling.

"Waitresses work hard. They shouldn't have to wait for their tips," he said, returning the smile.

The two couples walked to their cars, the men going ahead to see the doors were opened. Although the day was sunny, a light chill wind had begun to come off the water.

"Well," Hallock V said jovially, "I can't remember when I've enjoyed Sunday dinner so much. No offense, my dear," he noted to his wife. "Thank you, Tim! We shall look forward to seeing you on Thursday." He shook Tim's hand heartily. Then turning, he took Kathryn by the shoulders and kissed her on both cheeks. "He's a keeper, sister," he murmured so only she might hear.

Kathryn St. John's green eyes widened with surprise at her brother's words. "See you on Thursday," she managed to say as he turned away from her. "Debora, good-bye."

She climbed into Tim's old Ford. Debora waved. "What is this magic you have, Principal Blair, that has turned my brother into a human being?" she asked Tim as they drove out of the inn parking lot and onto the coast road back to the village.

Tim laughed. "I told you. I like Hallock. I understand him. My father was like your brother. It's a nineteenth-century mind-set, love. Now let's go home. You can help me exercise Rowdy while we walk off that incredible dinner."

"The inn isn't fancy," she noted.

"No, it isn't. Just well-cooked food from decent ingredients. I'm not much into pretentious cuisine, love."

Home, he had said. But of course it wasn't her home. Still, she liked the sound of it, and she liked the idea of walking that silly shaggy dog named Rowdy. Of course they would be seen by everyone on Wood's End Way, and the gossip would start. But it didn't matter anymore. They were a couple, and her brother actually approved, although why that mattered to her Kathryn couldn't say.

And everyone was out on Wood's End Way raking up the last of their leaves. They smiled and greeted Kathryn and Tim as they passed by, Rowdy galloping ahead the full length of his long lead. And when they returned home again, she helped him rake up the few leaves left on his little front lawn. Then as it got dark he took her home, where he made passionate, tender love to her in her canopied bed before kissing her good night and leaving. It had been a perfect day, Kathryn thought, but it would have been more perfect if Tim had not had to leave. If she woke up Monday morning with him by her side.

It was a new and disturbing thought for her. She was an independent woman. She had her own income. A career and home of her own. She had never needed a man. Had never wanted one after Jonathan died. The Channel had given her everything she needed. Sex when she wanted it with no strings attached. Yet knowing the kind of woman she was, she wondered now if marriage in her youth to Jonathan Curtis would have been a good thing. But here she was in the late summer, or maybe even early autumn, of her life. Was she changing enough to really share herself with a man like Timothy Blair? And was he even interested in more than what they had? Being a couple. Being friends with benefits. And why was she questioning herself? Was she changing?

Monday came, and the week went quickly. She delivered her traditional St. John family poultry stuffing to Debora on Wednesday afternoon. The table was already set for eight in the dining room with a separate children's table. There was a beautiful arrangement on the main table, filled with large and small yellow and bronze mums, orange bittersweet berries, and colored leaves. Kathryn remarked on it.

"Tim sent it," Debora said. "He called me Monday and asked if he might. Wasn't that sweet of him? He said it was his hostess gift."

"It's darned thoughtful," Kathryn remarked. "And better than a box of candy the kids would mongrel down."

"Hallock can't stop talking about what a good time he had on Sunday," Debora continued. "I actually think those two might become friends."

"Terrific," Kathryn said dryly.

Debora laughed. "Hey, it can't hurt to have them be friends. As long as my husband, your sibling, continues to approve of Tim Blair, he won't notice what you're doing with him." Debora's blue eyes were twinkling.

"Oh shut up!" Kathryn said, but she was smiling.

Tim picked her up on Thanksgiving Day at three forty-five and they drove to the St. John house. Hallock was out in the backyard playing tag football with Jeremy Peabody and his children. After greeting the other guests Tim joined them. Watching them, Kathryn shook her head in wonder. When her three-year-old niece, Coralyn, managed to get the ball, Tim picked up the little girl, ran to the goal, and then set her down, dancing a victory dance with her.

"That is so sweet," said Mavis, who was standing next to Kathryn.

"He likes Hallock. He actually gets on with Hallock," Kathryn replied.

"A catch," Rina Seligmann remarked. "Grab him while you can."

"I agree," Debora said.

"Suddenly you all want me . . . what?" Kathryn challenged the trio.

"Married!" they chorused.

"Why now?" she wanted to know. "I've lived a perfectly happy adult life without a husband. Why now?"

"Because this is the right guy, Kathy," Mavis answered her.

The other two nodded solemnly.

Dinner was served at four thirty. Hallock stood at the head of the table carving the turkey, setting the thin sliced pieces of breast and dark meat on the hot plates for his guests while the children waited expectantly at their table. "All right, children," he finally said. "You may lift your plates. Who has the Indian-head pennies?"

"I do, Daddy!" six-year-old Samuel St. John piped up.

"I do too, Daddy," ten-year-old Anne St. John, one of the twins, called out.

"Then you get the drumsticks," their father announced as he put one on each of two plates. "Hallock the Sixth, come and serve your brothers and sisters."

"Yes, sir," said Hallock VI, jumping from his place at the children's table and hurrying to take the two plates.

"Family custom," Kathryn explained to the guests. "Whoever among the children finds those pennies beneath their plate on Thanksgiving are awarded the drumsticks."

"What an excellent idea," Dr. Sam remarked. He was Egret Pointe's beloved family doctor, as his antecedents had been since colonial times. For one hundred and fifty years his had been the only Jewish family in the town. Wives had had to be imported for the Seligmann men from Europe until the early 1900s. And over the years, until a small temple was built in the village, his family had celebrated their Sabbath in their homes. Now Temple Yakov David, named for the first Seligmann men to come to Egret Pointe, served its people and the community. His wife, Rina, came from the city.

When all the plates at both tables had been filled everyone joined hands, and Hallock recited the poet Robert Burns's grace: "Some hae meat and canna eat, And some wad eat that want it; But we hae meat, and we can eat, and sae the Lord be thank it."

At the children's table there was a sudden burst of hilarity. Hallock St. John looked sharply at his offspring. "Something you'd like to share?" he asked them.

"Sam had another grace, Dad," Hallock VI said.

"Samuel, would you like to say your grace to us?" his father asked.

"Yeah, Sam, go ahead." Hallock VI goaded his little brother.

"Over the teeth, and through the gums, look out stomach, here it comes!" Samuel said with a wide grin. "My friend Freddy told it to me, Dad."

The adults were snickering softly.

"It's an old grace, Samuel, but perhaps not as elegant

as the Burns grace. Thank you for sharing it with us, but do not repeat it again in this house," Hallock V told his son.

"Yes, sir," Samuel said. He glared at his older brother.

"Ah, sibling rivalry," Kathryn said.

"What is this in the stuffing?" Hallock V suddenly asked, poking at the dressing with his fork.

"Cranberries," Kathryn said.

"Our traditional stuffing is celery and onions, sister," Hallock noted.

"It is celery and onions, but I tossed a few cranberries in for flavor and for color," Kathryn responded. "Try it. I think you'll like it. Our ancestors used cranberries in their poultry stuffing, Hallock. Quite traditional," she assured him.

Mavis had baked six pies for dessert: two apple, two pumpkin, and two pecan.

A quarrel broke out at the children's table when Hallock VI snitched some of Sam's pie, claiming his younger brother's piece was larger than his. Hallock VI was sent from the table, and when the twins snickered and stuck out their tongues at him they too were told to go by their displeased father.

"I don't know how you keep them all in order, Hallock," Rina Seligmann. "They really are good children. Their table manners are wonderful. I wish my grandchildren had such wonderful table manners."

"Let's have our coffee and tea in the living room," Debora said.

By eight P.M. they were stuffed, and talked out. Mavis and Jeremy left first, followed by Dr. Sam and Rina. A few

minutes later Kathryn and Tim were ready to make their
escape.

"Don't call me in the morning, Hallock, unless it's an
emergency. I intend sleeping in. We've got the book fair
next Saturday, and this coming week is going to be very
busy. Debora, it was all delicious, and I thank you." Kathryn hugged her sister-in-law. "Now get off your feet. The
housekeeper is cleaning up nicely."

"Good night, Hallock, Debora," Tim said. "Thank
you for including me."

"Come for Christmas dinner," Hallock said.

"No," Tim said. "You, Debora and the kids come to
my place. Your wife is going to be delivering soon, Hallock. She will not want to cook a big Christmas dinner. As
it happens cooking is my hobby."

"If I weren't married already, I'd marry you myself,"
Debora said. "Say yes, Hallock! For heaven's sake, say
yes!"

Hallock St. John V chuckled and looked fondly at his
wife. "Very well, yes," he said. "Most thoughtful of you,
Tim. Most thoughtful!"

When they were in the car, Kathryn said, "Are you
mad? Your living room isn't big enough for a formal dinner. Where are you going to put the kids?"

"At the kitchen table," he said. "It will be fine, Kathy."
He pulled away from the curb. "Now enough about to-
day, and Christmas yet to come. We're going home, and
I'm taking you to bed. Okay, love?"

"Okay," she agreed. She was certainly ready. They
hadn't been together since Sunday night, and she wanted
that nice big cock of his plundering her cunt. With a sigh of

contentment Kathryn sat back while he brought them safely home. She was wearing sexy underwear, and had a small discreet duffel with some clothing and her toothbrush.

Rowdy greeted them enthusiastically. Tim let him out back, and then pulled a small packet of deboned turkey from his jacket pocket. "Debora wanted the dog to have his Thanksgiving too," he told Kathryn, emptying the turkey into the dog's bowl and setting it down on the mat by the kitchen door into the dining room.

"She really is much too good for my brother," Kathryn said.

"I disagree," Tim responded. "She's the perfect wife for him. She loves him, treats him like the lord of the manor he thinks he is, and manages their home and their children so his life runs smoothly. Investments are a tough business, and your brother has kept ahead of the wave, which means his clients didn't suffer greatly in the recession."

"No," Kathryn said thoughtfully. "I know I certainly didn't."

Hearing Rowdy whining at the back door, Tim went and let him in. The dog headed directly for his bowl and began eating.

"Let's sit by the fire for a while," Kathryn said. "Your house is so wonderfully peaceful. And I like the smell of the wood smoke. Gas is more practical for my cottage."

The fire was ready to light, and after Tim had put a match to it they sat together on the couch. The blaze caught, and the firelight filled the room with a warm glow. Rowdy came and stretched out in front of the hearth. Only the sound of the clock ticking on the mantel broke the silence. Tim held her hand.

What was it about this man, and this house? Kathryn wondered to herself. She felt so different, so changed since they had met. He had turned her life upside down, and while she thought she shouldn't be enjoying it, she was. Her world was no longer bound by her work and The Channel. She was even beginning to see her older brother in an entirely different light. She sighed softly.

"What are you thinking about, Kathy?" he asked her.

"I'm thinking how much you've changed everything for me since we met," Kathryn said candidly. "I'm thinking I like being a couple."

"Good," he replied. Then he pulled her into his arms and began kissing her.

Oh God! It was wonderful! His lips were warm, and his kisses excited her. He slid his hand beneath her sweater and into her bra, fondling her breast.

Suddenly he stopped kissing her. "There's lace on your bra," he said.

"Yes," she answered him.

"Are you wearing naughty underwear, Kathy?" he inquired.

"Yes, Tim, I am," she admitted. "Would you like to see it?"

"Into the bedroom with you, Kathy St. John! I don't intend sharing you with the neighbors. A little canoodling on the couch is one thing, but a fashion show with naughty underwear is another thing entirely." He stood up, pulling her with him, and practically dragged her down the hallway to the bedroom.

"Get my bag," she said to him.

"Later."

"No, now. I have high heels in it, and naughty underwear shows best in high heels," Kathryn told him.

"Woman, I am going to swoon if you keep offering me these tantalizing word pictures," he said. He pushed her into the bedroom and dashed back to get her little duffel. When he got back into the bedroom Kathryn was already in the bathroom with the door shut. "Where do you want your bag?" he called to her.

"Give it to me," she said, a hand reaching out from the bathroom. She took it, and then the door closed. "I'll be out in a minute, Tim. Get out of your clothes, and stretch out on the bed."

He hurried to comply, pulling his shoes and socks off; stripping off his slacks, sweater, shorts and tee. Then he lay down on the bed. "I'm ready," he called to her.

The bathroom door opened and she stepped out. She was wearing a low-cut underwire bra made of soft silk fuchsia lace. Her round breasts were barely contained.

The matching bikini and a pair of black stiletto pumps completed her outfit. She paraded slowly about for him, looking coyly over her shoulder at him at one point. "The bikini has a very neat little feature," she told him as she walked over to the bed. "Give me your hand, Tim." And when he did he found there was a slit in the crotch of the panties.

"How's that for convenient?" she teased him, whirling away.

His mouth had dropped open when he discovered the opening. "Get over here, Kathy," he said in a tight voice. "Let's utilize that little convenience."

She smiled wickedly. He was hard already, and his

cock was thrusting forward. "Try and be a good boy, and let me have my way with you," she teased as she climbed onto the bed, and atop him. He pulled her over his head, his tongue pushing through the slit to lick her and suck her clit. After a moment she wiggled away. Taking his penis, she rolled it between her hands. From the look in his eyes she could see he was struggling to control himself. Bending, she kissed the head of his dick, then lowered herself slowly onto it. It slid through the soft lace and into her wet cunt. She sheathed him all the way, then, leaning over, she kissed him, purring, "Now isn't that nice, love?"

Reaching out he grabbed her tempting ass with both of his hands, and squeezed.

Releasing her butt, he moved to unhook her bra, and tossed it to the floor. Her breasts spilled out, and he pulled her down to bury his face in her deep cleavage. She rode him gently, letting him enjoy her breasts, which he fondled, licking her nipples, then sucking and biting them. Then suddenly he rolled her over, gaining the dominant position. Her legs, feet still in the black stilettos, wrapped around him, and he fucked her hard and fast until she climaxed with a scream. But he was still hard and he began to fuck her once more, pushing her legs over his shoulders so he could go deeper.

"You're going to kill me." Kathryn gasped.

"I ought to spank you for looking so damned exciting, I couldn't wait to fuck you," he told her. He thrust with slow deep strokes until he managed to hit her G-spot. The sharp gasp told him he had it right. He worked her hard, his throbbing cock swelling as she clenched and released it, giving him the utmost pleasure. He didn't know how a woman who hadn't had sex in years could be so damned facile at it, but he didn't care.

"Tell me when you're ready," he gritted through his teeth.

"Anytime, love," she husked back at him.

And with that he took them to Nirvana and back again. He could hear himself almost howling with his pleasure, and her soft scream in return. Then he collapsed.

When he came to himself again, Kathryn was sprawled on her belly, her long hair spread all over the pillows. She was still wearing that enticing lace bikini, and looking at her perfectly rounded ass, he decided it was as delicious as her breasts. Leaning over he bit it gently, and she stirred slightly.

Tim grinned. He knew without a doubt that this was the woman he had been waiting for all his life. He meant no disrespect to Phoebe. She had been a wonderful girl, and he had loved her. And maybe one day she might have grown into a wonderful woman. But she wasn't Kathy St. John, pronounced *Sin Gin,* and with a definite emphasis on the sin. He wasn't certain how he was going to convince her, but sooner or later they were going to be a whole lot more than just a couple.

CHAPTER NINE

They woke up Friday morning to find it was snowing. It was an early snow, and left about two inches on the ground by mid-morning. It was the perfect excuse not to go out. On Saturday the sun shone brightly, and the snow melted, for the ground was still warm. Kathryn had turned off her cell, but she did check it now and again. There were no calls, much to her relief. Finally on Sunday afternoon they went out, driving to the East Harbor Inn for dinner. Then he took her home, kissed her chastely at the door, and then turned to head back to his car.

She watched him walk slowly down the path through the garden almost as if he didn't want to leave. She hadn't had these feelings welling up in her since she had fallen in love with Jonathan Curtis. Was it possible for a woman of forty-eight to actually fall in love? Or was it just that he was simply the best damned lay she had ever had? Yet they had done more than just fuck this delicious long weekend. He had cooked for her, and got her to help him. She could pare carrots now. And until Saturday she had never pared a carrot in her life.

And they had talked, and talked and talked about everything. They had shared their lives, and their likes and dislikes. And they had laughed together, watching old Britcoms. He had several entire series including one called 'Allo 'Allo! that turned out to be both his and her favorite, followed by another titled Are You Being Served? On Saturday night they had watched Casablanca, with Bogart and Bergman, and at the end, when Bogart says, "Here's looking at you, kid," Tim had kissed her, and they had made very tender love to each other. Watching him walk away from her cottage now, Kathryn wondered if the weekend had been just as good for him as it had been for her.

Tim thought he felt her eyes on him as he walked, but he didn't look back. If she wasn't there he would feel like a fool. He could already sense the loneliness creeping in as he got into his car. It had been a wonderful weekend, and he hadn't wanted it to end. For the first time since Phoebe died, he was considering what it would be like to share his life with another person. He and Kathy had so much in common, and yet they were very different. But would a woman alone for all those years be ready to give up a life with which she was apparently comfortable to marry?

My God, he thought, *I want to marry her. I've only known her a few months, but I want to marry her. It isn't just the sex either. I've lived a celibate life, and it's not the end of the world.* Only marry for love, he recalled his mother telling him when he was a boy. And he had loved Phoebe Hunter. And now he realized he was falling in love with Kathryn St. John. He loved her, and he wanted to share his life with her here in this small town that her ancestors had helped to found. He suddenly realized he didn't miss the city or his old life there at all. Now all he had to do was convince Kathy that they could make an absolutely wonderful life together if she would marry him.

The week after Thanksgiving flew by. The holiday season was just beginning to rev up, and the Egret Pointe Library Christmas Book Fair was upon them. On Thursday morning, booths lining the front walk from the street to the front door of the library were set up. Library patrons went around to the side door of the building during this time. Then Peter Potter's theatrical friends from the city arrived to set up facades on each booth resembling an early nineteenth-century street. Fake streetlamps were erected. A facade was also place before the front door and windows. A sign reading TEA SHOPPE was painted into it. And inside in the library's square foyer, the tables with their red and green paper cloths and napkins were set up along with folding chairs. Directly opposite the front door, on the far wall, a small kitchen space had been erected.

The rooms to the right of the foyer entrance would be where all the wonderful new books for sale were set up. In the Children's section, which was to the left of the front door, the Ghost of Christmas Present would be seated, reading stories to the children. There would also be games, supervised by Mistress Merryman. By late afternoon it had almost all come together. On Friday an electrician would run a line along each side of the front walk so those manning the shops could keep warm with electric heaters. And tonight the whole site would be guarded by a security firm hired by Hallock St. John V himself.

"I know it's a small town," he told his sister, "but no use taking chances."

Kathryn didn't argue. She thanked him and then hurried off for a final costume fitting. Her brother was suddenly less irritating, and she wasn't certain why that was. Tim seemed to have some magical effect on both of them. He had now officially joined St. Luke's, and Hallock had immediately drafted him to serve on the church's Christian Education Committee. It was as if Timothy Blair had lived in Egret Pointe his whole life.

He stayed with her Friday night before the fair, but they contained their passion to a single episode. In the morning he fixed breakfast, but Kathryn would only eat her blueberry yogurt and drink a little tea.

"How are you going to survive on that stuff?" he wanted to know.

"I have to wear a corset beneath my gown," she told him. "All I need is one of your yummy breakfasts being squished as I walk about all day. I'll need you to lace me up, love." She had taken to using the appellation he used. It was comfortable.

"I will enjoy that." He grinned, helping himself to several pancakes and spoonfuls of scrambled eggs along with some bacon. "Fortunately I don't have to worry about being squished in my loose velvet robes."

It had still been dark when they got up. Now as they dressed in their costumes, the sky began to lighten. It wasn't quite seven A.M., but the fair began at nine o'clock. The vendors were probably already in their booths unpacking their wares and warming the stalls where they would remain until four thirty in the afternoon, when it would once again be dark. The forecast was for a sunny day, which would bring people out, and keep them out.

Tim watched amazed as Kathryn donned a pair of lace-trimmed cotton and wool drawers and a knee-length chemise with short sleeves. He laced her into a demi-corset with garters, and rolled her stockings up her legs, attaching them. She then added a hoop cover with four petticoats. The one closest to her was soft brushed flannel. It was followed by a padded horsehair petticoat, a calico stiffened with cord, and finally one of starched muslin. The bodice and skirt of her gown were sewn together. It was velvet, silver-blue in color and embroidered with flowers of yellow, pink and green on the full skirt. The style was off the shoulder, the sleeves quite full and coming to just above her elbow. She had a long matching satin shawl lined in fur for when she went outside.

"Wow!" Tim said as she pinned her hair up into her usual chignon, and fastened a pair of antique drop earrings of gold studded with sapphires into her ears. Then she slid her feet into a pair of embroidered silk slippers.

"You're beautiful," he said, "but I still like my voluminous green velvet robes better, love." He picked up a thick wreath of greenery, gilded apples, and dried berries, and set it atop his head at a slightly rakish angle.

Together they left the cottage, entering the library through the back door. Mavis was already there in a pink-and-violet-striped gown. "Good morning!" she said, not saying, but definitely noticing, that they had come in together, and obviously from the cottage.

"It's just after eight, and the crowds are lining up to get in already," Mavis said. "Shall we open early, Kathy?"

"No. We advertised nine A.M. and there are families who are going to get here then. And they'll clean the vendors out of the best merchandise and books before our local people have a chance. If we let people in early, then the others will feel shut out. Besides, you know it's weekend people and people from the other towns around us who are out there waiting. In Egret Pointe, people know that when I say nine A.M. it's nine A.M. Not a moment earlier or later," Kathryn replied.

And when the clock in the library tower chimed nine, Kathryn St. John went outside wrapped in her fur-lined shawl, and personally unhooked the thick red velvet rope blocking the walkway. "Welcome to the Egret Pointe Library Christmas Book Fair," she said, greeting them. "Please remember this is for the benefit of the library."

The crowd surged in and around her. Kathryn walked back into the building.

"It will be a while before the tearoom gets busy," she said. "They're more interested in buying right now."

People began to come into the library now, looking for books. There were oohs and aahs as they looked through the titles piled neatly upon the tables. Emily Devlin, a.k.a. Emilie Shann, was there signing her latest title, *The Reluctant Princess*. Her publisher had sent along two dozen copies. In the children's wing of the library, Tim was seated upon his throne. There was a little girl in his lap, and at least eight other children seated in small chairs gathered about him as he read.

Soon the tearoom tables were all filled with people coming in from the cold to sip hot chocolate, tea, and mulled cider. Their plates were filled with meat pasties, mini-quiches, and tiny pies. Their shopping bags were filled with merchandise. Every shopper carried at least one red canvas tote with the words Egret Pointe Library Christmas Book Fair in red-and-white candy stripe. As this was the library's personal contribution, everyone wanted at least one bag to show their support.

Hallock St. John came by to congratulate his sister on the apparent success of this year's fund-raiser. He complimented her costume. And then he said, "Tim was seen coming out of your cottage this morning with you, sister." He let the unasked question hang in the air.

"He came to pick me up," Kathryn said without a moment's hesitation. "After all, Hallock, we are a couple now."

"Just a word of warning, sister. We do have our good name to consider," her brother said. "Knowing Tim I realize there was nothing untoward going on, but people will talk, Kathryn. This is Egret Pointe, and we are a prominent family."

Nothing untoward. Kathryn almost laughed. Well, maybe not this morning. "Thank you, Hallock, for bringing this to my attention. People, however, will have to get past my having a gentleman caller. No one on Wood's End Way seems distressed when I visit Tim. We walk Rowdy in broad daylight too."

"You've been to his home?" Hallock didn't know if he

should be shocked. His sister was hardly a slip of a girl. Indeed, she was approaching the autumn of her years.

"Yes, and he has lovely taste, Hallock, but then you will see at Christmas," Kathryn said quietly.

"You like him, don't you?" her brother said.

"I like him," she answered quietly. "And he likes me."

Hallock nodded. "Well," he said, "I realize I am inclined to be overprotective of you, Kathryn, but you are my younger sister. Still, both you and Tim are responsible enough not to cause a scandal."

"Why, Hallock, I do believe this is the first time in our adult lives you have given me credit for being intelligent," Kathryn said, and she kissed her brother on his cheek. "Thank you, dear."

He snorted and moved off, finding his way to the children's wing, where his children were listening to Tim read a Christmas tale about a donkey. He listened, smiling, and when the story had concluded and the children ran off to play some games, Hallock St. John said to Timothy Blair, "I trust your intentions towards my sister are honorable, Tim. You were seen coming from her cottage with her this morning. And Kathryn has told me she has visited your home."

Timothy Blair was surprised but he didn't show it. "My intentions are quite honorable, Hallock, but you know your sister requires careful handling. I don't want to spook her and scare her off."

His words told Hallock St. John what he wanted to know. "Of course not, of course not!" he said. My God! If this were one of Kathryn's romance novels he would have said that the schoolmaster was coming up to scratch. Was it possible, really possible that his sister might finally be married?

"How is Debora?" Tim asked. "I haven't seen her today."

"A bit under the weather. She's due in another six weeks," Hallock replied. "Well, I had best gather up my brood, and get them home. See you in church tomorrow."

The day progressed. The crowds didn't seem to lessen any. The tearoom ran out of food about two thirty, and was left with only cookies to serve. Several groups of carolers walked about at different hours singing, which seemed to encourage the Christmas spirit. Several of the local vendors, namely Ashley Mulcahy, and those who had brought handmade garments and knitted goods were completely sold out. All the homemade breads, muffins, rolls, and sweet goods were gone by noon. And there wasn't a book left to sell. When it finally concluded, and the library staff sat in the boardroom counting the monies taken in, they discovered they totaled a little over nine thousand dollars and change.

"I'll kick in a check to make it an even ninety five hundred," Kathryn said.

"And I'll make it an even ten thousand," Tim Blair said pulling his checkbook out of his jeans pocket.

"You don't have to do that," Kathryn quickly said.

"I want to," he answered her. "I can't remember a day when I had such fun as I had today. Count me in for next year's fund-raiser. Make the check an anonymous donation. I don't need social credit."

Kathryn nodded. "Agreed. Me too. The rest of you are sworn to secrecy."

"Agreed," everyone around the table chorused.

"I'll put our loot in the night deposit at the bank," Kathryn said.

"I'll drive you," Tim quickly spoke up.

The meeting broke up. Dickens the library cat was fed for the night. Kathryn locked up the library and changed out of her costume, and Tim brought her to the bank, where she used the night deposit. He had already shed his robe. They ate at their favorite little Italian restaurant in the mall, driving home to Tim's house afterward. Rowdy was eagerly awaiting them, wagging himself in delight at the sight of the doggie bag, which contained two meatballs Tim had requested as a treat for the animal.

"You spoil that mutt," Kathryn teased him.

"Yeah, I do," he agreed. "Now, let's talk Christmas. My family always had beef. How about yours?"

"Is there anything else?" Kathryn said. "Turkey for Thanksgiving, beef for Christmas, and ham on the New Year for luck."

"Baked stuffed potatoes, green beans, creamed onions and turnip?" he asked.

"Love it! What's for dessert?"

"Plum pudding for those of us who like it. An ice-cream bombe and Christmas cookies for those who don't," Tim answered her.

"Where have you been all my life?" Kathryn asked him. "And you're going to do this all by yourself?"

"Nope. You're going to help me," he told her.

"You know I'm no good in the kitchen," she protested.

He laughed. "I taught you to pare carrots, didn't I? Now I'm going to teach you to French cut beans."

"Ohhh, *French cut*," Kathryn exclaimed. "Sounds dirty to me."

He shook his head, laughing, pulling her into his arms to kiss, and Kathryn found herself sighing with absolute pleasure as his lips met hers. She was so happy. Thinking back, she couldn't remember a time when she had been happier. "I suppose," he said, looking down into her face, "I'm going to have to keep doing the cooking when we're married, Kathy, but you are simply going to have to learn how to do prep for me."

"*What?*" What had he just said? She couldn't possibly have heard right.

His big hand caressed her face. "I believe in my own clumsy way I have just asked you to marry me," Tim said.

"Why?" Her heart was pounding so loud she could hear it in her ears. And worse, she couldn't, didn't, want to move from the shelter of his arms.

"Because I love you," he said without hesitation.

"I love you too," she heard herself answering back. *And she did!* It wasn't just the incredible sex. It was him. He was funny and kind, generous and compassionate. And second best of all, because the sex did come first, her brother liked him. And while Kathryn St. John was absolutely an independent woman, her family was important to her. After Jonathan Curtis she had never expected to really love again, but she did.

"You aren't going to make me get down on one knee, are you?" he asked her.

"Yes!" Kathryn said. "Yes, damn it! If you want to marry me, then you have to ask me properly. Remember,

I'm a St. John." She sat up, positioning herself straight on the couch, legs together, ankles crossed, the bottoms of her jeans just touching her low boots. Her hands were folded neatly in her lap. A tendril of her red hair had come loose.

He stood up, and then kneeling down on his right knee, he took one of her hands in his. "Miss St. John," he said gravely, "will you do me the honor of becoming my wife?"

"Why, Mr. Blair, this is quite unexpected," she trilled at him.

"Yes, or no, Kathy!" he growled.

"Yes," she answered him simply.

Then to her surprise he dug into his pocket and pulled out a small box. It was a faded green velvet. Opening it, he presented it to her. "This was my mother's, Kathy. Will you wear it? Not the traditional diamond, but I thought it suited you."

The ring setting was diamond shaped, a pearl surrounded by sparkling diamonds.

"It's beautiful," Kathryn said, holding out her left hand for him. He slid the ring on her third finger of her hand. It fit perfectly. And suddenly she began to cry softly. "Oh God! I didn't think I was that sentimental," she sobbed.

He rejoined her on the couch, taking her into his arms. "I think I may cry too," he said, and the truth was, he did feel misty. But then Tim said, "Now, I'm going to take you home, Kathy. And tomorrow morning I will come to your cottage to pick you up. We will go to church together, and tell your brother."

"Hallock will like the idea I'm making an honest man of you, Tim," she teased.

"I don't want to wait to get married," he told her candidly. "We're too old for a big to-do. You don't want one, do you?"

"No," Kathryn answered him. "Just family and a few friends. Before or after Christmas?" she inquired.

"Before. I want to wake up Christmas morning with my wife, love. Then we can welcome the family for dinner together."

"Where are we going to live?" she asked him. "I love my cottage."

"And I have a two-year lease with an option to buy this house," he said.

"We can work that out later then," Kathryn heard herself saying.

He pulled his wallet from his jeans pocket and drew out a tiny calendar. "The Saturday before Christmas is December eighteenth," Tim told her. "Does that sound like a good day for a wedding, Kathy?"

"It sounds perfect," she agreed. Her head was spinning with excitement. She was getting married! Kathryn Victoria Lucretia St. John was, at the advanced age of forty-eight, taking a husband who was five years her junior. What were people going to think?

To hell with what people thought! She loved him, and that was all that counted.

"Does the inn have a private dining room?" he asked her.

"A little one, yes," she responded.

"We'll speak with them tomorrow when we have dinner about booking it for a private dinner reception," Tim said.

It was all happening so fast, but she wasn't afraid. He took her home, and in the morning arrived as promised to pick her up for church. They met Hallock as he arrived with his children. "Anne, Elizabeth, take Samuel and Coralyn down into the Sunday School. Hallock the Sixth, wait for me in our pew," he told his children.

"Debora still feeling poorly?" Kathryn asked.

"Dr. Sam says she has to have bed rest from now on," Hallock V answered. "There's a chance she may deliver early. She's a game girl, my wife."

"I've asked Kathy to marry me," Tim said softly, so only her brother might hear. "She's accepted. We're not going to wait. December eighteenth is the day."

Hallock St. John V grinned the biggest grin Kathryn had ever seen in all their lives. "Splendid!" he said. He shook Tim's hand, and kissed his sister. "Debora will be delighted with this news. She can use a little cheering up. The service will be here, of course. It's customary for St. John women to be married from St. Luke's."

"I'll speak with Father Porter after services," Tim said.

"We'll speak with Father Porter," Kathryn murmured. She was getting married, but she didn't intend losing her independence. "It is *our* wedding, after all. Hallock, do you like my ring? It was Tim's mother's." She held out her hand.

Hallock St. John did like his sister's engagement ring, and said so. Then as the bells began to peal, the trio headed into the church for services. Afterward, when St. Luke's had emptied of parishioners, Tim and Kathryn sought out Father Jim Porter in his office. He had already changed out of his robes.

"Kathy, Tim, come in. That was some Christmas fair yesterday. How did the library make out?" He gestured them into the two chairs in front of his desk.

"Ten thousand dollars," Kathryn said, smiling.

"Well, praise the Lord!" the Episcopal priest exclaimed. "Marge thought it was going to do well. She said the quality and variety of goods were exceptional, and everyone loved the tea shop. Now, what can I do for you?"

"You can make a little time the Saturday before Christmas to marry us," Tim said.

"Marry you?" He looked to Kathryn.

She held out her hand. "Marry us," she replied.

"Well, bless my soul," the priest said. "This is wonderful! I've always thought that a Christmas wedding was an especially blessed event. What time?"

"Two thirty in the afternoon, and we'll want you and Marge to come to our reception. We're hoping to get the little private dining room at the inn," Kathryn said. "I'll let you know when it's all set. We're keeping it small. Just my family, Mavis, and Jeremy. Tim doesn't have any family left."

"I'd like Gloria Sullivan and her husband to come as she's been especially helpful in getting me settled into the school," Tim said. "And my friend from the city, Ray Pietro d'Angelo and his wife. He was the one who tipped me off to Egret Pointe's search for a new Middle School principal early last June. We used to play squash a couple of times a week. If he and Rose are willing to come, I'd like it. Actually, I was going to ask him to be my best man. Hallock has to give Kathy away, so he's already got a task."

Father Porter looked at his calendar. "The eighteenth

is fine. We have the carol service the next afternoon, but I'm free Saturday. I'll pencil it in for two thirty."

It was done. The ring was on her finger, the church was booked, and when they went for Sunday dinner at East Harbor Inn, they booked the little private dining room for the afternoon of the eighteenth.

"What's the occasion?" asked Felicity Clarence, the owner of the inn, as she pulled out her appointment book and a pad.

"We're having a dinner party for a few friends," Kathryn quickly said.

Felicity raised a bushy gray eyebrow and looked directly at Kathryn's ring.

"Engagement party?" she said tartly.

"Wedding, and it's a secret," Tim quickly put in. "Kathy wants to keep it quiet until we've had time to make an official announcement."

"Well, I'm not one to gossip," Felicity Clarence said, sounding offended. "How many? And what kind of a menu are we talking about?"

"I'm not entirely certain yet of the number, a dozen probably," Kathryn said. "Maybe a nice roast loin of pork?"

"I can do one stuffed with apricots and prunes," Felicity replied. We'll serve it with thin slivers of sweet-potato pie, and steamed broccoli. Our house Waldorf salad, and small fresh baked raised rolls. And wedding cake. I'll bake it myself."

"A wedding cake?" Kathryn sounded reluctant. A wedding cake made it sound so fussy. She knew it was traditional, but for an older couple?

"I'm not letting a St. John get married without a wedding cake. Your brother would have my hide," Felicity said. "We do things proper here."

"Don't put one of those cutesy brides and grooms on the cake," Kathryn said.

"I should say not," Felicity responded. "I've got an idea for an entirely different kind of topper for your cake. You'll like it, I promise you. Now what's your color scheme, and who's doing the flowers?"

Kathryn St. John looked positively panic-stricken. "Color scheme? Flowers?" she managed to gasp. "I'm trying to keep everything simple, Felicity."

"Mavis going to stand up for you?" Felicity asked.

"Yes."

"Have Mavis call me. We'll take care of everything, dear, and it will be simple and lovely, just the way you want it," Felicity responded.

Tim struggled not to chuckle as he helped Kathryn into the car. The very together and organized Miss St. John was entirely flummoxed by the idea of preparing her wedding. "I think we should go to Mavis's and tell her our news," he said.

"Yes, yes, good idea," Kathryn replied.

Mavis whooped and hugged her best friend upon learning of the impending marriage. Jeremy Peabody shook Tim's hand, grinning.

"We're doing a little dinner at the inn after the ceremony," Kathryn said. "Felicity says to call her. Something about color scheme and flowers. I don't know what she's talking about. It sounds like such a big deal." Her voice was edged with panic. "I don't want a big deal,

Mavis. I just want us to get married. We're too old for a big deal."

"I'll take care of everything," Mavis said soothingly. "All you have to do is show up. We'll have to go dress shopping immediately."

"No dress!" Kathryn said firmly.

"Kathy! It's your wedding day. You have to have a dress," Mavis said.

"No dress!" Kathryn repeated. "I have that beautiful winter white pantsuit I bought two years ago and have only worn once. I'm wearing that. It's perfect for an older bride. I don't want something chiffony and beige, or worse, mauve pink. Especially with my red hair. And you know that's what I'm going to find. Mother-of-the bride dresses, but I'm the bride. Now my question is, What are you going to wear? Nothing frou-frou, Mavis. I'm warning you."

"Okay, let's make it a Christmas wedding theme," Mavis said calmly. "I just bought a very simple forest green wrap dress. It will look perfect with your winter white. It's elegant enough for a wedding without being too *recherché*. That all right with you?"

"Terrific!" Kathryn said, looking less stressed now.

"And I'll take care of the flowers for you," Mavis offered.

"What do we need flowers for, damn it?"

"The altar at St. Luke's," Mavis answered calmly. "The table in the dining room. Boutonnieres for Tim, Hallock, and Tim's best man. Nosegays for us. Now tell me what color you want our nosegays to be. I'll do Christmas colors for the church and the inn, and white for the men's boutonnieres."

"Yellow?" Kathryn ventured. You know I love yellow."

"Okay," Mavis responded. "Yellow it is. You have to tell the staff at the library."

"Oh God! I should invite them to the wedding, but I just don't want a big deal, Mavis. I'm nervous enough as it is. I'm not certain I'm doing the right thing. Am I?"

"Do you love him?" Mavis queried.

"Yes! Yes, I do love him!" Kathryn said without hesitation. "I don't know how it happened, but when he asked me I knew it was the right thing."

"Love can be funny," Mavis told her longtime best friend. "Sometimes you know the second you meet your perfect match. Other times it just grows. Love is unexpected. Love happens. Don't question it, Kathy."

"No, I don't think I will, but I want to get this wedding stuff over and done with before I panic entirely," Kathryn said.

The next morning the staff of the library learned their boss was getting married in less than two weeks. They bubbled with excitement until Mavis told them to calm down.

But Kathryn found she was suddenly enjoying her staff's delight in her happiness. She and Tim went the next morning to the town hall to get their license. They then left it with Father Porter at the church. On Thursday half of the front page of the *Egret Pointe Gazette* was devoted to her upcoming marriage.

Miss Kathryn St. John, the town's beloved librarian, has at last found her own happy ending! Miss Kathy, as she is known to one and all, will be married on the eighteenth of this month to Mr. Timothy Blair, principal of Egret Pointe Middle School.

The wedding will be celebrated at St. Luke's Episcopal Church.

The article then went on to detail the St. John heritage as founders of the town, and their connection with the library. To Tim's surprise his history was printed for all to read as well. As Doris Kirk, the real estate agent, had told him, gossip was an important part of life in a small American town. And he found he couldn't go anywhere for the next few days without being congratulated and told what a fine woman Miss Kathy was, and what a lucky fellow he was. He bore it all with good humor. It was his Kathy who was suddenly nervous again.

"I know they mean well," she told him. "But I just wish everyone would shut up, and let us get married quietly. They're going to all show up at St. Luke's. I know it!"

"You're probably right," Tim agreed. "How terrible to be so loved by everyone."

She glared at him but when he made a face at her and stuck out his tongue, Kathryn burst out laughing. "You are so damned good, Timothy Blair," she told him.

He pulled her into his arms and kissed her soundly. "And you are so damned sexy, Kathy St. John." His hand slipped up beneath her sweater to unhook her bra.

Kathryn purred deep in her throat as he tweaked a nipple. Then she drew away from him and stood. "Let's go upstairs, love, so we can fuck each other into oblivion."

Then she ran up the stairs while he hurried behind her.

Each time they made love it seemed to get better and better between them, although how that was possible Kathryn didn't understand. She had been angry when Nicholas had taken The Channel away from her. Her fantasies had been lots of fun, and she would never deny them. But being in love with Timothy Blair, being made love to by Timothy Blair, and having him in love with her was far, far better. Nicholas had actually done her a favor banning her from The Channel. Had he known what would happen? Or had he just been showing his true nature, and being deliberately cruel?

Nora Buckley, back in Egret Pointe for the Christmas holiday, saw the story in the *Egret Pointe Gazette*. Flipping open her cell phone as she sat over her morning coffee she pushed 1.

"Good morning, Nora. What may I do for you, my dear?" Mr. Nicholas's smooth voice said as he answered.

"I thought you might be interested to learn that Kathy St. John is getting married, sir. The new Middle School principal, Timothy Blair," Nora reported to her employer.

"Indeed," Mr. Nicholas replied. "I really do dislike this time of year, Nora. It's rife with bad news of all kinds. Thank you for informing me."

"Can I do anything for you, sir?" Nora asked anxiously.

"No, no, my dear. You are on holiday." And Mr. Nicholas closed his own cell phone with a snap.

"What is it, Uncle?" Fyfe McKay asked as he lounged in a comfortable chair near the fireplace in Mr. Nicholas's elegant office.

"Kathy St. John is getting married," Mr. Nicholas replied. "I had hoped that being denied The Channel would eventually force her over to us. It seems, however, that she has come to prefer reality. Check the Fiend Finder for Timothy Blair, my boy, and let's see what we find."

Fyfe McKay got up and walked over to the computer station in his uncle's office. He typed in TIMOTHY BLAIR, MIDDLE SCHOOL PRINCIPAL, EGRET POINTE. The machine hummed softly, and then the required information came up. Fyfe scanned it, and then hit PRINT. When the document was ready he handed it to his uncle. "Dull as dishwater, but a big man with a big cock, Uncle. That is obviously Kathy's great—if you will forgive the pun—interest in the man. Clever little bitch, isn't she? You deny her The Channel, and she goes out and finds a man who is more than qualified to service her. She has a wonderful appetite for sex. We fucked every night she was at the island spa last time. She claws, and bites, and isn't one bit shy about screaming when you make her come. I quite enjoyed her. Did you enjoy her, Uncle, when you took her virginity?"

"I do not feel it necessary to discuss my sexual exploits, Fyfe, in order to justify my masculinity," Mr. Nicholas said heatedly. "And I know when to cut my losses. I miscalculated, and it has cost me Kathy St. John. The men in her family are easy pickings, but she was the first of their women I attempted to entrap."

"You have a soft spot for her, Uncle," Fyfe said. "And you played fair. You know better than to play fair. Give her back The Channel, and you will see how quickly she sheds the schoolmaster. Tell her it's a wedding present," he chuckled.

"The wedding is in two days," Mr. Nicholas said. "Besides, Kathy is intelligent, Fyfe. Did you think because she enjoys good sex that she has no brain? That she will toss her fiancé aside for the return of her fantasies? She would not marry him if she were not in love. And you cannot—*I* cannot—win out against love. The man, I am forced to admit, is perfect for her. He shares her values, her faith, and he too likes good sex. Let it go, my boy. We lose one now and again."

"I can get her back for you, Uncle," Fyfe insisted, his dark eyes gleaming maliciously. "Let me try!"

"You are ruthlessly ambitious, and I enjoy that in you," Mr. Nicholas said, "but I tell you to let it go, Fyfe."

"Let me try, Uncle," Fyfe McKay repeated.

Mr. Nicholas shrugged fatalistically. "I could stop you if I chose," he said. "But I can see you will not be satisfied until you do. But if you fail, Fyfe, I will punish you for your failure, and for going against my better judgment."

"But I won't fail, Uncle," Fyfe McKay said. "So what will you reward me with when I succeed?"

Mr. Nicholas smiled. "You need no incentive, Fyfe. But should you succeed we will discuss your prize then. I will give you the period from the winter solstice until the spring equinox to bring Kathy back to me. And, Fyfe, you may not take the easy way by killing her husband, or harming any she loves and cherishes. You will do this the old-fashioned way, by using irresistible temptation. Is that understood?"

"Yes, Uncle," came the answer. "But the winter solstice is three days after her wedding," Fyfe noted. "Shouldn't I begin before that happens?"

Mr. Nicholas sighed. These young people were in such a hurry today. They never stopped to consider anything. "Would your victory not be more painful for her, and triumphant for you if the marriage were destroyed? Do I have to explain everything to you, Fyfe? You are beautiful to the eye, and have great charm, my boy, but you think nothing out ahead of time. Would Kathy not succumb more easily if her lover were gone from her bed? Let her have her momentary happiness. Then strike! Now run along. You have a great deal of preparation to do before you can even consider success." And with a wave of his hand Mr. Nicholas gestured Fyfe McKay from his office.

When the young man he called his nephew, but who was actually one of his many sons, had gone, Mr. Nicholas pulled open one of his desk drawers. Reaching in, he pulled out a small photograph of Kathryn St. John and stared down at it. Fyfe was right, of course. He had always had a soft spot for Kathy. There had been so many women passing through his world over the centuries. Women who had borne his offspring, both male and female. And other innocents, like Kathy, whose virginity he had taken. But for some reason he had never understood, she had been the one he remembered best of all.

He realized it was a weakness on his part, and while he had told Fyfe that they had *lost* her the truth was that he had released her. And he didn't understand why. But he wanted her free to find her own happiness. Fyfe might try his best to win her back, but his nephew would fail. And when he did, Mr. Nicholas intended punishing him for his insolence in even trying.

Fyfe McKay, however, was already plotting. He had read Tim Blair's biography, and learned that he had left Kensington Academy because the headmaster, David Grainger, was just a few years older than he was. There was no chance for advancement, and Blair was obviously an intelligent man with some small ambition. But what if David Grainger was suddenly forced out? Kensington's board would most likely turn to their old assistant head, a man of impeccable credentials. And certainly a man who had lived his entire life in a big city would be delighted to return to it.

Fyfe McKay went to his own small office and activated the Fiend Finder to learn what he could learn about David Grainger. He was extraordinarily pleased with what he discovered. Grainger was a very handsome and vain man, and he had a libido that he hid, but that was ready to be tempted. Fyfe probed further, and discovered Ms. DuBois, the Kensington French teacher, who was a customer of The Channel. Viewing Ms. DuBois's fantasies, Fyfe knew he had found his pawn. The young woman wanted a husband and babies, and she wasn't particular how she got them as her thirty-third birthday was looming in January.

David Grainger suddenly found himself looking at Ms. DuBois with new eyes at the faculty's Christmas party that Friday afternoon, the seventeenth of December. Her high, pointed breasts excited him as did her tight, round ass. And Ms. DuBois, realizing his interest, began to flirt discreetly. She was the one who volunteered to do the cleanup as the party concluded. Her fellow teachers were only too glad to let her, as they hurried off to Christmas shop or go home to pack for their own vacations.

The headmaster of Kensington remained also to help. But his eyes kept straying to Irene DuBois's butt as she bent over, picking up bits of wrapping that had fallen to the floor during the secret Santa exchange. He couldn't take his eyes off of her, and his dick was swelling in his trousers as she dumped the final scraps in the garbage bag.

"There!" she said, standing up and turning about to face him. "That should do it."

Then she saw the bulge in his pants. Her eyes grew wide, but she said nothing.

David Grainger unzipped himself, and pulled out his turgid cock. "I have a little present for you, Mademoiselle DuBois," he said in a husky voice.

"Ohh, Mr. Grainger." She giggled. "You're a very naughty man!"

"The question is, are you a very naughty girl, Mademoiselle DuBois?"

Her little pink tongue touched her lip thoughtfully. "Do you want me to suck you off, or do you want to fuck me, Mr. Grainger?" she whispered.

"Both!" he groaned.

She carefully perused him. She could see he was very hard. If she took him into her mouth he was going to come like a shot, and that was no present. "I'm not wearing any panties," she told him as she pulled her skirt up. Then turning, she bent over the table in the faculty lounge, where the party had been held.

He was on her quickly, his prick nosing its way beneath her butt and ramming itself into her cunt. Fully sheathed he moaned with his excitement. Fyfe watched them on the screen of his Fiend Finder dispassionately, but he did make certain that Mr. Grainger's ordinary dick felt thick and long to his partner, and that Ms. DuBois's previously well-used cunt was tight and gave the kind of pleasure that neither of the couple had ever enjoyed. This was going to be the start of a very dangerous affair for them both. And when it concluded they would be quite ruined. Timothy Blair would succumb to temptation and return to Kensington as its new headmaster, and Kathy St. John would be Fyfe's for the taking.

Unlike his uncle, Fyfe McKay enjoyed the Christmas season. There were so many opportunities for deviltry. And he was not a man to miss a good opportunity.

CHAPTER TEN

Saturday, the eighteenth day of December, dawned sunny. Looking out of her bedroom window, Kathryn saw it had snowed in the night. Everything was covered in a pristine white. It was almost magical. She ate her favorite breakfast of yogurt and buttered rye toast. Drank her orange juice with a vitamin pill. She had switched to acid-reduced juice as her stomach had been a bit fussy of late. She had alternated between euphoria and panic for the last two weeks.

Out of habit she rinsed her dishes and put them in the dishwasher. Then she went back upstairs to shower and wash her hair. Then she lay down in an attempt to relax. She had slept late, but the wedding wasn't until two thirty in the afternoon. Her brother was coming to get her. A little after one as she dozed, she heard knocking on her front door. Getting up, she went downstairs to find Mavis and Miss Julie from the Egret Pointe Salon. Mavis was carrying a box with their nosegays.

"We've come to get you ready," she said.

"I don't need any help getting dressed," Kathryn said. Oh God! Mavis was going to fuss, and Kathryn was nervous enough.

"Honey," Miss Julie said as she stepped into the foyer of the cottage, "every bride needs someone to do her hair and makeup. You trying to put me out of business, Miss Kathy? Let's go upstairs now. I can see you washed your hair already." She gently urged Kathryn back up the stairs, Mavis following.

"I didn't want a fuss," Kathryn said.

"Wait until you get the ring on your finger, and through his nose, before you stop fussing, honey," the hairdresser advised.

Kathryn had to laugh. "Okay," she said. "I give up. Do your worst, and I promise not to complain."

"Where's your suit?" Mavis wanted to know as she headed for the big walk-in closet across the room.

"Left side, in a garment bag. I'm wearing my mother's single strand of pearls for the something old, okay?" Kathryn sat still while Miss Julie began to do her hair first.

"My underwear is new."

Miss Julie giggled. "Something naughty from *Lacy Nothings*, I hope, and not a Walmart special."

"Suitably bridal, and yes, from Ashley's shop," Kathryn answered, grinning.

"What's borrowed and blue?" Mavis wanted to know.

Kathryn shrugged. "I didn't get any further than something old, something new," she admitted.

"I figured as much." Mavis opened the small bag she had been carrying. She pulled out a pair of beautiful gold-and-pearl clip earrings. "Wear these," she said. "They were Mom's. She'd be so happy to see this day. She always thought of you as her other daughter, Kathy. And tuck this in your pocket."

Kathryn took the earrings, and put the box on her dressing table. She was just slightly teary. "I wish your mom were here today," she said. "Thank you." Then she looked at Mavis's outstretched hand. In it rested a small irregular-shaped piece of pale blue bottle glass. "Oh God," she said softly. "I can't believe you still have it!"

"First present you ever gave me," Mavis said softly. "How old were we that summer? Four? Five? Of course I kept it. It was from my best friend, and I want it back after the wedding, Kathy."

Now Kathryn did cry.

"Good thing I haven't done your makeup yet," Miss Julie said. Now wasn't this just the sweetest story to tell her customers next week? "Mavis, go get a cold washcloth for me. Can't make up puffy eyes."

"Happy tears don't make you puffy," Kathryn said between sobs.

"Whoever told you that, honey, wasn't your friend," Miss Julie said tartly. Then the cosmetologist finished twisting Kathryn's beautiful red-gold hair into a French twist and pinned it firmly. "Mavis, where's that comb the florist made up for her hair?"

"Flowers in my hair?" Kathryn sounded dubious.

"You're much too old for a veil, and hats are too old for you," Miss Julie said.

"Here it is." Mavis held out a small tortoiseshell comb decorated with a spray of fragrant cream-colored freesia. "It's not fussy. See?"

Kathryn nodded as Miss Julie fixed the comb at the top of the French twist. Then Miss Julie put on Kathryn's makeup. Knowing the lady well, and her dislike of too much, Miss Julie applied a light foundation to even out the bride's porcelain skin, a touch of blush on her cheekbones, a delicate stroke of dark green eye shadow on her eyelids, and a bit of mascara to her lashes. Last, she brushed on some coral pink lipstick. "Blot," Miss Julie said, offering Kathryn a Kleenex. "There! You're finished, honey, and I'm going to be on my way. Good luck to you!" And she quickly packed up the tools of her trade, and was gone down the stairs. They heard the front door slam behind her.

"She canceled her entire schedule of appointments this afternoon so she could come and do this. She'll be in the church too. I think most of the town will be there for it, so don't panic, Kathy," Mavis said.

"Oh God, I should have had a big wedding and invited everyone," Kathryn said.

"No," Mavis replied. "You should have just what you wanted. A small wedding. You and Tim can hold a big party sometime in the next year, and invite everyone. But today is just for you, the family, and a few of us who are your especial friends. Incidentally, it was very sweet of Tim to ask Jeremy to stand up for him when his friend, Ray Pietro d'Angelo, couldn't make it. How come?"

"One of his daughters got engaged, and Rose had scheduled the party for today. She's been working on it for the last four months. We were kind of last minute. They'll probably be able to come when we give our big party for everyone who isn't coming today," Kathryn said.

"Who did you replace them with at the table?" Mavis wanted to know.

"Actually I invited the Devlins, Mulcahys, Seligmanns. Ashley's my cousin, and Tim seems to have hit it off with Mick Devlin," Kathryn said. "And I asked Mr. and Mrs. Bills. She's taken care of me since I moved into the cottage. I couldn't leave her out."

"That was nice," Mavis agreed.

The clock in the hallway struck two o'clock.

"I guess I'd better get dressed," Kathryn said. "You know my brother. He said two twenty, and he'll be here exactly on time."

"I'll get your suit," Mavis said, going to the closet and taking out the garment bag.

She lay it on the bed, opened it, and lifted it out. "Unconventional, but beautiful," she admitted. "The town will be agog."

"Let them," Kathryn said as she shed her fleece robe, and reached for the trousers. She was wearing a cream-colored lace garment that incorporated a low-cut strapless lace bra and panties with garters holding up her stockings. There were rosettes on the bra where her nipples fit, down the torso in a single line, and the garters.

"Holy cow!" Mavis exclaimed. "That is downright sexysexysexy!"

"Uh-huh," Kathryn agreed, nodding. "Just 'cause I'm the town librarian doesn't mean I have to wear a cotton bra and briefs all the time." She reached for the soft winter white wool trousers and pulled them on, zipping up the fly. Then she drew on the plain tunic top, which buttoned up the back with little pearl buttons. The tunic had a round neckline, and her mother's opera length pearls looked perfect when she fastened them about her neck. Mavis's gold-and-pearl earrings were the perfect complement. "Well," she said. "What do you think?" she asked her best friend as she slid into her shoes.

Mavis shook her head. "I didn't think it would work, Kathy, but the pantsuit is just perfect as a wedding outfit. But you're going to need something for outdoors. It's chilly with the snow last night, and there's a slight wind blowing in off the bay."

"I've got that fur-lined oatmeal-colored cape Hallock gave me a few Christmases ago," Kathryn said. "It should be perfect."

Mavis opened the box containing the flowers, and drew out a small bouquet in a silver holder. She handed it to Kathryn. "Cream-colored freesia, some little cream-colored roses touched with just a hint of pale yellow along their edges, and a wisp of lacy fern for greenery. Nothing fussy, Kathy. I got the fussy one."

Kathryn took the elegant bouquet. She held it to her nose, inhaling the fragrance of the freesia. "I love it," she said. "Thanks, best friend."

A knocking sounded at the front door downstairs.

"It's your brother, and he's right on time," Mavis said, picking up her own bouquet of yellow roses, freesia, and greenery.

The two women hurried downstairs, where they found Hallock V. "An unusual but most attractive ensemble, Kathryn. Only you would choose pants in which to be married, and somehow carry it off." His voice was amused more than censoring. "Get your coats on, ladies. We'll just make the church in time."

"Didn't anyone ever tell you it's good luck to be married as the minute hand is sweeping up, and not down, Hallock?" Mavis said as she put a dark wool cape on over her forest-green wrap dress.

"No, they did not," he replied, helping his sister on with her fur-lined cape. "Didn't I give this to you, Kathryn?" Hallock asked.

"Three years ago Christmas, Hallock, and it has been quite my favorite gift from you, even though I'm quite certain Debora picked it out. How is she today?"

"Actually quite well. She refused to miss your wedding, sister, and so we put her in a wheelchair for transport. Mr. Bills volunteered to transport her, our housekeeper, and the children in his van. Hallock the Sixth will push his mother's chair while the twins monitor the little ones. They will, of course, return home with Elsa after the service."

"Get me to the church on time," Kathryn sang slightly off key. "I feel an attack of nerves coming on, big brother."

They departed the cottage and Hallock drove while the two women sat in the backseat of his town car. When they reached the church Mavis quickly exited the car while Hallock V got out, hurrying around to escort his sister. To Kathryn's initial horror the church was packed. It would appear the entire town had come to see Miss Kathy and her swain married. Someone took her cape. Her hand went to her hair to make certain it was neat. Her other hand grasped the bouquet.

She had decided that "Here Comes the Bride" was perhaps meant more for someone younger. She had chosen a lovely Baroque piece instead. The music began, and Mavis moved out ahead of the bride. Kathryn clutched her older brother's arm. To her surprise he reached over and patted her hand with a reassuring smile. Then he walked her down the aisle past a sea of faces, all of which she recognized. Hallock handed her off to Tim, and the ceremony began.

My God! He looked so handsome in his gray pin-striped suit. There was a small rose like the one in her bouquet in his buttonhole. And when he smiled at her, the corners of his blue eyes crinkling, all the nerves that had been threatening to explode dissolved into a pile of mush. He loved her. She loved him. And this was the absolutely right thing they were doing.

The music stopped.

"Dearly beloved," Father Porter began, "we are gathered here together in the sight of God, and in the face of this company to join together this man and this woman in holy matrimony. . . ."

How many times had she heard these words spoken, but never in all the years since Jonathan Curtis had been killed expected to hear them spoken for her? She struggled to focus on the words, her heart hammering when Tim answered, "I will," and Father Porter turned to ask her the same question.

"Kathryn, wilt thou have this man to be thy wedded husband, to live together after God's ordinance in the holy estate of matrimony? Wilt thou love him, comfort him, honor and keep him in sickness and health; and forsaking all others, keep thee only unto him, so long as ye both shall live?"

My God! What a serious commitment. Had she ever really listened to those words before? Understood them? Tim gently squeezed her hands, which were in his. "I will," she answered, and everyone in the church heard her say it.

"Who giveth this woman to be married to this man?" Father Porter asked.

"I do!" Hallock St. John V said loudly, and there was a ripple of soft laughter.

They then pledged themselves to each other. The plain gold rings they had purchased just this week in Mr. Jacobs's jewelry shop were blessed. Mr. Jacobs had even gotten the inscriptions engraved for them with the words TIMOTHY TO KATHRYN and KATHRYN TO TIMOTHY, with the date. There were a few more prayers.

Their hands were joined, and Father Porter declared, "Those whom God hath joined together let no man put asunder." He began the end of the ceremony. "Forasmuch as Kathryn and Timothy have consented together in holy wedlock . . ." Then came the blessing, and Father Porter declared, "You may kiss your bride, Tim."

And Timothy Blair did so most enthusiastically, as the music of the traditional wedding recessional swelled and filled the church. They broke off kissing to hurry back down the aisle to the back of the church, where they stood greeting all their well-wishers.

"It's a damned good thing we set dinner for four o'clock," Mavis murmured to her husband. "We'll just make it."

And they did. The sun was setting behind the hills edging the bay. The chill wind blowing over the snow was dying down as they entered the East Harbor Inn to be greeted by Felicity Clarence, who had managed to get to the church and back before the bridal party. She ushered them into the private dining room with its view of the bay. The bright evening star had already risen, and was hanging over the water. There would be a moon later too. Everyone sat down. Wine was poured, and the wedding dinner began.

The started with a pumpkin soup, hot, creamy, and rich. Then came the inn's famous Waldorf salad: chopped apples and walnuts in a sweet dressing on a bed of lettuce. There were four bread baskets with warm, fresh-baked mini-muffins on the table.

Because she had invited the Seligmanns Kathryn had changed the main course from roast loin of pork to a prime rib of beef with small potatoes roasted around the meat, and steamed broccoli. The wine was drunk to toast the newlyweds, but as everyone was driving home, at least one person per car had been designated a driver.

Finally the wedding cake was rolled into the room. It had two tiers with yellow flowers that tumbled from the top layer down the sides of the cake and around it. The topper was not a traditional bride and groom. Instead it was a small castle, a sign planted outside of it that read, AND THEY LIVED HAPPILY EVER AFTER. Kathryn saw it, and smiled. Nothing could have been a more perfect ending to a perfect day.

She looked to Felicity Clarence, who waited to carve and serve the cake. "Thank you!" she said, and Tim nodded in agreement.

The cake was consumed, but the top layer was carefully boxed. "Freeze it," Felicity said. "And have a party on your first anniversary."

No one wanted to be the first to leave. It had been such a wonderful day. And then suddenly Debora St. John said quite clearly, "*Oh merde!* My water has just broken!"

Dr. Sam was immediately at her side. "Pains?"

"Not yet," Debora said, "but I think I'm close."

"Hallock, get your car!" Dr. Sam said.

"I can't drive," Hallock said. "Debora said she would so I could have some wine at my sister's wedding."

"I'll drive," Tim spoke up.

"It's your wedding night," Hallock protested.

Tim gave him an amused look. "I'll drive," he said.

"You had wine," Dr. Sam said sternly.

"Two sips to toast the family," Tim said. "Look at my glass, Sam."

"All right then," Dr. Sam said. "I'll call the hospital to tell them we're coming in. They'll alert Dr. Lindeman. How many weeks early are you, Debora?"

"Five, six," she said, wincing.

"Pain?"

"Just the first one, although my back's been killing me all day," she answered.

"You've had five deliveries and you didn't realize you've been in labor all day?" Dr. Sam said. "Or did you know?"

"I didn't want to spoil Kathy's day," Debora admitted. "Ouch!"

"Let's get going!" Dr. Sam said.

"I'm coming," Kathryn said.

Tim had already gone for his car.

"I'm not a wine drinker," Mrs. Bills said. "Just had a bit of cider and some water. Same for the mister. We'll drive anyone who needs to go."

"Would you drive my car to the hospital?" Hallock asked Mr. Bills, tossing him the keys to his town car. "I want to ride with my wife, but I'll need to get home later."

"We'll stop and tell Elsa what's happening," Emily Devlin said.

Hallock nodded his thanks. Then he and Dr. Sam helped Debora into the front seat of the Contour. Hallock and Kathryn climbed into the back. They were met at the foot of the inn drive by a police car, for Dr. Sam had alerted the local police that they would need an escort. He and Rina came behind Tim's car while the rest of the guests went home. Mavis knew that Kathryn would call her when there was news.

"I'm glad I'm not carrying twins," Ashley Mulcahy said, touching her belly. "Just a nice quiet little girl." Then she remembered. "Sorry, Em."

Emily Devlin nodded. "Forgiven. I'm hoping for girls too," she said.

"You don't know yet?"

"You know my husband. He likes doing things the old-fashioned way," Emily said. "We'll know when I push the little darlings out, and not a moment before then."

"After the first I wanted to know right away," Ashley admitted. "Night, Em."

"Night, Ashley."

The moon had come up over the bay, sparkling on the

snow, lighting up the dark shore road. Tim drove carefully, very conscious of his new sister-in-law making funny little noises in the passenger seat. Hallock, seated behind her, kept talking as they drove.

"Breathe into the pain, my dear. That's it. We're almost there," he said.

"We damned well better be," Debora said, her Devonshire accent plain now.

"Hang on, Debora," Kathryn spoke up. "St. Johns don't get born in cars."

Debora snorted a laugh. "Then tell your husband to drive faster," she said.

The entrance to the hospital came into sight. Tim swung up the drive heading straight to the emergency entrance as Dr. Sam had instructed him when he went for his car. A group of nurses, male and female, was waiting. They helped the laboring woman onto a gurney and rushed her into the hospital, Hallock and Dr. Sam following quickly.

"Where's Lindeman?" Dr. Sam wanted to know.

"He's away this weekend," one of the nurses said, "and Dr. Wheeler, who was covering for him, came down with the flu."

"Then who the hell is on call?" Dr. Sam demanded. He was the small hospital's chief of staff, and highly respected.

"When was the last time you delivered a baby, Dr. Sam?" the nurse who had earlier spoken asked.

"Shit!" Dr. Sam swore. "All right, get Mrs. St. John into a delivery room. Find me a resident or intern who knows what he's doing, and let's go. There is no time left." He turned to Rina, Tim, and Kathryn. "Waiting room. I'll let you know."

"Oh my." Rina Seligmann chuckled. "He's having the time of his life. He always loved deliveries. And twins! He'll be in his glory. Back when he started as a G.P., did everything, but now everyone has to have a specialist. Listen, if you two want to go home I'll wait for Sam."

"No, we're here so I expect we'll wait," Kathryn said. "Tim?"

"We'll wait," he agreed. "It's kind of exciting. I'm here for the birth of my nephews." He put an arm about Kathryn.

"Where is home?" Rina inquired, curious.

They both laughed. "We haven't decided yet," Kathryn said. "Tim has an option to buy the Torkelson house, and I love my cottage."

"We'll work it out eventually," Tim told Rina. "And that will give Egret Pointe something to gossip about, won't it?"

Rina chuckled. "It will indeed. "You two going to have a honeymoon?"

"We haven't thought about it," Tim admitted. "I suppose during midwinter break we could go off somewhere warm, or go skiing up north."

"Seems to me there's a lot you haven't discussed yet," Rina said dryly.

"But, Rina, we love each other. Isn't that enough?" Kathryn replied.

Rina Seligmann laughed. "Actually it is," she agreed. "The rest will all fall into place eventually, Kathy."

"Where's my brother gotten to?" Kathryn wondered aloud.

"Oh, he's in with Debora," Rina told her. "He's always there for the birth of his children. Didn't you know that? It was the talk of the hospital the first time it happened. No one could believe that Hallock St. John the Fifth was in the delivery room coaching his wife as she gave birth."

"I never knew that!" Kathryn exclaimed.

They waited. An hour slipped by and suddenly the doors to the maternity waiting room swung open. Hallock St. John, grinning from ear to ear, stepped into the waiting room. In his arms were three swaddled infants. "Triplets!" he said. "Three identical boys. She had triplets!"

Kathryn burst out laughing. "Really, Hallock, don't you think that triplets are a bit excessive?" she teased him. Standing, she went over and looked down at the three tiny faces. "What are you going to call them?" she asked him.

"Evan, Maxwell and Jacob," Hallock replied. "Aren't they beautiful, sister?" His eyes were actually shining with tears.

Kathryn put a hand on her brother's arm. "Yes, Hallock," she said. "They are very beautiful. God bless them!"

Tim now stood next to his bride, admiring the trio.

Dr. Sam came into the waiting room. "Take those boys back to the nursery, Hallock, and go see your wife," he instructed.

"I thought she was having twins," Rina said to her husband.

"That's what the sonogram showed, but the third one was behind the other two. Until she went into labor, we didn't know. Hah! Lindeman and Wheeler are going to be sorry they missed this." He chortled. "And considering they were a mite early, their weights are good. Five pounds eight ounces, six, and six pounds one ounce. Their lungs are well developed. They'll survive quite nicely," Dr. Sam said. "You want to go see Debora before she goes to sleep?"

"Yes," Kathryn said.

They went to the pretty hospital room where Debora was now lying in bed.

The room was painted yellow with a mid-wall border of multicolored spring flowers. The furniture was cherry-wood, and the lamps green and white with light shades. There was a down comforter on the bed.

Kathryn went over and kissed her sister-in-law. "Congratulations! Is eight enough? You've assured that Egret Pointe will have its contingent of St. Johns for at least another generation. Maybe even into the next century."

"Sure fooled you all," Debora joked. She looked happy, but tired. "And I didn't steal your wedding day. I popped them out at three minutes after midnight, eight minutes after midnight, and ten minutes after midnight."

"Still," Tim told her, "we're not likely to forget."

Debora grinned.

"We're going to go," Kathryn said. "It's been a long day for everyone." She and Tim left the maternity wing of the hospital, finding their way to their car, which was parked in the ER parking lot. "Where to, my lord?" she asked him. "Your place or mine?"

"Let's spend the night at the Wood's End Way house," he said. "Rowdy will need to be let out before we can have any peace together, love."

"You want peace on our wedding night?" she teased him.

"Woman, you are in such trouble with me," he said. "Didn't you just promise to love, honor and obey me this afternoon?"

"No, darling, you weren't listening. I promised to love, honor and *cherish* you," Kathryn said mischievously.

He chortled, and drove them home. Rowdy greeted them enthusiastically, and then dashed out into the snowy backyard for a few minutes before coming in to be fed.

"We never brought any of my clothes over here," Kathryn said.

"You won't need clothing tonight," he told her. "I'll get what you want tomorrow. And I'll make you some space in the closet. We did this so quickly. I should move some stuff into the cottage too, because until we make up our collective mind what to do we're obviously going to be living in two different domiciles."

"Not really very practical," Kathryn admitted as they entered the bedroom.

"I'll do whatever you want, love," he told her. "I like this house, but I'm not invested in it yet."

"The cottage is small," Kathryn said slowly. "It was never meant for two people." She sighed. "Maybe we should look for something that we both love."

"There's time," Tim said quietly. He pulled her into his arms and kissed her slowly. "I love you, Mrs. Blair," he told her. Then turning her around he began to unbutton the little pearl buttons on her tunic.

Kathryn kicked off her low-heeled pumps, and slipped out of her trousers as he removed the soft wool tunic. His eyes widened, and she laughed.

"Holy cow!" Tim said. "Naughty underwear!"

"It's called a corselette. The rosettes are edible," Kathryn told him. •

"You're kidding!" His blue eyes were alight with amusement.

"Nope," she said. "Try one, darling."

He bent his head and his mouth closed over her left nipple. The pink and white rosette dissolved in his mouth. "Kathy, my Kathy," he said slowly as he raised his head. "Do not move," he said as he hurried to pull off his clothes. Naked, he bent to devour the rosette on the right nipple. Then he began to work down her torso, nipping off each delicate sugar flower as he went.

"The crotch is edible too," she told him as he moved lower and lower. She spread her legs for him.

He slipped beneath her to eat the soft fabric away until it was gone, and his tongue was pushing past her nether lips to lick her. "You are a very bad girl," he told her as she began to squirm beneath his facile tongue. "But I want a little attention too, love." He stood up. "Your turn, Kathy," he told her.

Kathryn unhooked the corselette, tossed it aside, and went down on her knees. He was only half-aroused. "Bad boy!" she scolded, taking him in her hand and moving his foreskin back and forth. "Open wide for your mistress now," she said, and sliding beneath him began to lick his balls, taking them in her mouth, and rolling his pouch about until he was groaning. Releasing him she knelt before him, and took his dick into her mouth, running the tip of her tongue around the head of it as she held the foreskin back.

Then she began to suck upon him, slowly, slowly,

slowly, awakening his sex gently, but completely and fully. His hand rested atop her head, the fingers•kneading it as she worked her magic.

"Enough," he finally groaned. He was fully aroused. So much so that she was near to gagging as the tip of his penis pressed against the back of her throat. He drew her up, pushed her back upon the edge of the bed and pulled her legs all the way out to rest against his shoulders as he thrust into her wet hot sheath as deeply as he could go.

"Oh God!" she moaned as she felt him fill her up. It was pure heaven. He was so thick and so damned long, and it was wonderful. "Fuck me, darling," she begged him.

"In a moment, love," he promised. "I just love feeling myself inside of you, Kathy. You are so deliciously tight, and, ahhh, when you squeeze me like that it is so incredible. It seems to me it gets better every time with us."

"Uh-huh," she agreed. "Oh God, Tim, do it to me! I'm going to die from wanting you so damned much. Fuck me! Fuck me!"

He began to move on her. Slowly at first, then with deep, hard strokes of his cock, then quickly, quickly, quickly, until she was dizzy with the pleasure coursing through every inch of her body. Even the soles of her feet were tingling. Then he slowed his pace again, and she protested, reaching out to claw at him, but he was standing. She was unable to reach him. "Okay, love," he said, seeing her distress. "I can do this again later, so let's fly." His tempo increased once again.

She was flying. Every stroke of his penis sent a thrill through her. She couldn't keep a thought in her head. There was only the heavenly sensation of being fucked. When he found her G-spot she shrieked, and within moments climaxed, bathing the head of his prick with her juices, feeling his juices spurting, spurting into her, and reveling in the perfect moment of union as they were joined not just in body, but soul.

And then it was over. He climbed onto the bed before he collapsed, pulling her into his arms, holding her tightly. "You are one helluva fuck, Mrs. Blair," he told her, kissing the top of her head. The French twist had come loose, scattering hairpins and her luxurious hair all over the pillows.

"You too, Mr. Blair," she said happily.

They slept after that until just before dawn, when she awakened to find his engorged cock nestled between the cheeks of her ass as she lay on her side. Aware she was awake he began to play with her round breasts, pinching the nipples and pulling them out as he rubbed his penis within the confinement of her tight butt cheeks. "This feels so good," he told her. Then one of his hands reached out to push between her nether lips and play with her clitoris, until they were both squirming excitedly as she came on his hand, and he came between her buttocks.

"I never realized you could do something like that," she said.

"Lots of fun things we can do," Tim promised, "and we have a lifetime in which to do them, love." He kissed the nape of her neck softly. "I love you, Kathy, and if anyone had told me a year ago how happy I would be today I wouldn't have believed them. You've become my world. You and Egret Pointe."

Kathryn cried happily in his arms. If someone had told

her a year ago what was going to happen, she would have laughed too. She had The Channel and the library. She didn't need love or a whole lot of reality in her life. But she did. Everyone needed someone to love, be it a husband, a lover, a child. "I'm so happy, Tim," she told him. "I never thought I would find love again, but I love you more than I could have ever loved anyone else, darling." She sniffled against his shoulder.

Kathryn had never thought to be so happy. At Christmas they entertained her brother and his large family. Debora had spent a little extra time in the hospital getting her tubes tied. Eight children were more than enough, and it was obvious to Kathryn that not only had she inherited the Kimborough libido, but her brother had too. She often wondered if he still paid weekly visits to the town dominatrix, but what if he did? He loved his wife, was a good husband and father. His sin was no worse than all the women in town playing in The Channel.

January passed, and then in February, Tim received a telephone call one evening.

Kathryn heard him say, "No, but thanks for thinking of me. No, I'm quite happy where I am, thanks."

"What was that?" she asked him afterwards.

"Job offer," he said. "But I'm content here. I'm not ever going to leave Egret Pointe. Hallock tells me the board already wants to extend my contract, and I'm happy to let them. It's a good little school, and they're letting me try some new stuff with the kids."

She let it go, but then that same February weekend, Ray Pietro d'Angelo showed up in Egret Pointe with his wife to ostensibly visit his cousin, Joe. Tiffany invited the

Blairs to dinner. It was after dinner that Kathryn saw her husband in deep conversation with Ray. Unable to control her curiosity, she walked over to where the two men were seated and heard her husband say, "No, Ray."

"Look, the board is ready to give you a long-term contract, and pay you a heck of a lot more than Egret Pointe is paying you. You'll have carte blanche to institute all those programs that Grainger wouldn't let you try. You'll have a housing allowance, and I hear your co-op deal fell through, so you can just move right back in and the school will be paying the taxes and maintenance."

"No," Tim Blair said. "Listen, Ray, I'm married now. I love Egret Pointe. I love my job, and I'm not going anywhere. Honestly, there is nothing you could offer me that would make me change my mind. I don't want to go back and be headmaster of Kensington. It was kind of the board to offer, and maybe if I hadn't fallen in love with Kathy and married, I might have considered it. But I did, and so my answer is no."

"Maybe your wife would like living in the city," Ray said.

Kathryn stood silent. Neither man had noticed her.

"Nope, she's Egret Pointe born and bred, Ray."

"Ask her," he said.

"I don't have to, Ray. I know my Kathy. This is our home. We have family. Did you know I have eight nieces and nephews now that include fraternal twin girls, and a set of identical triplet boys born right after our wedding last December? I've just been elected to my church's vestry. My life in the city was dull. My life here in Egret Pointe has been nothing but exciting. Besides, Rowdy would hate being cooped up again. He loves his big backyard. Thank the board for me, Ray, but tell them my decision is final."

"She's a lucky woman," Ray Pietro d'Angelo said.

"No, I'm a lucky man," Tim replied, and he reached out to draw Kathryn close, for he had realized she was standing there listening. "I'll explain later," he told her.

As they drove home afterward he told her. "It seems David Grainger, the headmaster of Kensington, has been fucking around with Irene DuBois, the thirty-three-year-old French teacher. He got her pregnant, and when she told him, he said if she would fuck around with him she would fuck around with other guys. She couldn't prove the kid was his. Of course she got a lawyer. She says he promised to leave his wife, and marry her."

"They all promise to leave their wives and marry the other woman," Kathryn said dryly. "They rarely if ever do. So what's happening?"

"Ms. DuBois went public. Claims Grainger raped her after the faculty Christmas party when she remained behind to clean up, but then he became her lover. He denied it all at first, until she claimed to be able to identify a specific mark on his body that she couldn't have seen unless they were engaged in sexual conduct. Her lawyer forced an examination for the mark. It was right where Ms. DuBois said it was. Grainger then admitted to having sex with her, but said the sex was consensual."

"They all say the sex was consensual," Kathryn remarked.

Tim laughed. "Unfortunately for both Grainger and Ms. DuBois, their contracts with the school include a morals clause. Both were clearly in violation of that clause.

They were fired. Jill Grainger has kicked her husband out of their apartment and filed for divorce. Of course she'll have to get out of the apartment with the kids sooner rather than later. The school owns it. They'll give her until the end of July, I imagine. The new head and his family will want at least a month before school starts to get settled."

"Are you certain you don't want to go back?" Kathryn asked him softly. "Until six months ago it was your life."

"I like this life better," Tim told his wife. "I know you heard what I said to Ray. I meant it, Kathy. I love you, and I'm happy right here in Egret Pointe, okay?"

"Okay," she agreed as the relief poured through her.

Watching the scene play out between Tim and Kathy on his Fiend Finder, Fyfe McKay swore irritably. He had been so certain he could break up the newlyweds. Timothy Blair had always wanted the headmaster's job at Kensington Academy, and Fyfe McKay had made it possible for him to have it. What had happened to him that he would turn down such a plum? The job he had coveted, his co-op with its upkeep paid. What else did the damned man want?

It had almost been embarrassingly easy to tempt David Grainger with the hot-blooded and ambitious Irene DuBois. Grainger was an egotistical fool who had just turned fifty and was beginning to doubt his virility. The little French teacher was looking for a husband, and an important man seemed better than an unimportant one. It had been a match made in hell. But his plan hadn't worked at all. He would have to take another tack. The spring equinox was coming up fast. And his uncle did not like failure.

And then it came to him in a flash. If he couldn't tempt

Timothy Blair, he would tempt Kathy. He knew the fantasies she had programmed into her six-button remote. He couldn't give her back The Channel right now, but he could certainly put those fantasies back into her libido. He could insinuate them into her dreams. When her husband saw the passion she exhibited in her sleep, it was certain to make him jealous and drive a wedge between them. He could make them both miserable. Tim would leave her. Kathy would become embittered and he would win his wager with his uncle.

That same night Kathryn St. John Blair began to dream. She found herself in Rapunzel's tower, and heard a man's voice pleading with her to let down her hair. Going over to the tower window she leaned out. "What do you want?" she demanded of the handsome prince who stood beneath in the shadows.

"Rapunzel, Rapunzel, let down your golden hair."

"Why?" Kathryn questioned.

"Because I want to fuck you, Rapunzel. I will make you scream with delight."

"Get lost!" Kathryn said. "I'm not interested."

"But I must fuck you, my beautiful princess!"

And suddenly of its own accord the long blond hair flung itself over the windowsill. The prince began to climb up it. When he was halfway to her Kathryn reached for a pair of shears lying near Rapunzel's embroidery frame. Leaning out the window she cut through the thick golden tresses, and the prince fell screaming to the ground.

She half woke but then fell back into sleep again.

"Milady St. Jean, open the door. 'Tis I, Porthos, and I have several friends with me."

"Go away!" Kathryn said. "I'm not interested."

"We'll have a four way. You can suck one of us while two of us fuck you in your cunt and your ass."

"No!"

The door was forced, and the three musketeers pushed their way into the chamber. Kathryn grabbed up two pistols from the table and shot Porthos and Athos dead. Then, flinging the pistols at Aramis, she pulled Porthos's sword from its scabbard and ran Aramis through his heart. He fell to the floor atop the other two. Once again, Kathryn attempted to awaken, but something forced her back into an even deeper sleep.

She found herself in the tent of Temur the barbarian. What the dickens was happening? Kathryn wondered. She had never had dreams like this. She didn't want dreams like this. She struggled to awaken even as Temur came toward her, waving a gigantic penis at her and smiling an evil smile. It was then she recognized the face of Fyfe McKay. She was naked. Helpless. But then she saw the dagger upon the mattress he was attempting to force her down upon. Grabbing it up she sliced his cock off, and he exploded in a burst of black dust. Kathryn woke up gasping, Tim's arms around her.

"Kathy! Kathy! Are you all right? You've been moaning and even shrieking in your sleep," her husband said. Concern was written all over his handsome face.

Tim! It was Tim. "I had the most horrific nightmare," she said. She was shaking. "I never had a nightmare in my whole life until now."

"Is it gone?" he asked. "Do you remember what it was all about?" he asked her.

"No," she lied, shaking her head. "But I somehow don't think I'll have another nightmare like it again. I haven't been feeling well lately. I think I may be coming down with the flu, Tim. I'm going to stay home tomorrow."

"Good girl!" he approved, kissing her gently, and cuddling her as she fell back asleep. She did feel a bit warm.

The next day Kathryn remained home alone. It was early afternoon when the doorbell rang. Going to it she was astounded to see Mr. Nicholas. "Nicholas!"

He stepped across her threshold. "My dear girl, I came to apologize for my nephew's disgraceful behavior last night." He took her by her shoulders and kissed her upon her forehead. "It was totally unconscionable, which I would approve, had it been anyone else but you, Kathy."

She brought him into the living room, where she had been lying upon the couch, and he sat down. "Why on earth did he give me such a nightmare, Nicholas?"

"Fyfe does not entirely understand human nature, my dear. The dark side of humanity, yes, but the good in people, no. I am who I am because I do understand both sides. When I cut you off from The Channel it was because, as I told you then, I should never be able to take your soul from you. You are too good. I felt you deserved what all people want, and what so many do not gain. Happiness."

"Did you put Tim in my path, Nicholas?"

"No, my dear, I can take no credit for that, I fear," he admitted. "Fyfe in his ignorance does not understand love, or the great power it has. He believed he could destroy your happiness with your bridegroom and turn you to me. I knew he could not, but to humor him I gave him from the winter solstice to the spring equinox to accomplish his goal. He has, of course, failed miserably."

"Did I kill him?" Kathryn asked nervously.

Mr. Nicholas chuckled wickedly. "No, but I believe he wishes that you did. It will take several hundred years to regrow that skillful cock of his, and of course during that time he will be of little use to me in his former capacity. I've assigned him to my accounting department, where he will weigh and balance souls. It's quite dull work, I fear. There is no glamour to it at all. But then the wages of sin . . ." and Mr. Nicholas chuckled once again. "I just wanted to pop in and assure you, Kathy, that you will not be plagued again by my people. Nothing is all black or all white in this universe, my dear, and even the devil can sometimes have a soft heart for a good woman. Good-bye, Kathryn St. John. It is very unlikely that we shall meet again."

Then Mr. Nicholas was gone in a flash, and she woke up on the couch, where she had been napping when the doorbell rang. Her stomach was roiling, and scrambling up, she headed for the bathroom, where she promptly threw up. When Tim came home, he called Dr. Sam. Dr. Sam came, told Tim to leave him with his patient, and then looked closely at Kathryn. He conducted a brief examination.

"When did you have your last period, Kathy?"

"They're irregular now," she answered.

"When?"

"Last September, I think," she answered him. "Why?"

"Could you pee for me now?" Dr. Sam said.

"Sure."

He reached into his bag, and pulled out what appeared to be a plastic stick. "Go pee on this, and then bring it back to me."

"No!" she said recognizing the pregnancy stick. "I'm too old."

"Maybe, but maybe not," Dr. Sam told her. "Go pee."

Kathryn brought the stick back a few moments later, and together they watched as the stick turned colors, and then read, YOU'RE PREGNANT! "It's got to be a mistake," Kathryn said to him. "I'm going to be forty-nine this summer."

"These things are usually pretty accurate, especially given that you may be coming out of your first trimester," Dr. Sam said. "But I'll want to run a few more tests. Be in my office tomorrow morning at ten," he said, standing. Then, opening the bedroom door, he called Tim. "Your wife has a little surprise for you." He chuckled as he left them. "I'll let myself out."

"Are you all right, love?" Tim asked anxiously, sitting on the edge of the bed.

"I'm pregnant," Kathryn said. "How do you feel about being a father?"

His jaw dropped. *"You're what?"*

"Dr. Sam wants to run a few more tests, but it seems I'm probably pregnant," she told him. "I never considered being a mother. You ever think of being a father?"

"We're going to have a baby!" His blue eyes were dancing with delight.

And when she saw his genuine happiness, Kathryn St. John Blair began to cry.

She didn't understand why such joy should be hers. Was Nicholas right about her? Was she a truly good woman? Or was this all just an incredible result of all the passionate pleasures that she and Tim shared? She didn't care. It was more than enough happiness to last her the rest of her life, however long that would be.

EPILOGUE

On the following July 12, Cora Nicole Blair was born at Egret Pointe General Hospital. She was delivered not by Drs. Lindeman or Wheeler, the local obstetricians, but by Dr. Sam Seligmann at her mother's specific request. She weighed in at seven pounds, seven ounces, was twenty-one inches long, and had a fuzz of red-gold hair and large blue eyes. She immediately tested ten on the Apgar scale. Her parents were totally besotted with her. Dr. Sam pronounced her a perfect baby.

"I know that Cora is a Blair family name," Hallock said to his sister as he sat in her hospital room. "But where does the Nicole come from, Kathy?"

"It's for a friend I used to have," Kathryn answered.

"Did I know her?" her brother asked, curious.

"No," Kathryn said. "You didn't." And she smiled to herself.

"Well," Hallock St. John V said, "I hope Cora Nicole grows up to be every bit the good woman her mother is!"

"So do I," Timothy Blair said, leaning over his daughter's basinette.

"Me too," Kathryn echoed, and then she laughed, for if she had been happy before, she was even happier now, if such a thing were possible. There might not be any more babies, given her age, but with Tim for a husband there would always be plenty of passionate pleasures for them to enjoy, she was absolutely certain. And she suspected that their one little miracle was going to be more than a handful if she was anything like her parents. Or—perish forbid!—her namesake.

ABOUT THE AUTHOR

Bertrice Small is a *New York Times* bestselling author and the recipient of numerous awards. In keeping with her profession, Bertrice Small lives in the oldest English-speaking town in the state of New York, founded in 1640. Her light-filled studio includes the paintings of her favorite cover artist, Elaine Duillo, and a large library. Because she believes in happy endings, Bertrice Small has been married to the same man, her hero, George, for forty-seven years. They have a son, Thomas, a daughter-in-law, Megan, and four wonderful grandchildren. Longtime readers will be happy to know that Nicki the Cockatiel flourishes along with his housemates: Finnegan, the long-haired, bad, black kitty; and Sylvester, the black-and-white tuxedo cat, who is the official family bad cat.

My dear Readers:

I am very happy to tell you that there will be one more book in the "Pleasures" series. Tentatively titled *Guilty Pleasures*, it is an anthology, and will be out in the summer of 2011.

I thought rather than telling you one story with one heroine and her adventures in The Channel, I would tell you five wickedly erotic little tales. The heroines involved are all, except one, characters you have met in previous books.

There is Carla from *Private Pleasures*, Tiffany and Nina from *Sudden Pleasures*, and J.P. from *Forbidden Pleasures*. The new character is Maureen Kelly, a nanny hired by Emilie Shann Devlin, my heroine from *Forbidden Pleasures*. Nanny Mo, as she is known to her charges, has a thing for brawny Celtic Warriors.

I hope you have enjoyed *Passionate Pleasures*, and that you will look forward to *Guilty Pleasures* in 2011. God bless and good reading from your most faithful author,

Bertrice Small